"I've Wanted You From The First Moment I Laid Eyes On You."

Tiffany laughed softly. "Now it's time for you to be serious."

"I am."

"You don't even know me—"

"I know you well enough to realize we're good together."

"In what ways?"

"All ways." He tugged on her arm, forcing her closer. As Zane looked down at her she felt as if he were stripping her bare. She smelled the clean, masculine scent of him, felt the warmth of his body, knew in a minute that he intended to kiss her.

"Let me love you," he whispered, refusing to let her go. She tried to deny the traitorous feelings burning in her breast. "I can't… I just…can't."

"You never will, unless you take a chance."

W9-CXK-648

Dear Reader:

Romance offers us all so much. It makes us "walk on sunshine." It gives us hope. It takes us out of our own lives, encouraging us to reach out to others. Janet Dailey is fond of saying that romance is a state of mind, that it could happen anywhere. Yet nowhere does romance seem to be as good as when it happens *here*.

Starting in February 1986, Silhouette Special Edition is featuring the AMERICAN TRIBUTE—a tribute to America, where romance has never been so wonderful. For six consecutive months, one out of every six Special Editions will be an episode in the AMERICAN TRIBUTE, a portrait of the lives of six women, all from Oklahoma. Look for the first book, *Love's Haunting Refrain* by Ada Steward, as well as stories by other favorites—Jeanne Stephens, Gena Dalton, Elaine Camp and Renee Roszel. You'll know the AMERICAN TRIBUTE by its patriotic stripe under the Silhouette Special Edition border.

AMERICAN TRIBUTE—six women, six stories, starting in February.

AMERICAN TRIBUTE—one of the reasons Silhouette Special Edition is just that—Special.

The Editors at Silhouette Books

LISA JACKSON
Devil's Gambit

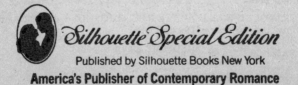

Silhouette Special Edition

Published by Silhouette Books New York

America's Publisher of Contemporary Romance

To Celia and Bate.

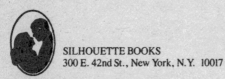

SILHOUETTE BOOKS
300 E. 42nd St., New York, N.Y. 10017

Copyright © 1985 by Lisa Jackson

ISBN: 0-373-09282-2

First Silhouette Books printing December 1985
Second printing January 1986

America's Publisher of Contemporary Romance

Printed in the U.S.A.

Books by Lisa Jackson

Silhouette Intimate Moments

Dark Side of the Moon #39
Gypsy Wind #79

Silhouette Special Edition

A Twist of Fate #118
The Shadow of Time #180
Tears of Pride #194
Pirate's Gold #215
A Dangerous Precedent #233
Innocent by Association #244
Midnight Sun #264
Devil's Gambit #282

LISA JACKSON

was raised in Môlalla, Oregon, and now lives with her husband, Mark, and her two sons in a suburb of Portland, Oregon. Lisa and her sister, Natalie Bishop, who is also a Silhouette author, live within an earshot of each other and do all of their work in Natalie's basement. Lisa and Natalie are both represented in the Silhouette Special Edition list this month.

Chapter One

Tiffany heard the back door creak open and then shut with a bone-rattling thud. *It's over,* she thought and fought against the tears of despair that threatened her eyes.

Hoping to appear as calm as was possible under the circumstances, she set her pen on the letter she had been writing and placed her elbows on the desk. Cold dread slowly crept up her spine.

Mac's brisk, familiar footsteps slowed a bit as he approached the den, and involuntarily Tiffany's spine stiffened as she braced herself for the news. Mac paused in the doorway. Tonight he appeared older than his sixty-seven years. His plaid shirt was rumpled and the lines near his sharp eyes were deeper than usual.

Tiffany knew what he was going to say before Mac had a chance to deliver his somber message.

"He didn't make it, did he?" she asked as her slate-blue eyes held those of the weathered ex-jockey.

There was a terse shake of Mac's head. His lips tightened over his teeth and he removed his worn hat. "He was a good-lookin' colt, that one."

"They all were," Tiffany muttered, seemingly to herself. "Every last one of them." The suppressed rage of three sleepless nights began to pound in her veins, and for a moment she lost the tight rein on her self-control. "Damn!" Her fist crashed against the desk before the weighty sadness hit and her shoulders slumped in defeat. A numb feeling took hold of her and she wondered if what was happening was real. Once again her eyes pierced those of the trainer and he read the disbelief in her gaze.

"Charlatan is dead," he said quietly, as if to settle the doubts in her mind. "It weren't nobody's fault. The vet, well, he did all he could."

"I know."

He saw the disappointment that kept her full lips drawn into a strained line. *She can't take much more of this,* he thought to himself. *This might be the straw that breaks the camel's back.* Everything that was happening to her was a shame—a damned shame.

"And don't you go blaming yourself," he admonished as if reading her thoughts. His crowlike features pinched into a scowl before he dropped his wiry frame into one of the winged side chairs positioned near the desk. Thoughtfully he scratched the rough stubble of his beard. He'd been awake for nearly three days, same as she, and he was dog-tired. At sixty-seven it wasn't getting any easier.

Tiffany tried to manage a smile and failed. What she felt was more than defeat. The pain of witnessing the last struggling breaths of two other foals had drained her. And now Charlatan, the strongest of the lot, was dead.

"It's just not fair," she whispered.

"Aye, that it's not."

She let out a ragged sigh and leaned back in the uncomfortable desk chair. Her back ached miserably and all thoughts of her letter to Dustin were forgotten. "That makes three," she remarked, the skin of her flawless forehead wrinkling into an uncomfortable frown.

"And two more mares should be dropping foals within the next couple of weeks."

Tiffany's elegant jaw tightened. "Let's just hope they're healthy."

Mac pushed his hands through his thinning red hair. His small eyes narrowed suspiciously as he looked out the window at the group of large white buildings comprising Rhodes Breeding Farm. Starkly illuminated by the bluish sheen from security lights, the buildings took on a sinister appearance in the stormy night.

"We've sure had a streak of bad luck, that we have."

"It almost seems as if someone is out to get us," Tiffany observed and Mac's sharp gaze returned to the face of his employer.

"That it does."

"But *who* and *why*...and *how*?" Nothing was making any sense. Tiffany stretched her tired arms before dropping her head forward and releasing the tight clasp holding her hair away from her face. Her long fingers massaged her scalp as she shook the soft brown tresses free of their bond and tried to release the tension in the back of her neck.

"That one I can't answer," Mac replied, watching as she moved her head and the honey-colored strands fell to her shoulders. Tiffany Rhodes was a beautiful woman who had faced more than her share of tragedy. Signs of stress had begun to age her fair complexion, and though Tiffany was still the most regally beautiful and proud woman he knew, Mac McDougal wondered just how much more she could take.

"That's just the trouble—no one can explain what's happening."

"You haven't got any enemies that I don't know about?" It was more of a statement than a question.

Tiffany's frown was pensive. A headache was beginning to nag at her. She shrugged her shoulders. "No one that would want to ruin me."

"You're sure?"

"Positive. Look, we can't blame anyone for what's happened here. Like you said, we've just had a string of bad luck."

"Starting with the loss of Devil's Gambit four years ago."

Tiffany's eyes clouded in pain. "At least we got the insurance money for him," she whispered, as if it really didn't matter. "I don't think any of the foals will be covered, not once the insurance company gets wind of the problems we're having."

"The insurance money you got for Devil's Gambit wasn't half of what he was worth," Mac grumbled, not for the first time. Why had Ellery Rhodes been so careless with the most valuable stallion on the farm? The entire incident had never set well with Mac. He shifted uncomfortably on the chair.

"Maybe not, but I'm afraid it's all water under the bridge." She pushed the letter to Dustin aside and managed a weak smile. "It really doesn't matter anyway. We lost the horse and he'll never be replaced." She shuddered as she remembered the night that had taken the life of her husband and his most treasured Thoroughbred. Images of the truck and horse trailer, twisted and charred beyond recognition, filled her mind and caused her to wrap her arms protectively over her abdomen. Sometimes the nightmare never seemed to go away.

Mac saw the sadness shadow her eyes. He could have kicked himself for bringing up the past and reminding her of the god-awful accident that had left her a widow. The last thing Tiffany needed was to be constantly reminded of her troubles. *And now there was the problem with the foals!*

The wiry ex-jockey stood and held his hat in his hands. He'd delivered his message and somehow Tiffany had managed to take the news in stride. But then she always did.

There was a stoic beauty and pride in Ellery Rhodes's widow that Mac admired. No matter how deep the pain, Tiffany Rhodes always managed to pull herself together. There was proof enough of that in her marriage. Not many women could have stayed married to a bastard the likes of Ellery Rhodes.

Mac started for the door of the den and twisted the brim of his limp fedora in his gnarled hands. He didn't feel comfortable in the house—at least not since Ellery Rhodes's death—and he wanted to get back to the foaling shed. There was still unpleasant work to be done.

"I'll come with you," Tiffany offered, rising from the desk and pursing her lips together in determination.

"No reason—"

"I want to."

"He's dead, just like the others. Nothing you can do."

Except cry a few wasted tears, Tiffany thought to herself as she pulled her jacket off the wooden hook near the French doors that opened to a flagstone patio.

Bracing herself against the cold wind and rain blowing inland from the coast, Tiffany rammed her fists into the pockets of her jacket and silently followed Mac down the well-worn path toward the foaling shed. She knew that he disapproved of her insistence on being involved with all of the work at the farm. After all, Ellery had preferred to leave the work to the professionals. But Tiffany wanted to learn the business from the ground up, and despite Mac's obvious thoughts that a woman's place was in the home or, at the very least, in the office doing book work, Tiffany made herself a part of everything on the small breeding farm.

The door to the shed creaked on rusty hinges as Tiffany entered the brightly lit building. Pungent familiar odors of clean straw, warm horses, antiseptic and oiled leather greeted her. She wiped the rain off her face as her eyes adjusted to the light.

Mac followed her inside, muttering something about this being no place for a woman. Tiffany ignored Mac's obvious attempt to protect her from the tragic evidence of Charlatan's death and walked with determination toward the short man near the opposite end of the building. Her boots echoed hollowly on the concrete floor.

Vance Geddes, the veterinarian, was still in the stall, but Felicity, the mare who just two days earlier had given birth to Charlatan, had already been taken away.

Vance's expression was grim and perplexed. Weary lines creased his white skin and bracketed his mouth with worry. He forced a weak smile when Tiffany approached him and he stepped away from the small, limp form lying in the straw.

"Nothing I could do," Vance apologized, regret and frustration sharpening his normally bland expression. "I thought with this one we had a chance."

"Why?" She glanced sadly at the dead colt and a lump formed in her throat. Everything seemed so...pointless.

"He seemed so strong at birth. Stood up and nursed right away, not like the others."

Tiffany knelt on the straw and touched the soft neck of the still-warm foal. He was a beautiful, perfectly formed colt—a rick chestnut with one white stocking and a small white star on his forehead. At birth his dark eyes had been keenly intelligent and inquisitive with that special spark that distinguished Moon Shadow's progeny. Tiffany had prayed that he would live and not fall victim to the same baffling disease that had killed the other recently born foals sired by Moon Shadow.

"You'll perform an autopsy?" she asked, her throat tight from the strain of unshed tears.

"Of course."

After patting the soft neck one last time, Tiffany straightened. She dusted her hands on her jeans, cast one final searching look at the tragic form and walked out of the stall. "What about Felicity?"

"She's back in the broodmare barn. And not very happy about it. We had a helluva time getting her away from the foal. She kicked at John, but he managed to get her out of here."

"It's not easy," Tiffany whispered, understanding the anxious mare's pain at the unexplained loss of her foal. Tiffany looked around the well-kept foaling shed. White heat lamps, imported straw, closed circuit television, all the best equipment money could buy and still she couldn't prevent the deaths of these last three foals.

Why, she wondered to herself. *And why only the offspring of Moon Shadow?* He had stood at stud for nearly eight years and had always produced healthy, if slightly temperamental, progeny. Not one foal had died. Until now. *Why?*

With no answers to her question, and tears beginning to blur her vision, Tiffany reluctantly left the two men to attend to the dead colt.

The rain had decreased to a slight drizzle, but the wind had picked up and the branches of the sequoia trees danced wildly, at times slamming into the nearby buildings. The weather wasn't unusual for early March in Northern California, but there was something somber and ominous about the black clouds rolling over the hills surrounding the small breeding farm.

"Don't let it get to you," Tiffany muttered to herself.

She shivered as she stepped into the broodmare barn and walked without hesitation to Felicity's stall.

The smell of fresh hay and warm horses greeted her and offered some relief from the cold night. Several mares poked their dark heads out of the stalls to inspect the visitor. Tiffany gently patted each muzzle as she passed, but her eyes were trained on the last stall in the whitewashed barn.

Felicity was still agitated and appeared to be looking for the lost foal. The chestnut mare paced around the small enclosure and snorted restlessly. When Tiffany approached, Felicity's ears flattened to her head and her dark eyes gleamed maliciously.

"I know, girl," Tiffany whispered, attempting to comfort the anxious mare. "It wasn't supposed to turn out like this."

Felicity stamped angrily and ignored the piece of apple Tiffany offered.

"There will be other foals," Tiffany said, wondering if she were trying to convince the horse or herself. Rhodes Breeding Farm couldn't stand to take many more losses. Tears of frustration and anxiety slid down her cheeks and she didn't bother to brush them aside.

A soft nicker from a nearby stall reminded Tiffany that she was disturbing the other horses. Summoning up her faltering courage, Tiffany stared at Felicity for a moment before slapping the top rail of the stall and walking back to the house.

Somehow she would find the solution to the mystery of the dying foals.

The first inquiry came by telephone two days later. Word had gotten out about the foals, and a reporter for a local newspaper in Santa Rosa was checking the story.

Tiffany took the call herself and assured the man that though she had lost two newborn colts and one filly, she and the veterinarian were positive that whatever had killed the animals was not contagious.

When the reporter, Rod Crawford, asked if he could come to the farm for an interview, Tiffany was wary, but decided the best course of action was to confront the problem head-on.

"When would it be convenient for you to drive out to the farm?" she asked graciously, her soft voice disguising her anxiety.

"What about next Wednesday? I'll have a photographer with me, if you don't mind."

"Of course not," she lied, as if she had done it all her life. "Around ten?"

"I'll be there," Rod Crawford agreed.

Tiffany replaced the receiver and said a silent prayer that the two mares who were still carrying Moon Shadow's unborn foals would successfully deliver healthy horses into the world, hopefully before next Wednesday. A sinking feeling in her heart told her not to get her hopes up.

Somehow, she had to focus Rod Crawford's attention away from the tragedy in the foaling shed and onto the one bright spot in Rhodes Breeding Farm's future: Journey's End. He was a big bay colt, whose career as a two-year-old had been less than formidable. But now, as a three-year-old, he had won his first two starts and promised to be the biggest star Rhodes Farm had put on the racetrack since Devil's Gambit.

Tiffany only hoped that she could convince the reporter that the story at Rhodes Breeding Farm was not the three dead foals, but the racing future of Journey's End.

The reputation of the breeding farm was on the line. If the Santa Rosa papers knew about the unexplained deaths of the foals, it wouldn't be long before reporters from San Francisco and Sacramento would call. And then, all hell was sure to break loose.

The doorbell chimed at nine-thirty on Wednesday morning and Tiffany smiled grimly to herself. Though the reporter for the *Santa Rosa Clarion* was a good half an hour early, Tiffany was ready for him. In the last four years she had learned to anticipate just about anything and make the most of it, and she wouldn't allow a little time discrepancy to rattle her. She couldn't afford the bad press.

Neither of the broodmares pregnant with Moon Shadow's offspring had gone into labor and Tiffany didn't know whether to laugh or cry. Her nerves were stretched as tightly as a piano string and only with effort did her poise remain intact. Cosmetics, for the most part, had covered the shadows below her eyes, which were the result of the past week of sleepless nights.

She hurried down the curved, marble staircase and crossed the tiled foyer to the door. After nervously smoothing her wool skirt, she opened the door and managed a brave smile, which she directed at the gentleman standing on the porch.

"Ms. Rhodes?" he asked with the slightest of accents.

Tiffany found herself staring into the most seductive gray eyes she had ever seen. He wasn't what she had expected. His tanned face was angular, his features strong. Raven-black hair and fierce eyebrows contrasted with the bold, steel-colored eyes staring into hers. There was a presence about him that spoke of authority and hinted at arrogance.

"Yes...won't you please come in?" she replied, finally finding her voice. "We can talk in the den...." Her words trailed off as she remembered the photographer. Where was he? Hadn't Crawford mentioned that a photographer would be with him this morning?

It was then she noticed the stiff white collar and the expensively woven tweed business suit. A burgundy silk tie was knotted at the stranger's throat and gold cuff links flashed in the early-morning sunlight. The broad shoulders beneath his jacket were square and tense and there was no evidence of a note pad, camera or tape recorder. Stereotyping aside, this man was no reporter.

"Pardon me," she whispered, realizing her mistake. "I was expecting someone—"

"Else," he supplied with a tight, slightly off-center smile that seemed out of place on his harsh, angular face. He wasn't conventionally handsome; the boldness of his features took away any boyish charm that might have lingered from his youth. But there was something about him, something positively male and sensual that was as magnetic as it was dangerous. Tiffany recognized it in the glint of his eyes and the brackets near the corners of his mouth. She suspected that beneath the conservative business suit, there was an extremely single-minded and ruthless man.

He extended his hand and when Tiffany accepted it, she noticed that his fingers were callused—a direct contradiction of the image he was attempting to portray.

"Zane Sheridan," he announced. Again the accent.

She hesitated only slightly. His name and his face were vaguely familiar, and though he looked as if he expected her to recognize him, she couldn't remember where she'd met him...or heard of him. "Please come in, Mr. Sheridan—"

"Zane."

"Zane," she repeated, slightly uncomfortable with the familiarity of first names. For a reason she couldn't put her finger on, Tiffany thought she should be wary of this man. There was something about him that hinted at antagonism.

She led him into the den, knowing instinctively that this was not a social call.

"Can I get you something—coffee, perhaps, or tea?" Tiffany asked as she took her usual chair behind the desk and Zane settled into one of the side chairs. Placing her elbows on the polished wood surface, she clasped her hands together and smiled pleasantly, just as if he hadn't disrupted her morning.

"Nothing. Thank you." His gray eyes moved away from her face to wander about the room. They observed all the opulent surroundings: the thick pile of the carpet, the expensive leather chairs, the subdued brass reading lamps and the etchings of Thoroughbreds adorning the cherry-wood walls.

"What exactly can I do for you?" Tiffany asked, feeling as if he were searching for something.

When his eyes returned to hers, he smiled cynically. "I was an acquaintance of your husband."

Zane's expression was meant to be without emotion as he stared at the elegant but worried face of Ellery Rhodes's widow. Her reaction was just what he had expected—surprise and then, once she had digested his statement, disbelief. Her fingers anxiously toyed with the single gold chain encircling her throat.

"You knew Ellery?"

"We'd met a few times. In Europe."

Maybe that was why his face and name were so familiar, but Tiffany doubted it. A cautious instinct told her he was lying through his beautiful, straight white teeth.

She was instantly wary as she leveled her cool blue gaze at him. "I'm sorry," she apologized, "but if we've met, I've forgotten."

Zane pulled at the knot of his tie and slumped more deeply and comfortably into his chair. "I met Ellery Rhodes before he was married to you."

"Oh." Her smile was meant to be indulgent. "And you're here because...?" she prompted. Zane Sheridan unnerved her, and Tiffany knew instinctively that the sooner he stated his business and was gone, the better.

"I'm interested in buying your farm."

Her dark brows arched in elegant surprise. "You're kidding!"

"Dead serious." The glint of silver determination in his eyes emphasized his words and convinced her that he wasn't playing games.

"But it's not for sale."

"I've heard that everything has a price."

"Well in this case, Mr. Sheridan, you heard wrong. The farm isn't on the market. However, if you're interested in a yearling, I have two colts that—"

"Afraid not. It's all or nothing with me," was the clipped, succinct reply. Apparently Zane Sheridan wasn't a man to mince words.

"Then I guess it's nothing," Tiffany replied, slightly galled at his self-assured attitude. Who the hell did he think he was, waltzing into her house uninvited, and offering to buy her home—Ellery's farm?

Just because he had been a friend of Ellery's—no, he hadn't said friend, just acquaintance.

It didn't matter. It still didn't give him the right to come barging in as if he owned the place. And there was more to it. Tiffany sensed that he was here for another reason, a reason he hadn't admitted. Maybe it was the strain in the angle of his jaw, or the furrows lining his forehead. But whatever the reason, Tiffany knew that Zane Sheridan was hiding something.

Tiffany stood, as if by so doing she could end the conversation.

"Let me know if you change your mind." He rose and looked past her to the framed portrait of Devil's Gambit; the painting was mounted proudly above the gray stone fireplace.

Just so that Mr. Sheridan understood the finality of her position on the farm, she offered an explanation to which he really wasn't entitled. "If I change my mind about selling the place, I'll give Ellery's brother Dustin first option. He already owns part of the farm and I think that Rhodes Breeding Farm should stay in the family."

Zane frowned thoughtfully and rubbed his chin. "If the family wants it—"

"Of course."

Shrugging his broad shoulders as if he had no interest whatsoever in the Rhodes family's business, he continued to gaze at the portrait over the mantel.

"A shame about Devil's Gambit," he said at length.

"Yes," Tiffany whispered, repeating his words stiffly. "A shame." The same accident that had claimed the proud horse's life had also killed Ellery. Mr. Sheridan didn't offer any condolences concerning her husband, the man he'd said he had known.

The conversation was stilted and uncomfortable, and Tiffany felt as if Zane Sheridan were deliberately baiting her. But why? And who needed it? The past few weeks had been chaotic enough. The last thing Tiffany wanted was a mysterious man complicating things with his enigmatic presence and cryptic statements.

As she walked around the desk, shortening the distance between the stranger and herself, she asked, "Do you own any horses, Mr. Sheridan?" His dark brows quirked at the formal use of his surname.

"A few. In Ireland."

That explained the faint accent. "So you want to buy the farm and make your mark on American racing?"

"Something like that." For the first time, his smile seemed sincere, and there was a spark of honesty in his clear, gray eyes.

Tiffany supposed that Zane Sheridan was the singularly most attractive man she had met in a long while. Tall and whip-lean, with broad shoulders and thick, jet black hair, he stood with pride and authority as he returned her gaze. His skin was dark and smooth, and where once there might have been a dimple, there were now brackets of strain around his mouth. He had lived a hard life, Tiffany guessed, but the expensive tweed jacket suggested that the worst years had passed.

It would be a mistake to cross a man such as this, she decided. Zane Sheridan looked as if he were capable of ruthless retribution. This was evidenced in the tense line of his square jaw, the restless movement of his fingers against his thumb and the hard glint of determination in those steel-gray eyes. Zane was a man to reckon with and not one to deceive.

The doorbell rang, and Tiffany was grateful for the intrusion.

"If you'll excuse me," she said, taking three quick steps before pausing to turn in his direction.

"We're not through here."

"Pardon me?" Tiffany was taken aback. She expected him to show some civility and leave before Rod Crawford's interview. Instinctively Tiffany knew that having Zane in the same room with the reporter would be dangerous.

"I want to talk to you—seriously—about the farm."

"There's no reason, Mr...Zane. You're wasting your time with me. I'm not about to sell."

"Indulge me," he suggested. He strode across the short distance separating them and touched her lightly on the arm. "Hear what I have to say, listen to what my offer is before you say no."

The doorbell chimed again, more impatiently this time.

"I really do have an appointment," she said, looking anxiously through the foyer to the front door. The grip on her arm tightened slightly.

"And I think you should listen to what I have to say."

"Why?"

He hesitated slightly, as if he weren't sure he could trust her and the skin tightened over his cheekbones. His rugged features displayed a new emotion. Anger and vengeful self-righteousness were displayed in the thrust of his jaw. All traces of his earlier civility had disappeared. Tiffany's heart began to pound with dread.

"Why are you here?" she asked again, her voice suddenly hoarse.

"I came to you because there is something I think that you should know."

"And that is?" Her heart was pounding frantically now, and she barely heard the doorbell chime for the third time.

"I'm not so sure that Devil's Gambit's death was an accident," he stated, gauging her reaction, watching for even the slightest trace of emotion on her elegant features. "In fact, I think there's a damned good chance that your horse is still alive."

Chapter Two

The color drained from Tiffany's face. "You...you think that Devil's Gambit might be alive?" she repeated, her voice barely a whisper. "You're not serious...."

But she could tell by Zane's expression that he was dead serious.

"Dear God," she whispered, closing her eyes. She wanted to dismiss what he was saying as idle conjecture, but he just didn't seem the type of man who would fabricate anything so bizarre. "I don't know if I can deal with this right now...." Devil's Gambit alive? But how? She'd been to the site of the accident, witnessed the gruesome truth for herself. Both the horse and the driver of the truck had been killed. Only Dustin had survived.

It was difficult to speak or to think rationally. Tiffany forced herself to look into Zane's brooding gaze and managed to clear her throat. "Look, I really do have an interview that I can't get out of. Please wait.... I...I want to talk to you. Alone." She extracted her arm from his grasp and made her way to the door. Her mind was running in crazy circles. What did he mean? Devil's Gambit couldn't possibly be alive. And Ellery—what about Ellery? Dear Lord, if what Zane was suggesting was true, there might be a chance that Ellery was still alive. But how? *Don't think like this,* she told herself. *What this man is suggesting can't possibly be true.*

Her knees were weak, and she leaned against the door for several seconds, trying to recover her lost equilibrium before the bell chimed for the fourth time. "Get hold of yourself," she murmured, but she was unable to disguise the clouds of despair in her eyes. Why now? Why did Zane Sheridan pick this time when everything at the breeding farm was in turmoil to enter her life with rash statements about the past? Forcing her worried thoughts to a dark corner of her mind, she straightened and braced herself for the interview.

With a jerk, she tugged on the brass handle and the door swung inward. Despite the storm of emotions raging within her, she forced what she hoped would appear a sincere and pleasant smile. Only the slightest trembling of her full lips hinted at her ravaged emotions.

"Mr. Crawford?" Tiffany asked the agitated young man slouching against a white pillar supporting the roof. "Please accept my apologies for the delay. My housekeeper isn't in yet and I had an unexpected visitor this morning." Her voice was surprisingly calm, her gaze direct, and she disguised the trembling in her fingers by hiding her hands in the deep pockets of her wool skirt.

The bearded, blond man eyed her skeptically, motioned to someone in the car and then handed her a card that stated that he was Rod Crawford of the *Santa Rosa Clarion.*

A petite, dark-haired woman climbed out of the car and slung a camera over one shoulder. Tiffany stepped away from the door to let the two people enter her home. In the distance she heard the familiar rumble of Louise's old

Buick. The noise was reassuring. Once the housekeeper took charge of the kitchen, some of the disorder of the morning would abate. *Except that Zane Sheridan was in the den, seemingly convinced that Devil's Gambit and, therefore, Ellery were still alive.*

"Could I offer you a cup of coffee...or tea?" Tiffany asked with a weak smile.

"Coffee—black," Crawford stated curtly, withdrawing a note pad from his back pocket.

Tiffany trained her eyes on the photographer. "Anything," the pleasant-featured woman replied. She flashed Tiffany a friendly grin as she extended her small hand. "Jeanette Wilkes." Jeanette's interested eyes swept the opulent interior of the house and she noted the sweeping staircase, gleaming oak banister, elegant crystal chandelier and glossy imported floor tiles. "I was hoping to get a couple of pictures of the farm."

"Wonderful," Tiffany said with a smile that disguised her inner turmoil. "Please, have a seat in the living room." She opened the double doors of the formal room and silently invited them inside.

"You have a beautiful home," Jeanette stated as she looked at the period pieces and the Italian marble of the fireplace with a practiced eye. Everything about the house was first class—no outward sign of money problems.

"Thank you."

"Is this where you work?" Crawford asked skeptically.

"No..."

"If you don't mind, Jeanette would like to get some shots of the inside of the farm as well as the outbuildings. You know, give people a chance to see whatever it is you do when you're working. Don't you have an office or something?" He eyed the formal living room's expensive formal furniture with obvious distaste.

"Of course." The last thing Tiffany could afford was any bad press, so she had to accommodate the nosy reporter.

She decided she would have to find a way to get rid of Zane Sheridan. His story was too farfetched to be believed; and yet there was something forceful and determined about him that made her think the Irishman wasn't bluffing.

Zane was still in the den and Tiffany wanted to keep Rod Crawford, with his probing questions, away from the visitor with the Irish accent. If the two men with their different perspectives on what was happening at Rhodes Breeding Farm got together, the results would be certain disaster. Tiffany shuddered when she envisioned the news concerning Moon Shadow's foals and a rumor that Devil's Gambit was still alive being splashed across the front page of the *Santa Rosa Clarion*. The minute the combined reports hit the front page, she would have reporters calling her day and night.

Tiffany's mind was spinning miles a minute. What Zane had suggested was preposterous, and yet the surety of his gaze had convinced her that he wasn't playing games. But Devil's Gambit, alive? And Ellery? Her heart was beating so rapidly she could barely concentrate. She needed to talk to Zane Sheridan, that much was certain, just to find out if he were a master gambler, bluffing convincingly, or if he really did mean what he was saying and had the facts to back him up. But she had to speak to him alone, without the watchful eyes and ears of the press observing her.

Holding her back stiffly, she led Rod and Jeanette back through the foyer to the den, which was directly opposite the living room. Zane was standing by the fireplace, his eyes trained on the painting of the horse over the mantel. He had discarded his jacket and tossed it over the back of one chair, and the tight knot of his tie had been loosened. He looked as if he intended to stay. That was something she couldn't allow, and yet she was afraid to let him go. There were so many questions whirling in her mind. Who was he? What did he want? How did he know Ellery? Why did he want her to believe that Devil's Gambit might still be alive after four long years?

Without hesitation, Tiffany walked toward him. He turned to face her and his eyes were as cool and distant as the stormy, gray Pacific Ocean. If he had been lying a few moments before, he showed no trace of deceit. Yet his story couldn't possibly be true; either it was a total fabrication or he just didn't know what he was talking about.

The steadiness of his glare suggested just the opposite. Tiffany knew intuitively that Zane Sheridan rarely made mistakes. Cold dread took hold of her heart.

"Mr. Sheridan, would it be too much trouble to ask you to wait to finish our discussion?" she asked with an unsteady smile. *What if he wouldn't leave and caused a scene in front of the reporter from the* Santa Rosa Clarion? *His story was just wild and sensational enough to capture Rod Crawford's attention.*

Zane's eyes flickered to the other two people and quickly sized them up as reporters. Obviously something was going on, and the widow Rhodes didn't want him to know about it. His thick brows drew together in speculation.

"How long?"

"I'm not sure.... Mr. Crawford?"

"Call me Rod."

Tiffany made a hasty introduction, while the bearded man came to her side and shook Zane's outstretched hand. The image of the reporter's hand linked with Zane's made her uneasy.

"I don't know," Rod was saying, rubbing his bearded chin. "I suppose it will take...what?" He eyed Jeanette for input. "An hour, maybe two. I want to ask you some questions and then we need a quick tour of the buildings."

Tiffany's throat went dry. No matter how crazy Zane's story seemed, she had to talk to him, find out what he wanted and why he thought that Devil's Gambit might still be alive.

"I have a meeting at noon," Zane stated, his calculating gaze never leaving the worried lines of her face. There was something in Tiffany Rhodes's manner that suggested it would be to his advantage to stay. But he needed to be with her alone in order to accomplish everything he had planned for six long years. He'd given her the bait, and she'd swallowed it hook, line and sinker. The satisfaction he had hoped to find was sadly lacking, and he felt a twinge of conscience at the worry in her clouded eyes.

"Look, Ms. Rhodes—can we get on with it? We've got another story to cover this afternoon," Crawford interjected.

"Of course." Tiffany returned her attention to Zane's proud face. She hoped that she didn't sound nearly as desperate as she felt. "Could you come by tomorrow, or would it be more convenient to meet you somewhere?"

"I have to catch an early flight." His angular jaw was tense, his muscles rigid, but there was the glimmer of expectancy in his eyes. *He's enjoying this,* she thought and she had to work to control her temper. She couldn't blow up now, not with Rod Crawford in the room, but there was something infuriating in Zane's arrogant manner.

Trying not to sound condescending she asked, "Then tonight?" He couldn't just waltz into her life, make outrageous statements, and then disappear as if nothing had happened. She had to know the truth, or what he was attempting to portray as the truth. She wanted to forget about him and his wild imaginings, but she couldn't dismiss him as just another publicity seeker. What did he want—*really want* from her?

Zane's gray eyes narrowed a fraction. "All right. What time?"

"How about dinner—seven-thirty?"

"I'll be here."

He picked up his jacket and flung it over his arm. Tiffany escorted him to the door and let out a long sigh of relief when he was gone. At least he had no inkling why the reporter was there, although it wouldn't be too hard to figure out, especially once the article was printed. "Maybe he'll be back in Ireland where he belongs by then," she muttered with false optimism.

Louise was serving coffee and scones when Tiffany returned to the den. After accepting a cup of black coffee, Tiffany seated herself at her desk, feeling uncomfortably close to Rod Crawford, who sat across the desk. While Jeanette snapped a few "candid" shots of Tiffany at work, Rod began the interview.

"How long have you actually managed the farm?" he asked.

"About four years."

"Ever since your husband's death?"

Tiffany felt her back tighten. "That's right. Before that I helped Ellery on the farm, but he ran it."

"I don't mean to bring up a sore subject," the wily reporter went on, "but ever since you took over, you've had quite a few bad breaks."

Tiffany smiled grimly. "That's true, but I don't like to dwell on them. Right now I'm concentrating on Journey's End."

"The three-year-old, right?"

"Yes. He has all the potential of being one of the greatest horses of the decade."

Rod Crawford laughed aloud. "I doubt if you're all that objective about your own colt."

"Obviously you've never seen him run," Tiffany replied with a slow-spreading grin. The tense air in the room dissolved, as she talked at length about Journey's End's impressive career.

"What about the recent string of death's in the foaling shed?" Rod asked when the conversation waned. Though Tiffany had been bracing herself for the question, she found no easy answer to it.

"Three foals died shortly after birth," she admitted.

"And you don't know why?" Skepticism edged Rod's question.

Tiffany shook her head. "So far the autopsies haven't shown anything conclusive, other than that the cause of death was heart failure."

Rod settled into his chair and poised his pencil theatrically in the air. "Were the foals related?"

Here it comes, Tiffany thought. "They had different dams, of course, but both colts and the filly were sired by Moon Shadow."

"And he stands at stud here, on the farm."

"Yes, although we're not breeding him...until all this is cleared up." Tiffany's hands were beginning to shake again, and she folded them carefully over the top of the desk.

"You think he might be the cause?"

"I don't know."

"Genetic problem?"

Tiffany pursed her lips and frowned thoughtfully. "I don't think so. He's stood for almost eight years, and until now he's proved himself a good sire. Devil's Gambit and Journey's End are proof of that."

"Moon Shadow was the sire of both stallions?"

"And many more. Some not as famous, but *all* perfectly healthy and strong horses."

"So, what with Journey's End's success, you must be getting a lot of requests for Moon Shadow's services."

"That's right. But we're turning them down, at least for a while, until we can prove that whatever is happening here is not a genetic problem."

"That must be costing you—"

"I think it's worth it."

"Then you must think he's the cause."

"I don't know what's the cause. It may just be coincidence."

Rod snorted his disbelief, and Tiffany had to press her hands together to keep from losing her temper. To Rod Crawford, Moon Shadow was just another story, but to Tiffany he was a proud stallion with an admirable reputation as a racehorse and a sire. She would do anything she had to—short of lying—to protect him and the reputation of the farm.

"Have you had him tested?" Rod asked.

"Moon Shadow?" When Rod nodded, Tiffany replied, "Of course. He's been given a complete physical, and we've taken samples of his semen to be analyzed."

"And?"

"So far, nothing."

Rod twirled his pencil nervously. "What about mares that were brought to Moon Shadow and then taken home?"

Tiffany felt a headache beginning to pound. "As far as I know, only the horses on this farm have been affected. However, it's still early in the year and there are several mares who haven't yet dropped their foals."

"Have you been in contact with the owners of the mares and explained the problem to them?"

"Mr. Crawford," Tiffany stated evenly, "I'm not certain there is a problem, or exactly the nature of it. I'm not an alarmist and I'm not about to warn other owners or scare them out of their wits. What I have done is written a letter inquiring as to the condition of the foals involved. I've had seven responses, and all of them indicate that they have beautiful, healthy horses. Two owners want to rebreed their mares to Moon Shadow."

Rod frowned. "And have you?"

"Not yet."

"Because you're afraid?"

"Because I want to be certain of what is happening before I do anything that might cause any stress or trauma to the horses or the owners." Tiffany looked him squarely in the eye. "This is more than a business for me; it's a way of life and there's more at stake than money." Rod's blank stare told Tiffany that he didn't understand anything she was saying. Perhaps no one did. Rod Crawford, or anyone else for that matter, couldn't know about the agonizing years she had spent growing up in musty tack rooms and dingy stables where the smell of ammonia had been so strong it had made her retch. No one knew that the only comfort she had found as an adolescent child was in working with the Thoroughbreds her father had been hired to train.

Before her thoughts became too vivid and painful, Tiffany spread her hands expressively over the desk and forced a frail smile at the reporter. "Look, until I know for certain what exactly it is that's happening, I'm not about to make any rash statements, and I would appreciate your cooperation—"

Rod raised a dubious blond brow. "By withholding the story?"

"By not sensationalizing the deaths and *creating* a story. I agreed to this interview because I know of the *Clarion*'s reputation."

"I have to report the truth."

Tiffany smiled stiffly. "That's all I can ask for. Now, if you have any further questions about the horses involved, you can call Vance Geddes, the veterinarian who was with the mares when they delivered the foals."

"Fair enough," Rod replied.

Tiffany led the reporter and his assistant through the broodmare barn and the foaling shed, before returning outside to the brisk March air. While Rod asked questions, Jeanette took some outside shots of a field where mares grazed and spindly-legged foals ran in the shafts of late-morning sunlight.

Tiffany's face lifted with pride as she watched the dark foals run and shy behind the safety of their mothers' flanks. The newborns always held a special place in her heart. She loved to watch them stand and nurse for the first time, or run in the fields with their downy ears pricked forward and their intelligent eyes wide to the vast new world. Maybe that was why the deaths of the foals affected her so deeply.

"I'll send you a copy of the article," Rod promised just before he and Jeanette left.

"Thank you." Tiffany watched in relief as the sporty Mazda headed out the long drive. The interview hadn't been as bad as she had expected, but nonetheless, she felt drained from the ordeal.

After changing into comfortable jeans and a sweatshirt, Tiffany returned to the den and pulled out the checkbook. But before she could concentrate on the ledgers she let her eyes wander to the portrait of Devil's Gambit, the horse that Zane Sheridan insisted was alive.

"It can't be," she murmured to herself. Devil's Gambit had been a beautifully built colt with a short, sturdy back, and powerful hind legs that could explode into a full stride of uncanny speed and grace. Jet-black, with one distinctive white stocking, Devil's Gambit had taken the racing world by storm, winning all of his two-year-old starts by ever-increasing margins. As a three-year-old his career had taken off with a flourish, and he had been compared to such greats as Secretariat and Seattle Slew.

Then, a month before the Kentucky Derby, it had all ended tragically. Devil's Gambit suffered a horrible death while being transported from Florida to Kentucky.

Tiffany had learned that Ellery had been driving and had apparently fallen asleep at the wheel. Dustin, his brother, had been a passenger in the truck. Miraculously, Dustin had survived with only minor injuries, by being thrown out of the cab as the truck tumbled end over end down an embankment, where it exploded into flames that charred beyond recognition the bodies of Ellery Rhodes and his fleet horse. Dustin's injuries had included a broken leg and minor concussion, which were treated at a local hospital. He had been out of the hospital in time to stand by Tiffany's side at Ellery's funeral.

Tiffany swallowed against the painful memory and shook her head. It had taken her several months to come to accept the death of her husband and his brave horse. And now a total stranger, a man by the name of Zane Sheridan, was trying to make her believe that it had all been a treacherous mistake.

But he didn't state that Ellery was alive, she reminded herself with a defeated smile, only Devil's Gambit. And when Zane had mentioned Ellery, it had been with a look of barely veiled contempt on his rugged black-Irish features.

What can it all mean? She slanted a glance at the portrait of Devil's Gambit and frowned. How could someone hide a horse of such renown? And who could have come up with such a scheme? And why? Certainly not for kidnapping ransom. *Get hold of yourself,* she cautioned, *you're letting your imagination run away with you, all because of some stranger's outlandish remarks.*

With a grimace she turned her attention back to the checkbook and finished paying the month-end bills. She wasn't exactly strapped for money, but each month her assets seemed to diminish. There was still a large, outstanding mortgage against the property, and several major repairs to the barns couldn't be neglected much longer.

If she regretted anything, it was allowing Ellery to build the expensive house. "You can't be a horse breeder unless you look the part," he had said with the confidence of one who understands the subtleties in life. "No one will bring their mares here if we don't *look* like we know what we're doing."

"It's not the house that counts, it's the quality of the stallions and the care of the horses," Tiffany had argued uselessly. In the end, Ellery had gotten his way. After all, it had only taken a quick signature at the bank—his signature—to get the loan to rebuild the house into a grand, Southern manor.

"This is California, not Kentucky," she had reminded him. "No one cares about this sort of thing." But her protests had fallen on deaf ears and Ellery had taken up wearing suits with patches on the sleeves and smoking a pipe filled with blended tobaccos.

The house was finished only six months before the accident. Since that time she had lived in it alone. It was beautiful and grand and mortgaged to the hilt. Ellery hadn't seen fit to purchase mortgage insurance at the time he took out the loan. "Money down the drain," he had commented with a knowing smile.

"I must have been out of my mind to have listened to him," Tiffany thought aloud as she pushed the ledgers aside and stood. How many years had she blindly trusted him, all because he had saved her life? She shuddered when she remembered the time she had seen Ellery, his face contorted in fear, as he dived in front of the oncoming car and pushed her out of its path.

Maybe it had been gratitude rather than love that she had felt for him, but nonetheless they had been married and she had depended upon him. *And now there was a chance that he was still alive.* The thought made her heart race unevenly.

After grabbing her jacket, she sank her teeth into her lower lip, walked outside and turned toward the broodmare barn. A chilly wind was blowing from the west and she had to hold her hair away from her face to keep it from whipping across her eyes. Mac was leaning over the railing of one of the stalls in the barn. His sharp eyes turned in her direction when she approached.

"I was just about to come up to the house," he stated, a worried expression pinching his grizzled features.

"Something wrong?"

"No...but it looks like this lady here—" he cocked his head in the direction of the black mare restlessly pacing her stall "—is gonna foal tonight."

Instead of the usual expectation Tiffany always felt at the prospect of new life, she now experienced dread. The mare in question, Ebony Wine, was carrying another of Moon Shadow's foals.

"You're sure?" she asked, surveying the mare's wide girth.

"Aye. She's a week overdue as it is, and look." He pointed a bony finger at the mare's full udder. "She's waxed over and beginning to drip."

"Has she starting sweating?"

"Not yet. It will be a while—sometime after midnight unless I miss my guess."

"But everything else looks normal?" Tiffany asked, her knowing gaze studying the restless horse.

"So far."

"Let me know when the time comes," Tiffany ordered, patting the mare fondly.

"You're not going to wait up again?"

"Of course I am."

Mac took off his hat and dangled it from his fingers as he leaned on the railing of the stall. "There's nothing you can do, you know. What will be, will be."

"You can't talk me out of this. I'll give Vance a call and ask him to come over." She took one last glance at the heavy-bellied mare. "Come up to the house and get me if anything goes wrong, or if it looks like the foal will be early."

Mac nodded curtly and placed his frumpy fedora back on his head. "You're the boss," he muttered, placing his hands in the back pockets of his trousers. "I'll be in the tack room if ya need me."

"Thanks, Mac." Tiffany walked outside but didn't return to the house. Instead, she let herself through a series of gates and walked through the gently sloping paddocks away from the main buildings.

When she neared the old barn, she halted and studied the graying structure. Once the barn had been integral to the farm, but the vacant building hadn't been used for years. Ellery had insisted that the horses needed newer, more modern facilities, and rather than put money into modernizing the old barn, he had erected the new broodmare barn and foaling shed.

The weathered building with the sagging roof was little more than an eyesore, and Tiffany realized that she should have had it torn down years before. Its only function was to store excess hay and straw through the winter.

She walked toward the barn and ignored the fact that blackberry vines were beginning to ramble and cling to the east wall. The old door creaked on rusty rollers as she pushed it aside and walked into the musty interior.

It took a few minutes for her eyes to adjust to the dim light. How many years had it been since she had first seen Ellery? She had been standing near the stalls, making sure that the horses had fresh water when he had startled her.

Before that fateful day, she had seen him only from a distance. After all, she was only a trainer's daughter. A nobody. Tiffany doubted that Ellery Rhodes realized that when he hired Edward Chappel, he took on Edward's eighteen-year-old daughter as well.

Perhaps her mistake had been to stay with her father, but Edward Chappel was the only family she had known. Her mother, Marie, had abandoned them both when Tiffany was only five. She could remember little of Marie except that she had thick, golden hair and a beautiful but weary face that very rarely smiled.

Fragments of life with her mother had come to mind over the years. Tiffany remembered that Marie insisted that her daughter's hair always be combed and that her faded clothes always be neatly starched. And there was a tune...a sad refrain that Marie would sing when she helped Tiffany get dressed in the morning. Twenty years later, Tiffany would still find herself humming that tune.

The day that her mother had walked out of her life was still etched vividly in her mind. "You must remember that Mommy loves you very much and I'll come back for you," Marie had whispered to Tiffany, with tears gathering in her round, indigo eyes. "I promise, pumpkin." Then Marie had gathered her daughter close to her breast, as if she couldn't bear to walk out the door.

Tiffany had felt the warm trickle of her mother's tears as they silently dropped onto the crown of her head.

"Mommy, don't leave me. *Please....* Mommy, Mommy, don't go. I'll be good...Mommy, I love you, please..." Tiffany had wailed, throwing her arms around her mother's neck and then sobbing with all of her heart for hours after Marie's car had disappeared in a plume of dust.

Her father's face was stern, his shoulders bowed. "Don't blame her, Tiffy," he had whispered hoarsely, "it's all my fault, you know. I haven't been much of a husband."

Tiffany had never seen Marie Caldwell Chappel again.

At first she couldn't believe that her mother had left her, and each night she would stare out the window and pray that the tall man with the big car would bring her mother home. Later, in her early teens, Tiffany was angry that she didn't have a mother to help her understand the changes in her body and the new emotions taking hold of her. Now, as an adult, Tiffany understood that a woman who had been brought up with a taste for the finer things in life could never have been happy with Edward Chappel.

Edward had always been irresponsible, going from job to job, breeding farm to breeding farm, working with the animals he loved. But each time, just when Tiffany thought they had settled down for good and she had made one or two friends in the local school, he would lose his job and they would move on to a new town, a new school, a new set of classmates who would rather ignore than accept her. To this day, she had never made any close friends. She had learned long ago that relationships were fragile and never lasted for any length of time.

After Marie had left him, Edward had sworn off the bottle for nearly three years. Tiffany now realized that his abstinence was because of the hope that Marie would return to him rather than because of his new responsibility as a single parent.

When she was just eighteen and trying to save enough money to go to college, they'd moved to the Rhodes Farm. Edward was off the bottle again and he had promised his daughter that this time he would make good.

It was in this very barn that her life had changed. While she'd been softly talking to one of the yearlings, Ellery Rhodes had walked in on her.

"Who are you?" he'd asked imperiously, and Tiffany had frozen. When she'd turned to face him, the look on his even features was near shock.

"I'm Tiffany Chappel," she had replied, with a faltering smile.

"Ed's daughter?"

"Yes."

Ellery had been flustered. "I thought that you were just a little girl." His eyes moved from her face, down the length of her body and back again. An embarrassed flush crept up his neck. "Obviously, I was mistaken."

"Dad seems to think that I'm still about eleven," she explained with a shrug and turned back to the horses.

"How old are you?"

"Eighteen."

"Why aren't you out on your own?" It was a nosy question, but Ellery asked it with genuine concern in his gold eyes. His brows had pulled together and a thoughtful frown pulled at the corners of his mouth. For a moment Tiffany thought that he might fire her father because of her. Maybe

Ellery Rhodes didn't like the idea of a girl—young woman—on his farm. Maybe one of the grooms had complained about a woman on the farm. She had already had more than her share of male advances from the stable boys.

Tiffany couldn't explain to her father's employer that she had to look after him, or that a good share of his work was done by her strong hands. Edward Chappel would be fired again. Instead she lied. "I'm only helping him out for a little while. Until I go back to college—"

Ellery's practiced eyes took in her torn sweatshirt, faded jeans and oversized boots. Tiffany knew that he saw through her lie, but he was too much of a gentleman to call her on it.

Two days later she was called into his office. Her heart pounded with dread as she entered the old farmhouse and sat stiffly in one of the chairs near his desk.

Ellery looked up from a stack of bills he had been paying. "I've got a proposition for you, young lady," he stated, looking up at her and his gold eyes shining. "Your father has already approved."

"What do you mean?"

Ellery smiled kindly. It wasn't a warm smile, but it was caring. He explained that he had worked out a deal with her father. He liked the way she handled the horses, he claimed, and he offered to send her to school, if she promised to return to the farm and work off the amount of money her education would cost once she had graduated.

Tiffany had been ecstatic with her good fortune, and Edward, feeling that he had finally found a way to rightfully provide for his daughter, was as pleased as anyone.

She had never forgotten Ellery's kindness to her, and she had held up her part of the bargain. When she returned to the farm four years later, she found that her father was drinking again.

"You've got to leave," he said, coughing violently. The stench of cheap whiskey filled the air in the small room he had been living in on the farm.

"I can't, Dad. I've got a debt to pay."

Edward shivered, though he was covered by several thick blankets. "You should never have come back."

"Why didn't anyone tell me you were sick—"

Edward raised a feeble hand and waved away her concerns. "It wouldn't help anything now, would it? You were so close to finishing school, I didn't want you to know."

"I think you should be in a hospital."

Edward shook his head and another fit of racking coughs took hold of him. "I want you to leave. I've got a little money. Get away from this farm, from Ellery Rhodes—"

"But he's been so good to me."

Her father's faded blue eyes closed for a second. "He's changed, Tiff...." Another fit of coughing took hold of him, and he doubled up in pain.

"I'm getting you to a hospital, right now."

Despite her father's protests, Tiffany managed to get him out of the stifling room and to the main house. When she knocked on the door, Stasia, the exotic-looking woman Ellery was living with, answered the door.

"My father needs help," Tiffany said.

Stasia's full lips pulled into a line of disgust at the sight of Tiffany and her father. Her dark eyes traveled over Tiffany, and she tossed her hair off her shoulders. "He needs to dry out—"

"He's sick."

"Hmmph."

Pulling herself to her full height, Tiffany looked the older woman directly in the eye. "Please. Call Ellery."

"He's not here."

"Then find someone to help me."

Edward's coughing started again. His shoulders racked from the pain. "I don't know why Ellery keeps him around," Stasia muttered, as she reached for her coat and begrudgingly offered to drive them into town.

Tiffany remained at her father's side for two days until the pneumonia that had settled in his lungs took his life.

"You stupid, lovable old fool," Tiffany had said, tears running down her face. "Why did you kill yourself—why?" she asked, as her father's body was moved from the hospital room to the morgue.

Refusing help from the hospital staff, Tiffany had run out of the building, blinded by tears of grief and guilt. If she hadn't gone away to school, if she had stayed on the farm, her father would still have been alive.

She didn't see the oncoming car as she crossed the street. She heard the blast from an angry horn, smelled the burn of rubber as tires screamed against the dry asphalt and felt a man's body push her out of the way of the station wagon.

The man who had saved her life was Ellery. He'd gathered her shaken form into his arms and muttered something about being sorry. She didn't understand why, and she didn't care. Ellery Rhodes was the only person she had ever known who had been kind to her with no ulterior motives.

Within two weeks, Stasia was gone and Ellery asked Tiffany to marry him.

Tiffany didn't hesitate. Ellery Rhodes was the first person she had met that she could depend on. He cared for her, and though he seemed distant at times, Tiffany realized that no relationship was perfect.

She wondered now if she had married him out of gratitude or grief. The love she had hoped would bloom within her had never surfaced, but she supposed that was because passionate, emotional love only existed in fairy tales.

Inexplicably, her thoughts returned to Zane Sheridan, with his knowing gray eyes and ruggedly hewn features. He was the last person she needed to complicate her life right now, and the idea that he could shed any light on what had happened to Devil's Gambit or Ellery was preposterous.

But what if there's a chance that Ellery's alive?

Without any answers to her questions, Tiffany headed back to the house to remind Louise that there would be a guest for dinner.

"You're asking the impossible!" John Morris stated as he eyed his client over the clear rims of his reading glasses.

"It's a simple document," Zane argued, rubbing the back of his neck and rotating his head to relieve the tension that had been building ever since he had met Tiffany Rhodes. He'd known she was beautiful; he'd seen enough pictures of her to understand that her exotic looks could be any man's undoing. But he hadn't counted on the light of intrigue and mystery in her intense gaze or the serene beauty in the curve of her neck....

"A deed of sale for a breeding farm? You've got to be joking."

Zane's eyes flashed like quicksilver. He pulled at the bothersome knot in his tie and focused his eyes on the attorney. "Just get me a paper that says that for a certain amount of money—and leave that blank—I will purchase all of the assets and the liabilities of Rhodes Breeding Farm."

The lawyer let out a weary sigh. "You're out of your mind, Zane. That is if you want anything legal—"

"I want it to be binding. No loopholes. It has to be so tight that if the buyer decides she wants out of the deal, she has no legal recourse. None whatsoever." His square jaw tightened, and the thin lines near the corners of his eyes deepened with fresh resolve. Revenge was supposed to be sweet. So where was the satisfaction he had been savoring for nearly six years?

"You're asking the impossible. We're not talking about a used car, for God's sake."

"It can't be that difficult." Zane paced in the prestigious San Francisco lawyer's office and ran impatient fingers through his raven-black hair in disgust. "What about a quitclaim deed?"

The lawyer leaned back in his chair and held on to his pen with both hands. "I assume that you want to do this right."

"Of course."

"No legal recourse—right?"

"I already told you that."

"Then be patient. I'll draw up all the legal documents and do a title search...take care of all the loose ends. That way, once you've agreed upon a price, you can wrap it up and it *will* be binding. You can't have it both ways, not here anyway. You're not just talking about real estate, you know. There is personal property, equipment, the horses...."

"I get the picture." Zane stared out the window and frowned. The trouble was he wanted to get away from Tiffany Rhodes. Do what he had to do and then make a clean break.

There was something about the woman that got under his skin, and he didn't like the look of honesty in her slate-blue eyes. It bothered him. A lot. Whatever else he had expected of Ellery Rhodes's widow, it hadn't been integrity.

Zane shrugged as if to shake off the last twinges of guilt. "So how long will it take you?" he asked, hiding some of his impatience.

"Four weeks—maybe three, if we're lucky. I'll work out something temporary for the interim. Okay?"

"I guess it will have to be. Doesn't seem that I have much of a choice."

John drummed his fingers on the desk. "You're sure that this woman wants to sell? I've read a little about her; she seems to be...the plucky type. Not the kind to sell out."

"She just needs a little convincing."

John scowled at the blank piece of paper in front of him. "That sounds ominous—right out of a bad B movie."

Zane smiled despite his discomfiture. It was a rare smile, but genuine, and he flashed it on his friend in a moment of self-mockery. "I guess you're right."

"Aren't I always?"

"And humble, too," Zane muttered under his breath. "Come on, counselor, I'll buy you a drink."

"On one condition—"

Zane's brows quirked expectantly.

"That you quit calling me counselor. I hear enough of that in the courtroom."

"It's a deal."

John slipped his arms into his jacket and then straightened the cuffs before bending over his desk and pressing a button on the intercom. "Sherry, I'm going out for a few minutes with Mr. Sheridan. I'll be back at—" he cocked his wrist and checked his watch "—three-thirty."

John reached for the handle of the door before pausing and turning to face his friend. "There's just one thing I'd like to know about this transaction you requested."

"And that is?"

"Why the hell do you want to buy a breeding farm? I thought you learned your lesson in Dublin a few years back."

Zane's eyes grew dark. "Maybe that's exactly why I want it." With a secretive smile he slapped his friend fondly on the back. "Now, how about that drink?"

Chapter Three

Tiffany's fingers drummed restlessly on the desk as she stared at the portrait of Devil's Gambit. For so long she had believed that Ellery and his proud horse were dead. And now this man, this stranger named Zane Sheridan, insisted just the opposite. Her blue eyes were shadowed with pain as she studied the portrait of the horse. *Was it possible? Could Ellery still be alive?*

Shaking her head at the absurdity of the situation, she got up and paced restlessly, alternately staring at the clock and looking out the window toward the foaling shed. Ebony Wine would be delivering a foal tonight, Moon Shadow's foal. Would he be a normal, healthy colt or would he suffer the same cruel fate as three of his siblings?

She listened as the clock ticked off the seconds, and her stomach tightened into uneasy knots. Mac hadn't come to the house this afternoon, and Tiffany was beginning to worry. Between her anxiety for the unborn foal and worries about Zane Sheridan and his motives for visiting her, Tiffany's nerves felt raw, stretched to the breaking point.

Seven-thirty-five. Though Zane would arrive any minute, Tiffany couldn't sit idle any longer. She jerked her jacket off the wooden peg near the French doors and hurried outside, oblivious to the fact that her heels sank into the mud of the well-worn path. The darkness of the night was punctuated by the sharp wind that rattled the windowpanes and whistled through the redwoods.

Tiffany found Mac in the broodmare barn, examining the black mare. His face was grim, and Tiffany's heart nearly stopped beating.

"How's it going?" she asked, hoping that she didn't sound desperate.

Mac came to the outside of the stall and reached down to scratch Wolverine, the farm's border collie, behind the ears. Wolverine thumped his tail against the concrete floor in appreciation, but Tiffany had the impression that Mac was avoiding her gaze.

"So far so good," the ex-jockey replied, straightening and switching a piece of straw from one side of his mouth to the other. But his sharp brown eyes were troubled when they returned to Ebony Wine. The mare shifted uncomfortably in the large stall, and Tiffany noted that everything was ready for the impending birth. Six inches of clean straw covered the concrete floor, and a plastic bucket containing towels, antibiotics, scissors and other equipment necessary to help the mare give birth, had been placed near the stall.

"Might be a little earlier than I thought originally," Mac suggested. He took off his hat and straightened the crease with his fingers.

"Why?"

"This is her second foal. If I remember right, the last one came before midnight." He rammed the hat back on his head. "Could be wrong...just a feeling I've got."

"Have you called Vance?"

Mac nodded curtly. "He'll be here around eleven, earlier if we need him."

"Good."

Tiffany cast one final look toward the mare and then returned to the house. Wolverine padded along behind her, but she didn't notice. Her thoughts were filled with worry for the mare and anxiety about meeting Zane Sheridan again. He couldn't have picked a worse time to show up.

All afternoon her thoughts had been crowded with questions about him. Who was he? What did he want? How did he know Ellery? Why would he concoct such an elaborate story about Devil's Gambit being alive?

There was something about the man that was eerily familiar, and Tiffany felt that she had heard Ellery speak of him at least once. But it was long ago, before they were married, and she couldn't remember the significance, if there was any, of Ellery's remarks.

She had just returned to the house and stepped out of her muddied shoes when headlights flashed through the interior of the manor as if announcing Zane's arrival. "Here we go," she muttered to herself as she slipped on a pair of pumps and attempted to push back the tides of dread threatening to overtake her. "He's only one man," she told herself as the doorbell chimed. "One man with a wild imagination."

But when she opened the door and she saw him standing in the shadowy porch light, once again she experienced the feeling that Zane Sheridan rarely made mistakes. He was leaning casually against one of the tall pillars supporting the porch roof, and his hands were thrust into the front pockets of his corduroy slacks. Even in the relaxed pose, there was tension, strain in the way his smile tightened over his teeth, a coiled energy lying just beneath the surface in his eyes.

In the dim light, his mouth appeared more sensual than she had remembered and the rough angles of his face seemed

less threatening. His jet-black hair was without a trace of
gray and gleamed blue in the lamplight. Only his eyes gave
away his age. Though still a sharp, intense silver, they were
hard, as if they had witnessed years of bitterness. The skin
near the corners of his eyes was etched with a faint webbing
that suggested he had stared often into the glare of the
afternoon sun.

"Sorry I'm late," he said, straightening as his bold gaze
held hers.

"No problem," she returned and wondered what it was
about him that she found so attractive. She'd never been a
woman drawn to handsome faces or strong physiques. But
there was an intelligence in Zane's eyes, hidden beneath a
thin veneer of pride, that beckoned the woman in her. It was
frightening. "Please come in."

I can't be attracted to him, she thought. *He can't be
trusted. God only knows what he wants from me.*

He walked with her to the den. "I'm sorry for the inter-
ruption this morning—" she began.

"My fault. I should have called." A flash of a brilliant
smile gleamed against his dark skin.

Tiffany didn't bother to wave off his apology. Zane's
surprise appearance on her doorstep had thrown her day
into a tailspin. It had been a wonder that she could even
converse intelligently with the reporter from the *Santa Rosa
Clarion* considering the bombshell that this man had
dropped in her lap.

"Could I get you a drink?" she inquired as she walked
toward a well-stocked bar disguised in the bookcase behind
her desk. Ellery had insisted on the most modern of con-
veniences, the bar being one of his favorites. Tiffany hadn't
used it more than twice since her husband's death.

"Scotch, if you have it."

She had it all right. That and about every other liquor
imaginable. "You never can guess what a man might
drink," Ellery had explained with a knowing wink. "Got to

be prepared...just in case. I wouldn't want to blow a potential stud fee all because I didn't have a bottle of liquor around.'' Ellery had laughed, as if his response to her inquiry were a joke. But he had filled the bar with over thirty bottles of the most expensive liquor money could buy. ''Think of it as a tax deduction,'' he had joked.

''Oh, I'm sure I've got Scotch,'' she answered Zane. ''It's just a matter of locating it.'' After examining a few of the unfamiliar labels, Tiffany wiped away some of the dust that had collected on the unused bottles. *What a waste.*

It didn't take long to find an opened bottle of Scotch. She splashed the amber liquor into a glass filled with ice cubes and then, with a forced smile, she handed Zane the drink. ''Now,'' she said, her voice surprisingly calm, ''why don't you tell me why you think Devil's Gambit is alive?''

After pouring herself a glass of wine, she took an experimental sip and watched Zane over the rim of her glass. ''That is, if you haven't changed your mind since this morning.''

A gray light of challenge flashed in his eyes and his facade of friendly charm faded slightly. ''Nothing's changed.''

''So you still think that the horse is alive...and you're still interested in buying the farm, right?''

''That's correct.''

Tiffany let out a ragged sigh and took a chair near the desk. ''Please, have a seat.''

Zane was too restless to sit. He walked over to the window and stared into the black, starless night. ''I didn't mean to shock you this morning.'' Why the hell was he apologizing? He owed this woman nothing more than a quick explanation, and even that stuck in his throat. But there was something intriguing about her—a feminine mystique that touched a black part of his soul. Damn it all, this meeting was starting off all wrong. Ellery Rhodes's widow turned his thinking around. When he was with her, he started forgetting his objectives.

"Well, you did."

"Like I said—I should have called to make sure that we would have some time to talk."

Tiffany shifted uneasily in the chair. "We have all night," she said, and when a flicker of interest sparked in his eyes she quickly amended her statement. "Or however long it takes to straighten out this mess. Why don't you explain yourself?"

"I told you; I have reason to believe that Devil's Gambit is alive."

Tiffany smiled and shook her head. "That's impossible. I...I was at the scene of the accident. The horse was killed."

Zane frowned into the night. "*A* horse was killed."

"Devil's Gambit was the only horse in the trailer. The other two horses that had been stabled in Florida were in another truck—the one that Mac was driving. They were already in Kentucky when the accident occurred." She ran trembling fingers through her hair as she remembered that black, tragic night. Once again she thought about the terror and pain that Ellery and his horse must have gone through in those last agonizing moments before death mercifully took them both. "Devil's Gambit died in the accident." Her voice was low from the strain of old emotions, and she had to fight against the tears threatening her eyes.

"Unless he was never in that truck in the first place."

Tiffany swallowed with difficulty. "What are you suggesting, Mr. Sheridan?"

"I think that Devil's Gambit was kidnapped."

"That's crazy. My husband—"

Zane's eyes flashed silver fire. "Was probably involved."

Tiffany stood on trembling legs, her hands flattened on the desk to support her. A quiet rage began to burn in her chest. "This conversation is absurd. Why would Ellery steal his own horse?"

Zane shrugged. "Money? Wasn't Devil's Gambit insured?"

"Not to his full value. After he won in Florida, we intended to increase the coverage, as he proved himself much more valuable than anyone had guessed. I had all the forms filled out, but before I could send them back to the insurance company as Ellery had suggested, I had to wait until I saw him again. Several of the documents required his signature." She shook her head at her own foolishness. "Why am I telling you all of this?" After releasing a weary sigh, she rapped her knuckles on the polished desk and clasped her hands behind her back.

"Because I'm telling you the truth."

"You think."

"I know."

Tiffany's emotions were running a savage gauntlet of anger and fear, but she attempted to keep her voice steady. "How do you know?"

"I saw your horse."

She sucked in her breath. "You saw Devil's Gambit? That's impossible. If he were alive, someone would have told me—"

"Someone is."

There was a charged silence in the air. "It's been four years since the accident. Why now?"

"Because I wasn't sure before."

Tiffany shook her head in denial, and her honey-colored hair brushed her shoulders. "This is too crazy—where did you see the horse? And how did you know it was Devil's Gambit? And what horse was killed in the trailer—and...and...what about my husband?" she whispered. "His brother Dustin was with him. Dustin knows what happened."

"Dustin claimed to be sleeping."

Tiffany flinched. How did this man, this virtual stranger, know so much about her and what had happened that night? If only she could remember what Ellery had said about Zane Sheridan. Ellery had spent some time in Ireland—Dublin. Maybe that was the connection. Zane still spoke with a slight brogue. Ellery must have known Zane in Dublin, and that's why he was here. Something happened in Ireland, years ago. Any other reason was just a fabrication, an excuse.

"Dustin would have woken up if the truck was stopped and the horses were switched. Dear God, do you know what you're suggesting?" Tiffany took a calming swallow of her wine and began to pace in front of the desk. Her thoughts were scattered between Zane, the tragic past and the tense drama unfolding in the foaling shed. "Ellery would never have been involved in anything so underhanded."

"Didn't you ever question what happened?" Zane asked suddenly.

"Of course, but—"

"Didn't you think it was odd that Dustin had taken sleeping pills? Wasn't he supposed to drive later in the night—switch off with Ellery so that they wouldn't have to stop?"

Tiffany was immediately defensive. "Dustin's an insomniac. He needed the rest before the Derby."

"The Derby was weeks away."

"But there was a lot of work—"

"And what about your husband? Why did he decide to drive that night? Wasn't that out of the ordinary?" Bitterness tightened Zane's features, and he clutched his drink in a death grip.

"He was excited—he wanted to be a part of it." But even to her, the words sounded false. Ellery had always believed in letting the hired help handle the horses. Before that night, he had always flown—first class—to the next racetrack.

Zane saw the doubts forming in her eyes. "Everything about that 'accident' seems phony to me."

"But there was an investigation—"

"Thorough?"

"I—I don't know.... I think so." At the time she had been drowning in her own grief and shock. She had listened to the police reports, viewed the brutal scene of the accident, visited Dustin in the hospital and flown home in a private fog of sorrow and disbelief. After the funeral, Dustin's strong arms and comforting words had helped her cope with her loss.

"Were Ellery's dental records checked?"

Tiffany's head snapped up, and her eyes were bright with righteous defiance. "Of course not. Ellery was driving. Dustin was there. There didn't need to be any further investigation." Her eyes narrowed a fraction, and her voice shook when she spoke again. "What are you suggesting, Mr. Sheridan? That my husband is still alive—hiding from me somewhere with his horse?"

Zane impaled her with his silvery stare and then ran impatient fingers through his hair. "I don't know."

A small sound of disbelief came from Tiffany's throat and she had to lean against the desk for support. "I—I don't know why I'm even listening to this," she whispered hoarsely. "It just doesn't make any sense. Devil's Gambit is worth a lot more as Devil's Gambit—in terms of dollars at the racetrack and stud fees. Anything you've suggested is absolutely beyond reason." She smiled grimly, as if at her own foolhardiness. "Look, I think maybe it would be better if you just left."

"I can't do that—not yet."

"Why not?"

"Because I intend to convince you that your horse was stolen from you."

"That's impossible."

"Maybe not." Zane extracted a small manila envelope from his breast pocket and walked back to the desk. "There are some pictures in here that might change your mind." He handed Tiffany the envelope, and she accepted it with a long sigh.

There were three photographs, all of the same horse. Tiffany scanned the color prints of a running horse closely, studying the bone structure and carriage of the animal. The similarities between the horse in the photograph and Devil's Gambit were uncanny. "Where did you get these?" she asked, her breath constricting in her throat.

"I took them. Outside of Dublin."

It made sense. The horse, if he really was Devil's Gambit, would have to be hidden out of the country to ensure that no one would recognize or identify him. Even so, Zane's story was ludicrous. "This isn't Devil's Gambit," she said, her slate-blue eyes questioning his. "This horse has no white marks...anywhere." She pointed to the portrait above the fireplace. "Devil's Gambit had a stocking, on his right foreleg."

"I think the stocking has been dyed."

"To hide his identity?"

"And to palm him off as another horse, one of considerably less caliber."

"This is ridiculous." Tiffany rolled her eyes and raised her hands theatrically in the air. "You know, you almost convinced me by coming in here and making outlandish statements that I nearly believed. Heaven knows why. Maybe it's because you seemed so sure of yourself. But I can tell you without a doubt that this is not Devil's Gambit." She shook the prints in the air before tossing them recklessly on the desk. "Nothing you've said tonight makes any sense, nor is it backed up with the tiniest shred of evidence. Therefore I have to assume that you're here for another reason, such as the sale of the farm. My position hasn't altered on that subject, either. So you see, Mr. Sheridan, any further discussion would be pointless."

Louise knocked softly on the door of the den before poking her head inside. "Dinner's ready." She eyed Tiffany expectantly.

"I don't think—"

"Good. I'm starved," Zane stated as he turned his head in the housekeeper's direction. A slow-spreading, damnably charming grin took possession of his handsome face. Gray eyes twinkled devilishly, and his brilliant smile exposed a dimple on one tanned cheek.

"Whenever you're ready," Louise replied, seemingly oblivious to the tension in the room and returning Zane's smile. "I have to be getting home," she said apologetically to Tiffany, who nodded in response. Louise slowly backed out of the room and closed the door behind her.

"I didn't think you'd want to stay," Tiffany remarked, once Louise had left them alone.

"And miss a home-cooked meal? Not on your life."

Tiffany eyed him dubiously. "Something tells me this has nothing to do with the meal."

"Maybe I'm just enjoying the company—"

"Or maybe you think you can wear me down and I'll start believing all this nonsense."

"Maybe."

"There's no point, you know."

Zane laughed aloud, and the bitterness in his gaze disappeared for a second. "Try me."

"But we have nothing more to discuss. Really. I'm not buying your story. Not any of it."

"You're not even trying."

"I have the distinct feeling that you're attempting to con me, Mr. Sheridan—"

"Zane."

"Whatever. And I'm not up to playing games. Whether you believe it or not, I'm a busy woman who has more important things to do than worry about what could have happened. I like to think I deal in reality rather than fantasy."

Zane finished his drink with a flourish and set the empty glass down on the corner of the desk. "Then you'd better start listening to me, damn it. Because I'm not here on some cock and bull story." His thick brows lifted. "I have better things to do than spend my time trying to help someone who obviously doesn't want it."

"Help?" Tiffany repeated with a laugh. "All you've done so far is offer me vague insinuations and a few photographs of a horse that definitely is *not* Devil's Gambit. You call that help?"

Zane pinched the bridge of his nose, closed his eyes and let out a long breath. "If you weren't so blind, woman," he said, his black-Irish temper starting to explode.

"Look—"

Zane held up one palm and shrugged. "Maybe you just need time to think about all of this."

"What I don't need is someone to march into my life and start spewing irrational statements."

Zane smiled, and the tension drained from his face to be replaced by genuine awe of the woman standing near the desk. In the past six years, he'd imagined coming face to face with Ellery Rhodes's widow more often than he would like to admit, but never had he thought that she would be so incredibly bewitching. His mistake. Once before Ellery Rhodes and Zane Sheridan had been attracted to the same woman, and that time Zane had come out the loser, or so he had thought at the time. Now he wasn't so sure.

"Come on," he suggested, his voice becoming dangerously familiar. "I wasn't kidding when I said I was starved."

Tiffany backed down a little. "I won't change my mind."

With a nonchalant shrug, Zane loosened the knot of his tie and unbuttoned the collar of his shirt. His chin was beginning to darken with the shadow of a day's growth of beard, and he looked as if he belonged in this house, as if he

had just come home from a long, tiring day at the office to
share conversation and a drink with his wife.... The unlikely turn of her thoughts spurred Tiffany into action. As
a slight blush darkened the skin of her throat, she opened
the door of the den. Knowing it to be an incredible mistake, she led Zane past a formal dining room to a small al-
cove near the kitchen.

Louise had already placed the beef stew with gravy on the
small round table.

"Sit," Tiffany commanded as she pulled out a bottle of
wine and uncorked it before pouring the rich Burgundy into
stemmed glasses. Zane did as he was bid, but his face reg-
istered mild surprise when Tiffany took the salads out of the
refrigerator and set them on the table.

After Tiffany sat down, Zane stared at her from across a
small maple table. "Your housekeeper doesn't live in?"

"No."

"But she manages to keep the place up?"

Tiffany released an uneasy laugh. "I'm not that messy. I
do pick up after myself, even do my own laundry and cook
occasionally," she teased. What must he think of her? That
she was some princess who wouldn't get her fingers dirty?
Did his preconceived notions stem from his relationship—
whatever that was—with Ellery? "Actually, Louise only
comes in twice a week. Today I asked her to come over because of the interview with Rod Crawford. I thought I might
need another pair of hands. But usually I can handle whatever comes up by myself."

"That surprises me," Zane admitted and took a sip of his
wine.

Tiffany arched her elegant dark brows. "Why?"

"Because of the house, I suppose. So formal."

"And here you are stuck in the kitchen, without the ben-
efit of seeing the crystal and silver," Tiffany said with a
chuckle. "Disappointed, Mr. Sheridan?"

His gray eyes drove into hers and his voice was low when he spoke. "Only that I can't persuade you to call me by my first name."

"I don't think I know you that well—"

"Yet." He raised his glass in mock salute and his flinty eyes captured hers. "Here's to an independent woman," he announced before taking another long drink.

She was more than a little embarrassed by the intimate toast, and after a few silent moments when she alternately sipped the wine and twirled the glass in her fingers, she decided she had to level with him. Against her wishes she was warming to him, and that had to stop. "Look, *Zane.* As far as I'm concerned, you're close enough to certifiably crazy that I doubt if I'll associate with you again," she said half-seriously as she poured them each another glass of wine and then began to attack her salad. "There's no reason for first names."

"I'm not crazy, **Ms.** Rhodes—"

"Tiffany." Gentle laughter sparkled in her eyes. "Just concerned, right?" Her smile faded and she became instantly serious. "Why? Why are you here, now, telling me all of this?"

"It took me this long to be sure."

"Then you'll understand why I'm having trouble accepting what you're suggesting as the truth. You've had four years to think about it. I just found out this morning."

Tiffany pushed her plate aside, crossed her arms over her chest and leveled serious blue eyes in his direction. "Let's quit beating around the bush," she suggested. "So what's in this for you? You don't impress me as the kind of man who would go traipsing halfway around the world just to set the record straight and see that justice is served."

"I'm not."

"I didn't think so."

"I have an interest in what happens here."

Dread began to hammer in her heart. "Which is?"

"Personal."

"What does that mean? A grudge—revenge—vendetta—what?" She leaned on one hand and pointed at him with the other. "This morning you said you knew Ellery. I got the impression then, and now again, that you didn't much like him." Her palm rotated in the air as she collected her scattered thoughts. "If you ask me, all this interest in my horse has to do with Ellery. What's the point, Mr. Sheridan? And why in the world would you want to buy this farm? There must be a dozen of them, much more profitable than this, for sale."

Zane set aside his fork and settled back in the chair. As he pondered the situation and the intelligent woman staring beguilingly at him, he tugged on his lower lip. "The reason I want this farm is because it should have been mine to begin with. That your husband got the capital to invest in this parcel of land was a...fluke."

"Come again," she suggested, not daring to breathe. What was he saying? "Ellery's family owned this land for years."

"I don't think so. The way I understand it, he was a tenant farmer until a few years ago. The two hundred thousand dollars that your husband put into this farm as a down payment—"

"Yes?" Tiffany asked.

"He stole it from me."

"Oh, dear God," Tiffany whispered, letting her head fall forward into her waiting hands. She didn't know whether to laugh or to cry. Obviously Zane thought he was telling the truth, and he didn't seem like a dangerous psychotic, but what he was saying was absolutely ridiculous. Ellery might have been many things, but Tiffany knew in her heart he wasn't a thief.

"I think it's time for you to leave, Mr. Sheridan," she said, her voice as cold as ice. "You've been saying some pretty wild things around here—things that could be construed as slander, and—''

Footsteps on the back porch interrupted her train of thought. Panic welled in Tiffany's mind and she snapped her head upward as the familiar boot steps drew near. Within a minute, Mac was standing in the kitchen, worrying the brim of his fedora in his fingers, his dark eyes impaling hers. ''You'd better come, Missy,'' he said, his voice uncommonly low.

''Ebony Wine?''

''Aye.''

''The foal is here?''

''Will be soon, and...'' His eyes shifted from Tiffany to Zane and back again. Tiffany's heart began to thud painfully in her chest. She could read the silent message in Mac's worried gaze.

''No...'' she whispered, pushing the chair back so hard that it scraped against the hardwood floor. Her fearful eyes darted to Zane. ''If you'll excuse me, we have an emergency on our hands.'' She noticed the glimmer of suspicion in Zane's eyes, but didn't bother to explain. Time was too imperative.

In seconds she was away from the table and racing toward the den. ''Have you called Vance?'' she called over her shoulder.

Mac pushed his hat onto his head and nodded. ''He's on his way. Damn, but I should have seen this coming. I'll meet you in the shed.''

Tiffany kicked off her pumps, pulled on a pair of boots and yanked her jacket off the wooden hook. Mindless of the fact that she was dressed in wool slacks, angora vest and silk blouse, she opened the French doors and raced into the dark night. She had taken only three breathless strides, when she felt the powerful hand on her arm, restraining her in its hard grasp.

"What's going on?" Zane demanded as Tiffany whirled to face the man thwarting her. Her hair tossed wildly around her face, and even in the darkness Zane could see the angry fire in her wide eyes. He hadn't been able to decipher the silent messages passing from Mac to Tiffany in the kitchen, but Zane knew that something horrible was taking place and that Tiffany felt she could do something about it.

Tiffany didn't have time to argue. She was trying to free herself. "A mare's gone into labor."

"And that upsets you?"

She jerked her arm free of his imprisoning grasp. "There might be complications. If you'll excuse me—" But he was right beside her, running the short distance from the house to the foaling shed with her, his strides long and easy.

With a sinking feeling, Tiffany realized that there was no way she could hide her secret from him any longer, and she really didn't care. The only thing that mattered was the mare in labor and the unborn colt.

Chapter Four

The soft overhead lights of the foaling shed were reflected in the sweat-darkened coat of Ebony Wine. As the mare paced restlessly in the stall, she alternately snorted in agitation and flattened her dark ears against her head in impatience.

Mac's arms were braced on the top rail of the gate to the foaling stall and his anxious brown eyes studied the horse. A matchstick worked convulsively in the corner of his mouth.

He spoke softly in quiet tones filled with years of understanding. "Simmer down, lady." His gravelly voice was barely audible as the distressed mare shifted under the intense pressure of an abdominal contraction.

Tiffany's heart was pounding more rapidly than her footsteps on the cold concrete floor as she walked rapidly down the length of the corridor to the foaling stall. The acrid smells of sweat and urine mingled with antiseptic in the whitewashed barn. One look at Mac's tense form told her that the birth of Ebony Wine's foal was going no better than he had expected.

Zane was at Tiffany's side, matching her short strides with his longer ones. His dark brows were drawn over his slate gray eyes. He kept his thoughts to himself as he tried to make head or tail of the tense situation. Something was very wrong here. He could feel it. Though it hadn't been stated, he had witnessed fear in Tiffany's incredible blue eyes when Mac had entered the kitchen and made the announcement that one of the mares had gone into labor. Zane had noticed something else in Tiffany's worried expression—determination and pride held her finely sculpted jaw taut but worry creased her flawless brow. A sense of desperation seemed to have settled heavily on her small shoulders.

"Has her water broken?" Tiffany asked as she approached Mac and leaned over the railing of the stall.

Mac shook his head and ran bony fingers over the stubble on his jaw. "Not yet."

Ebony Wine was moving restlessly in the stall. Her sleek body glistened with sweat, and her ears twitched warily.

"Come on, lady," Mac whispered softly, "don't be so stupid. Lie down, will ya?"

"She didn't get off her feet the last time," Tiffany reminded the trainer.

"She'd better this time," Mac grumbled, "or we'll lose this one, sure as I'm standing here." He shifted the matchstick from one side of his mouth to the other. "Moon Shadow's colts need all the help they can get. Come on, Ebony, be a good girl. Lie down."

"Moon Shadow?" Zane asked. "He's the sire?"

Mac's troubled gaze shifted from the horse to Tiffany in unspoken apology. "That he is."

Zane's eyes narrowed as he studied the anxious mare. "Where's the vet?"

"He was at another farm—said he'd be here on the double," Mac replied.

At that moment, Ebony Wine's water broke and the amniotic fluid began cascading down her black legs.

"Looks like he might be too late," Zane observed wryly.

Without asking any further questions, he rolled up his shirt sleeves, walked to a nearby basin and scrubbed his arms and hands with antiseptic.

"What're you doing?" Tiffany demanded.

His gaze was steady as he approached her. "I'm trying to help you. I've spent most of my life with horses and seen enough foals being born to realize when a mare's in trouble. This lady here—" he cocked his dark head in the direction of the anxious horse "—needs a hand."

Mac looked about to protest, but Tiffany shook her head to quiet him. "Let's get on with it."

Ebony Wine stiffened as Mac and Zane entered the stall. Her eyes rolled backward at the stranger. Mac went to Ebony Wine's head and talked to the horse. "Come on, Ebony, girl. Lie down, for Pete's sake."

Zane examined the horse and the bulging amniotic sac beginning to emerge below her tail. "We've got problems," he said with a dark frown. "Only a nose and one leg showing. Looks as if one leg has twisted back on itself."

"Damn!" Mac muttered. His hands never stopped their rhythmic stroking of Ebony Wine's head.

Tiffany felt her heart leap to her throat. Moon Shadow's foals were having enough trouble surviving, without the added problems of a complicated birth. Against the defeat slumping her shoulders, Tiffany forced her head upward to meet the cruel challenge fate had dealt the mare. Her vibrant blue eyes locked with Zane's. "What do you want me to do?"

"Help with supplies." He pointed in the direction of the clean pails, scissors and bottles of antiseptic. "We've got to get that foal out of there, and my guess is that this lady isn't going to want our help."

The sound of the door to the foaling shed creaking open caught her attention and brought Tiffany's head around. Vance Geddes, his round face a study in frustration, let the door swing shut and hurried down the corridor to Ebony Wine's stall.

He took one look at the horse and turned toward the basin. "How long has she been at it?" he asked, quickly washing his hands.

"Over half an hour," Mac replied.

"And she won't lie down?"

"Not this one. Stubborn, she is."

"Aren't they all?" Vance's gaze clashed with the stranger attending to Ebony Wine. Zane responded to the unspoken question. "Zane Sheridan."

"'Evening," Vance said.

"I was here on other business, but I thought I'd help out. I've worked with Thoroughbreds all my life, and I think we've got problems here. One leg's twisted back. The foal's stuck."

"Great," Vance muttered sarcastically, entering the stall as quietly as possible. "Just what we need tonight." His eyes traveled over the mare. "How're ya, gal? Hurtin' a little?" he asked as he studied the glistening horse.

"How can I help?" Tiffany asked, forcing her voice to remain steady as she noticed the tightening of Vance's jaw.

"Be ready to hand me anything I might need," Vance replied and then positioned himself behind the mare to confirm what Zane had told him. "Damn." He shook his blond head and frowned. "All right, let's get him out of there."

Ebony Wine moaned as her womb contracted, and the foal remained stuck in the birth canal.

"This is gonna be touchy," Vance whispered, as warning to the tall man standing next to him.

Zane's body tensed and he nodded curtly, before he helped Vance carefully push the foal back into the mare so that there was less danger of breaking the umbilical cord and to give more room to coax the bent leg forward. Time was crucial, and both men worked quickly but gently, intent on saving the mare and her offspring.

Tiffany assisted with the towels and antiseptic, silently praying for the life of the unborn horse. Her throat was hot and tight with the tension in the confining stall. Sweat began to bead on Zane's forehead, and his intent eyes never left the mare. The muscles in his bronze forearms flexed as he worked on righting the foal. Tiffany's heart was hammering so loudly, it seemed to pound in her ears.

Ebony Wine pushed down hard with all the muscles of her abdomen. As the mare pushed, Vance and Zane stood behind her and pulled down steadily toward her hocks in rhythm with the birth contractions.

With the first push, the tiny hooves and the head of the foal emerged. On the second contraction, the mare gave a soft moan, and the men were able to pull the shoulders, the broadest part of a foal's body, through Ebony Wine's pelvis. Once the shoulders emerged, the rest of the foal followed.

The umbilical cord broke.

Zane dropped to the floor and, mindless of the fluid pooling at his knees, he ripped open the tough amniotic sac. Vance was beside him and worked on the colt's nose, so that it could breathe its first breaths of air.

Tiffany brought towels and held them near the foal so that Vance could take them as he needed them. Her eyes watched the little black colt's sides as she prayed for the tiny ribs to move. *Dear Lord, don't let him die. Please don't take this one, too.*

Because the colt had to be pulled out of the mare, the umbilical cord had broken early, and he was shortchanged of the extra blood in the placenta that should have passed into his veins. Both men worked feverishly over the small, perfect body.

The foal's lips and eyelids looked blue as it lay wet and motionless in the straw.

"Oh, God, no," Tiffany whispered, as she realized that it had been far too long already since the birth. She dropped the towels and her small hands curled into impotent fists. "Not this one, too."

Ebony Wine nickered, ready to claim her foal. Mac gently held the frustrated mare as she tried to step closer to the unmoving black body lying on the floor of the stall.

Zane held his hands near the colt's nose to feel for breath. There was none. "He's not breathing," he whispered, looking up for a second at Tiffany before bending over the colt and pressing his lips to the nostrils, forcing air into the still lungs.

Vance knelt beside Zane, checking the colt for vital signs, while Zane fruitlessly tried to revive the colt.

"It's no use," Vance said at last, restraining Zane by placing a hand on his shoulder. "This one didn't have a prayer going in."

"No!" Tiffany said, her voice trembling and tears building in her eyes. "He's got to live. He's got to!"

"Tiff..." Vance said wearily. The vet's voice trailed off. There were no adequate words of condolence. For a moment the only sounds in the building were the soft rain beating against the roof and the restless shifting of the mare's hooves in the straw.

Mindless of the blood and amniotic fluid ruining her clothes, Tiffany fell into the straw beside the inert body of the beautifully formed black colt. Her throat was swollen with despair, her eyes blurred with fresh tears. "You have to live, little one," she whispered in a voice filled with anguished desperation. She touched the foal's warm, matted coat. "Please...live."

Her fingers touched the small ears and the sightless eyes. "Don't die...."

"Tiffany." Zane's voice was rough but comforting as he reached forward and grabbed her shoulders. He felt the quiet sobs she was trying to control. "He was dead before he was born—"

Tiffany jerked herself free. "No!" Her hands were shaking as she raised them in the air. "He was alive and healthy and..."

"Stillborn."

That single word, issued softly from Zane's lips, seemed to echo against the rafters.

A single tear wove a solitary path down her cheek. Tiffany let her arms fall to her sides. "Oh, God," she whispered, pulling herself to her full height and shaking her head. Blood discolored her silk blouse, and straw stuck in her angora vest as well as her hair. "Not another one." Her small fist clenched and she pounded it on the rough boards of the stall. "Why? Why is this happening?" she demanded, hopelessly battling an enemy she couldn't see...didn't understand.

Ebony Wine snorted, and Tiffany realized she was disturbing the already distraught mare. She let her head drop into her palm, leaned against the wall and closed her eyes against the truth. *Why the foals? Why all of Moon Shadow's foals?*

"Come on, let's go back to the house," Zane suggested, placing his strong arms gently over her shoulders.

"I should stay," she whispered as cold reality began to settle in her mind. She felt a raw ache in her heart as she faced the tragic fact that another of Moon Shadow's foals was dead before it had a chance to live. It just wasn't fair; not to the mare, not to the farm, and not to the poor lifeless little colt.

"We'll take care of things," Mac assured her, giving Zane a look that said more clearly than words, "Get her out of here." Mac was holding the lead rope to Ebony Wine's halter, and the anxious horse was nickering to the dead foal.

"I'll make some coffee…up at the house," Tiffany murmured, trying to pull herself together. She was shaking from the ordeal but managed to wipe the tears from her eyes.

"Don't bother for me," Vance said, working with the afterbirth. "I'll stay with the mare until Mac can watch her and then I'll call it a night."

"Same goes for me." Mac's kind eyes rested on Tiffany. "You just take care of yourself, Missy. We'll handle the horses."

"But—"

"Shh, could be three, maybe four hours till I'm finished with this old gal here," Mac said, cocking his head sadly in the black mare's direction. "After that, I think I'll hit the hay. I'm not as young as I used to be, ya know, and the missus, she'll be looking for me." He winked at Tiffany, but the smile he tried to give her failed miserably.

Numbly, leaning against Zane's strong body, Tiffany slowly walked out of the foaling shed and into the night. The rain was still falling from the darkened sky. It splashed against the sodden ground, and the large drops ran through her hair and down her neck.

She felt cold all over, dead inside. Another of Moon Shadow's foals. Dead. Why? Her weary mind wouldn't quit screaming the question that had plagued her for nearly two weeks. She shuddered against the cold night and the chill of dread in her heart. Zane pulled her closer to the protective warmth of his body.

Hard male muscles surrounded her, shielded her from the rain as well as the storm of emotions raging in her mind. Lean and masculine, Zane's body molded perfectly over hers, offering the strength and security she needed on this dark night. For the first time in several years, Tiffany accepted the quiet strength of a man. She was tired of making decisions, weary from fighting the invisible demons that stole the lifeblood from innocent newborns.

The house was still ablaze with the lights she had neglected to turn off. Zane led her into the den and watched as she slumped wearily into the chair near the fireplace. The sparkle in her blue eyes seemed to have died with Ebony Wine's foal. Her arms were wrapped protectively over her breasts, and she stared sightlessly into the smoldering embers of the fire.

"I'll get you a drink," he offered, walking to the bookcase that housed the liquor.

"Don't want one."

He picked up a bottle of brandy before looking over his shoulder and pinning her with his intense gray gaze. "Tiffany, what happened?" he asked quietly. She continued to gaze dully at the charred logs in the stone fireplace. He repeated his question, hoping to break her mournful silence. "Just what the hell happened out there tonight?"

"We lost a colt," she whispered, tears resurfacing in her eyes.

"Sometimes that happens," he offered, waiting patiently for the rest of the story as he poured two small glasses of the amber liquor.

She lifted her gaze to meet his and for a moment he thought she was about to confide in him, but instead she shrugged her slim shoulders. "Sometimes," she agreed hoarsely as she watched his reaction.

How much could she trust this stranger? True, he had tried to help her with the unborn colt and in a moment of weakness she felt as if she could trust her life to him. But still she hesitated. She couldn't forget that he was here on a mission. Not only did he want to buy the farm, but he was filled with some insane theory about Devil's Gambit being alive.

Zane's stormy eyes glanced over her huddled form. Her soft honey-brown curls were tangled with straw and framed her elegantly featured face. Her tanned skin was pale from the ordeal. Dark, curling eyelashes couldn't hide the pain in her wide, innocent eyes.

She's seen more than her share of pain, Zane guessed as he walked over to her and offered the drink that she had declined.

"I don't want—"

"Drink it."

She frowned a little. "Just who do you think you are, coming in here and giving me orders?"

He smiled sternly. "A friend."

Tiffany found it difficult to meet the concern in his eyes. She remained rigid and ignored the glass in his outstretched hand.

With an audible sigh, Zane relented. Dealing with this beautiful woman always seemed to prove difficult. "All right, lady. Drink it. *Please.*"

Tiffany took the glass from his hand and managed an obligatory sip. The calming liquor slid easily down her throat, and as she sipped the brandy she began to warm a little. *Who was this man and why did he care?*

Zane walked over to the fireplace and stretched the tension out of his shoulders, before stoking the dying fire and finally taking a seat on the hearth. He propped his elbows on his knees and cradled his drink in his large hands.

She didn't follow his actions but kicked off her shoes, ignoring the mud that dirtied the imported carpet. Then she drew her knees under her chin as if hugging herself for warmth against an inner chill.

Zane's eyes never left her face. As he watched her he felt a traitorous rush of desire flooding his bloodstream and firing his loins. As unlikely as it seemed, he suddenly wanted Ellery Rhodes's beautiful widow and wanted her badly. The urge to claim her as his own was blinding. In a betraying vision, he saw himself kissing away the pain on her regal features, lifting the sweater vest over her head, slipping each button of her blouse through the buttonholes.

Zane's throat tightened as he imagined her lying beneath him, her glorious, dark-tipped breasts supple and straining in the moonlight....

"Stop it," he muttered to himself, and Tiffany looked upward from the flames to stare at him.

"Stop what?" she whispered, her eyes searching his.

Zane's desire was thundering in his ears, and he felt the unwelcome swelling in his loins. "Nothing," he muttered gruffly as he stood, walked across the room and poured himself another drink. He downed the warm liquor in one long swallow as if the brandy itself could quell the unfortunate urges of his body.

For God's sake, he hadn't reacted to a woman this way since Stasia. At the thought of his sultry Gypsylike ex-wife, Zane's blood went ice-cold, and the effect was an instant relief. The ache in his loins subsided.

He set his glass down with a thud, jarring Tiffany out of her distant reverie. "Do you want to talk?" he asked softly, walking back across the close room to face her. He placed himself squarely before her, effectively blocking her view of the fire.

She shook her head and ran trembling fingers through her hair. "Not now..."

His smile was sad, but genuine. "Then I think you should get cleaned up and rest. It's after midnight—"

"Oh." For the first time that night, Tiffany was aware of her appearance. She looked down at her vest and saw the bloodstains discoloring the delicate gray wool. The sleeves of her pink blouse were rolled over her arms and stained with sweat and blood. She felt the urge to cry all over again when she looked up from her disheveled clothing and noticed the concern in Zane's gentle gray eyes.

Instead of falling victim to her emotions, she raised her head proudly and managed a stiff smile. "I'll be fine in the morning. This night has been a shock."

"Obviously."

"If you'll excuse me..."

When she rose from the chair, her knees felt unsteady, but she managed to stand with a modicum of dignity despite her disheveled appearance.

Zane picked up her barely touched glass. "I don't think you should be alone."

Involuntarily she stiffened. Ellery's words from long ago, just after her father had died, echoed in her mind. "You shouldn't be alone, Tiffany," Ellery had insisted. "You need a man to care for you." In her grief, Tiffany had been fool enough to believe him.

She lifted her chin fractionally. "I'll be fine, Mr. Sheridan," she assured him with a calm smile. "I've been alone for over four years. I think I can manage one more night."

He noticed the slight trembling of her fingers, the doubt in her clear blue eyes, and realized that she was the most damnably intriguing woman he had ever met.

"I'll stay with you."

"That won't be necessary."

"The mare's not out of the woods yet."

Tiffany hesitated only slightly. Zane's presence did lend a certain security. She remembered his quick, sure movements as he tried to revive Ebony Wine's dead colt. With a shake of her head, she tried to convince herself that she didn't need him. "Mac can take care of Ebony Wine."

"And it wouldn't hurt to have an extra pair of hands."

She was about to protest. She raised her hand automatically and then dropped it. "Don't get me wrong, Zane," she said softly, her tongue nearly tripping on the familiarity of his first name. "It's not that I don't appreciate what you've done tonight. I do. But the foal is dead." She shuddered and hugged her arms around her abdomen. "And Mac will attend to Ebony Wine." She shook her head at the vision of the dead little colt lying on the thick bed of straw. "I...I think it would be best if you would just leave for now. I know that we still have things to discuss, but certainly they'll wait until morning."

"I suppose." Zane glanced at the portrait of Devil's Gambit hanging proudly over the mantel. He had the eerie feeling that somehow the tense drama he had witnessed earlier in the foaling shed was linked to the disappearance of the proud stallion. *Impossible.* And yet he had a gut feeling that the two tragic events were connected.

As if Tiffany had read his thoughts, she shuddered. Zane was across the room in an instant. Tiffany wanted to protest when his strong arms enfolded her against him, but she couldn't. The warmth of his body and the protection of his embrace felt as natural as the gentle rain beating softly against the windowpanes. He plucked a piece of straw from her hair and tenderly let his lips press a soft kiss against her forehead. The gesture was so filled with kindness and empathy that Tiffany felt her knees buckle and her eyes fill with tears.

"I...I think you should go," she whispered hoarsely, afraid of her response to his masculinity. *Damn him!* She wanted to lean on him. What kind of a fool was she? Hadn't she learned her lessons about men long ago from Ellery?

"Shh." He ignored her protests and led her gently out of the den, through the foyer and up the stairs. "Come on, lady," he whispered into her hair. "Give yourself a break and let me take care of you."

She felt herself melt inside. "I don't think, I mean I don't need—"

"What you need is to soak in a hot tub, wrap yourself in one of those god-awful flannel nightgowns and fall into bed with a glass of brandy."

It sounded like heaven, but Tiffany couldn't forget that the tenderness of the man touching her so intimately might be nothing more than a ploy to extract information from her. At this moment she was too tired to really give a damn, but she couldn't forget her earlier instincts about him. He was engaged in a vendetta of sorts; she could feel it in her bones. Try as she would, Tiffany couldn't shake the uneasy feeling that Zane Sheridan, whoever the hell he was, would prove to be the enemy.

Zane left Tiffany in the master bedroom. Once she was certain he had gone downstairs, she peeled off her soiled clothes, threw them in a hamper and walked into the adjacent bathroom.

As she settled into the hot water of the marble tub, her mind continued to revolve around the events of the past few weeks. If the first foal's death had been a shock, the second had been terrifying. Now two more foals by Moon Shadow had died mysteriously. Each foal had been only a few hours old, with the exception of Charlatan, who had survived for a few hope-filled days.

Just wait until Rod Crawford gets hold of this story, she thought as she absently lathered her body. The wire services would print it in a minute and she'd have more reporters crawling all over the place than she could imagine. If that wasn't enough, Zane Sheridan's theories about Devil's Gambit's fate would stir up the press and get them interested all over again in what was happening at Rhodes Breeding Farm. *And the scandal. Lord, think of the scandal!*

Tiffany sank deeper into the tub, and didn't notice that her hair was getting wet.

What about Zane Sheridan? Was he here as friend or foe? She sighed as she considered the roguish man who had helped her upstairs. One minute he seemed intent on some vague, undisclosed revenge, and the next his concern for her and the farm seemed genuine. *Don't trust him, Tiffany,* the rational side of her nature insisted.

"Men," she muttered ungraciously. "I'll never understand them." Her frown trembled a little as she thought about Ellery, the husband she had tried to love. Marrying him had probably been the biggest mistake of her life. The moment she had become Mrs. Ellery Rhodes, he seemed to have changed and his interest in her had faded with each passing day. "Dad warned you," she chided herself. "You were just too bullheaded to listen."

The distance between her and her husband had become an almost physical barrier, and Tiffany had foolishly thought that if she could bear Ellery a child, things might be different. He might learn to love her.

What a fool! Hadn't she already known from her own agonizing experience with her mother that relationships between people who loved each other were often fragile and detached? In her own naive heart, she had hoped that she would someday be able to reach Ellery. Now, if what Zane Sheridan was saying were true, Ellery might still be alive.

"Oh, God," she moaned, closing her eyes and trying to conjure Ellery's face in her mind. But try as she would, she was unable to visualize the man she had married. Instead, the image on her mind had the forceful features on a virtual stranger from Ireland. "You bastard," she whispered and wondered if she were speaking to Zane or Ellery.

Her tense muscles began to relax as she rinsed the soap from her body and then turned on the shower spray to wash her hair.

Once she felt that all of the grime had been scrubbed from her skin, she turned off the shower, stepped out of the tub and wrapped herself in a bath sheet. After buffing her skin dry, she grabbed the only nightgown in the room, an impractical silver-colored gown of thin satin and lace.

Just what I need, she thought sarcastically as she slipped it over her head and straightened it over her breasts. She smiled to herself, grabbed her red corduroy robe and cinched the belt tightly around her waist. She was still towel-drying her hair when she stepped into the bedroom.

As she did, her gaze clashed with that of Zane Sheridan.

"What are you doing here?" she asked, lowering the towel and staring at him with incredulous slate-blue eyes.

"I wanted to make sure that you didn't fall asleep in the tub."

She arched an elegant brow suspiciously. "Didn't you hear the shower running?" When a slow-spreading smile grew from one side of his face to the other, Tiffany's temper snapped. "I don't need a keeper, you know. I'm a grown woman."

His eyes slid over her body and rested on the gap in her overlapping lapels. "So I noticed."

Angrily, she tugged on the tie of her robe. "You're insufferable!" she spit out. "I could have walked in here stark naked."

"Can't blame a guy for hoping—"

"I'm in no mood for this, Zane," she warned.

He sobered instantly and studied the lines of worry on her beautiful face. "I know. I just thought I could get you to lighten up."

"A little difficult under the circumstances."

"You lost a foal. It happens."

Her lips twisted wryly. "That it does, Mr. Sheridan. That it does." She sat on the corner of the bed and supported herself with one straight arm while pushing the wet tendrils of hair out of her face with her free hand. "It's been a long day."

"I suppose it has." He strode across the room, threw back the covers of the bed and reached for a drink he had placed on the nightstand. "I checked on Ebony Wine."

Tiffany watched his actions warily. Why was he still here and why was she secretly pleased? She raised her head in challenge and ignored her rapidly pounding heart. "And?"

"You were right. Mac took care of her. She's a little confused about everything that went on tonight, still calling to the foal. But she's healthy. The afterbirth detached without any problem and Mac had already cleaned her up. He thinks she'll be ready to breed when she shows signs of foal heat, which should be the middle of next week. The veterinarian will be back to check her tomorrow and again before she goes into heat."

Tiffany nodded and accepted the drink he offered. "It's a little too much for me to think about right now," she admitted, swirling the brandy in her glass before taking a sip.

"It's the business you're in."

Tiffany stared into the amber liquor in her glass and moved her head from side to side. "And sometimes it seems like a rotten way of life."

Zane ran his hand around the back of his neck. "It's never easy to lose one, but it's the chance you take as a breeder."

"And the living make up for the dead?"

Zane frowned and shrugged. "Something like that. If it bothers you so much, maybe you should get out of the business," he suggested.

"By selling the farm to you?" Her eyes lifted and became a frigid shade of blue.

"I didn't think we would get into that tonight."

"You brought it up."

"I just voiced your concerns."

"Oh, God," she whispered, setting her unfinished drink aside. "Look, I'm really very tired and I can't think about all this tonight."

"Don't. Just try and get some sleep."

She managed a wan smile and walked around to her side of the bed. "I guess I owe you an apology and a very big thank-you. I...really appreciate all the help you gave in the foaling shed."

Zane frowned. "For all the good it did."

Tiffany raised sad eyes to meet his questioning gaze. "I don't think there was anything anyone could have done."

"Preordained?"

She sighed audibly and shook her head. The wet hair swept across her shoulders. "Who knows?" She sat on the edge of the bed, her fingers toying with the belt holding her robe together. "Goodbye, Zane. If you call me in the morning, we can find another time to get together and talk about your hypothesis concerning Devil's Gambit and my husband."

"I'll be here in the morning," he stated, dropping into a chair facing the bed and cradling his drink in his hands.

"Pardon me?" she asked, understanding perfectly well what he meant.

"I'm staying—"

"You can't! Not here—"

"I just want to check with Mac once more, and then I'll sleep downstairs on the couch."

Visions of him spending the night in her house made her throat dry. She couldn't deny that he had been a help, but the thought of him there, in the same house with her, only a staircase away, made her uneasy. Her fingers trembled when she pushed them wearily through her hair. "I don't know," she whispered, but she could feel herself relenting.

"Come on, Tiff. It's after two. I'm not about to drive back to San Francisco now, just to turn around and come back here in six hours."

Tiffany managed a smile. "I don't suppose that makes a whole lot of sense." Her blue eyes touched his. "You don't have to sleep in the den. There's a guest room down the hall, the first door to the left of the stairs."

He returned her hint of a smile and stood. For a moment she thought he was about to bend over the bed and kiss her. She swallowed with difficulty as their eyes locked.

Zane hesitated, and the brackets near the corners of his mouth deepened. "I'll see you in the morning," he said, his eyes darkening to a smoky gray before he turned out the lamp near the bed and walked out of the room.

Tiffany expelled a rush of air. "Oh God," she whispered, her heart thudding painfully in her chest. "I should have made him leave." He was too close, his rugged masculinity too inviting.

Maybe he would come back to her room, or maybe he would sift through the papers in the den looking for something, anything, to prove his crazy theories. But all the important documents, the computer data disks and the checkbook were locked in the safe; even if Zane rummaged through the den, he would find nothing of value.

That's not why you're concerned, her tired mind teased. *What scares you is your response to him.* She rolled over and pushed the nagging thoughts aside. Despite all of her doubts, she was comforted that Zane was still with her. Somehow it made the tragedy of losing the foal easier to bear.

Zane hiked his quickly donned jacket around his neck and felt the welcome relief of raindrops slide under his collar. He needed time to cool off. Being around Tiffany, wanting to comfort her, feeling a need to make love to her until the fragile lines of worry around her eyes were gone, unnerved him. The last thing he had expected when he had driven to Rhodes Breeding Farm was that he would get involved with Ellery Rhodes's widow.

He heard the roar of an engine as he started to cross the parking lot. Turning in the direction of the sound, Zane walked toward Mac's battered truck. Mac rolled down the window as Zane approached. Twin beams from the headlights pierced the darkness, and the wipers noisily slapped the accumulation of rain from the windshield.

"Everything okay?"

"Aye," Mac replied cautiously. "The mare's fine."

"Good." Zane rammed his fists into the jacket of his coat. "What about the colt?"

"Vance will handle that." The wiry trainer frowned in the darkness. "He'll give us a report in a couple of days."

"Good." Zane stepped away from the truck and watched as Mac put the ancient Dodge pickup into gear before it rumbled down the driveway.

Wondering at the sanity of his actions, Zane unlocked his car and withdrew the canvas bag of extra clothes from the back seat. He always traveled with a change of clothes, his briefcase and his camera. He slung the bag over his shoulder and considered the briefcase. In the leather case were the papers his attorney had toiled over. According to John Morris, every document needed to purchase Rhodes Breeding Farm was now in Zane's possession. So why didn't owning the farm seem as important as it once had?

Zane cursed angrily and locked the briefcase in the car. Knowing that he was making a grave error, he walked back into the house, locked the doors and mounted the stairs. After throwing his bag on the guest bed, he took off his shoes and turned down the covers.

Then, on impulse, he went back to her room. He paused at the door and then strode boldly inside. His blood was thundering in his eardrums as he lowered himself into the chair near the bed. It took all of his restraint not to go to her.

Zane watched the rounded swell of her hips beneath the bedclothes, and the smoldering lust in his veins began to throb unmercifully. *You're more of a fool than you thought,* Zane chastised himself silently.

He noticed the regular rhythm of her breathing and realized that she had fallen asleep. The urge to strip off his clothes and lie with her burned in his mind. He fantasized about her response, the feel of her warm, sleepy body fitted to his, the agonizing glory of her silken fingers as they traced an invisible path down his abdomen....

A hard tightening in his loins warned him that his thoughts were dangerous; still he couldn't help but think of slowly peeling off her bedclothes and letting the shimmery nightgown peeking from the edges of her robe fall silently to the floor. He wanted to touch all of her, run his tongue over the gentle feminine curves of her body, drink in the smell of her perfume as he touched her swollen breasts....

Quietly he placed his drink on the table and walked over to the bed.

Tiffany moaned in her sleep and turned onto her back. In the dim light from the security lamps, with the rain softly pelting against the windows, Zane looked down at her. How incredibly soft and alluring she appeared in slumber. All traces of anxiety had left the perfect oval of her face. Her still-damp hair curled in golden-brown tangles around her shoulders and neck.

The scarlet robe had gaped open to display the silvery fabric of a gossamer gown and the soft texture of her breasts beneath. Tiffany shifted slightly and the hint of a dark nipple shadowed the silvery lace covering it.

Zane clenched his teeth in self-restraint. Never had he wanted a woman more, and he told himself that she was there for the taking. Hadn't he seen her vulnerability? Hadn't he witnessed the way she stared at him? Deep within her, there was a need to be taken by him; he could sense it.

He closed his eyes against the pain throbbing in his loins and dropped to his knees by the bed. "What have you done to me?" he whispered as he lovingly brushed a strand of hair from her eyes.

This woman was once the wife of Ellery Rhodes, a person he had intended to destroy. Zane couldn't help but wonder, as he stared into the sleep-softened face of Ellery Rhodes's widow, if just the opposite were true.

Would he be able to carry forth his plans of retribution, or would Ellery Rhodes's wife reap her sweet vengeance on him?

Chapter Five

When Tiffany opened her eyes she noticed that the first purple light of dawn had begun to filter into the room. With a muted groan, she stretched between the cool sheets and rolled over, intent on returning to sleep.

Her cloudy vision rested on the chair near the bed and her breath got lost somewhere in her throat.

Zane was in the room. The realization was like an electric current pulsing through her body, bringing her instantly awake. What was he doing here?

He was slumped back in the chair, his head cocked at an uncomfortable angle, his stocking feet propped against the foot of the bed. He had thrown a spare blanket over himself, but it had slipped to the floor. His unfinished drink sat neglected on the bedside table.

"You wonderful bastard," she whispered quietly, before a silent rage began to take hold of her. Why hadn't he left as he had promised? Why had he decided to stay here—in her bedroom? Conflicting emotions battled within her. On the one hand, she was pleased to see him; it was comforting to watch his beard darkened face relaxed in quiet slumber. There was something slightly chivalrous in the fact that he had stayed with her on the pretense of caring for her. She supposed that in all honesty she should consider his actions a compliment, an indication that he cared for her—if only a little.

On the other hand, she was quietly furious that he would force himself so boldly into her life. Whatever it was that he wanted at Rhodes Breeding Farm, he obviously wanted very badly. Badly enough to pretend interest in Tiffany and her horses.

The smile that had touched the corners of her mouth began to fade. Zane stirred in the chair, and Tiffany knew that he would soon be awake. No better time than the present to take the bull by the horns! She slipped out of the bed and cinched her robe tightly under her breasts before planting herself in front of his chair.

"Liar!" she whispered loudly enough to disturb him.

The muscles in Zane's broad shoulders stiffened slightly. He grumbled something indistinguishable and his feet dropped to the floor as he tried to roll over.

"What the hell?" he mumbled, before opening his eyes. He awoke to find himself staring up at Tiffany's indignant blue gaze. Stretching in the uncomfortable chair, he tried to rub the stiffness from his neck and cramped shoulders. "What're you going on about?" he asked.

"You said you'd sleep downstairs or in the guest room."

A devilish grin stole across his features. "So I did."

Her blue eyes narrowed. "Don't you have any shame?"

"None." He pulled himself out of the chair and stretched his aching muscles. God, he hurt all over. It had been years since he'd slept sitting up; and never in his thirty-six years had he kept vigil on a beautiful woman, a woman who obviously didn't appreciate his efforts.

"I should have known."

"Known what?" He rubbed his hands over the stubble of his beard and then threw his head back and rotated his neck to relieve the tension at the base of his skull. "Don't you have any coffee around here?" he asked once he'd stretched.

Tiffany crossed her arms self-righteously over her breasts and glared up at her unwelcome visitor. She was still wearing her robe, Zane noticed, though the gap of the lapels had been pulled together when she had tied the belt around her small waist. "Known you'd end up here."

"It's too early in the morning for this outraged virgin routine, Tiff," he said, rubbing the stubble on his chin. "We're both adults."

Her lips pressed together in anger. "Virginity isn't the issue."

He raised a brow in overt disbelief. "Then what is? Morality?"

"Sanity," she shot back. "Your being in here borders on the insane. I don't know who you are, what you want, where you live, why you're here in the first place.... God, Zane, for all I know you could be married with a dozen kids."

His dark glare silenced her. "I'm not married," he said gruffly.

"Good. Because I certainly wouldn't want some outraged wife calling me and demanding to talk to her husband." He looked as if she had slapped him.

"I came in here to check on you last night and you're acting as if I'm some kind of criminal, for God's sake."

She let out a ragged breath and her hands dropped to her sides. "It's just that I don't really know you," she said softly.

"Sure you do," he cajoled, his slate-colored eyes warming slightly when he noticed the flush of indignation on her cheeks.

Tiffany attempted to remain angry, but it was nearly impossible as she stared into Zane's incredible gray eyes. They were a reflection of the man himself, sometimes dark with anger, other times filled with a compelling intimacy that touched her heart and caused her pulse to jump. Slowly, by calculated inches, this man was working his way into her heart. She felt more vulnerable and naked than she had in years. The emotions beginning to blossom within her had to be pushed aside. She couldn't chance an involvement with him; it was far too dangerous.

Zane rubbed his eyes and stretched before smiling lazily. "Has anyone ever told you you're beautiful when you're angry?"

"Dozens," she returned sarcastically.

"Or that you're gorgeous when you wake up?"

Tiffany swallowed back a lump in her throat. "Not quite as many." She ran her long fingers through her knotted hair and slowly expelled a sigh. Arguing with him would get her nowhere. "I guess I haven't been very hospitable this morning," she conceded, lowering herself to a corner of the bed.

"Some people wake up in a bad mood."

"Especially if they find a stranger in their room?"

His gray eyes touched hers and his voice lowered to an intimate whisper. "We're not strangers."

Her elegant brows arched skeptically. "No?"

"No." He shook his head and frowned decisively.

"Then tell me," she suggested as one long, nervous finger began tracing the line of delicate stitching on the hand-pieced quilt. "Just how would you describe our relationship?"

A mischievous light gleamed in his eyes and his voice lowered suggestively. "How about two strong-willed people thrown mercilessly together by the cruel tides of fate?"

Tiffany couldn't help but laugh. "Seriously—"

"Seriously?" He sobered instantly. "Why don't we start as friends?"

She nodded silently to herself as if agreeing with an earlier-drawn conclusion. "Ah. Friends." Looking up, she found Zane staring intensely at her. "Friendship isn't formed in one night. Not when one of the 'friends' doesn't know anything about the other."

"Or suspects that he's holding out on her?"

She stiffened slightly. "Right." Folding her hands in her lap, she forced her eyes to meet the stormy gray of his. "You came here yesterday and announced that you intended to buy this farm. You also insisted that Devil's Gambit was alive. These aren't the usual kinds of statements to kick off an amiable relationship."

Before he could respond, she pointed an accusing finger up at him and continued, "And there's more to it than you've told me. I get the distinct impression you're here for other reasons, that you were probably involved with Ellery in the past and you're holding a grudge against him...or what used to be his before he died...."

Zane didn't deny it, but the mention of Ellery's name caused his face to harden. An unspoken challenge flashed from his eyes.

"My husband is dead—"

"You think." He rammed his fists into his pockets and walked over to one of the tall, paned windows. Leaning one shoulder against the window frame, he surveyed the farm. From his vantage point he could look past the white buildings near the house to the gently rolling hills in the distance. It was barely dawn. A gentle drizzle was falling, and wisps of fog had settled in the pockets between the hills to color the lush green meadows a hazy shade of blue.

Standing apart from the main buildings, its shape barely visible in the clinging fog, was the sagging skeleton of an old weather-beaten barn, the one structure on the farm that was in sharp contrast to the rest of the modern facilities. The old relic was out of sync with the times. Why had Ellery kept it?

Tiffany watched Zane with new fear taking hold of her heart. What was he saying? Did he really believe that Ellery could still be alive after all these years?

Her voice was suddenly hoarse and she was forced to clear her throat. "Look..."

He continued to stare at the rain-washed countryside.

"If you think that Ellery is alive, I want to know about it and I want to know now. This minute. No more stalls."

Zane lifted his hands dismissively. "I don't really know. The only thing I'm certain about is the horse."

"But you said—"

He whirled to face her, his burning hatred resurfacing in his eyes. "What I said was that I don't know what happened to your husband, but I wouldn't rule out the possibility that he could very well be alive and hiding out somewhere."

Tiffany's dark brows drew together, and she shook her head as if she could physically deny the doubts and fears beginning to plague her. "That doesn't make any sense!"

Zane's scathing eyes slowly traveled up her body to rest on her troubled face. He shook his head as if he couldn't begin to understand what was happening between himself and Ellery Rhodes's wife. "If your husband did leave you, then he's not only a crooked bastard, he's crazy to boot."

"You didn't much like him, did you?"

"I didn't like him at all." Zane uttered the words without any trace of emotion, as if he were simply stating a fact. He noticed the worry clouding her gaze, the weariness in the slump of her shoulders, and he silently wondered how such a beautiful woman could have linked up with the likes of Ellery Rhodes. Stasia's passion for money was understandable, but Tiffany? The bitter thought of Stasia heightened his curiosity and got the better of him. "Tell me, what kind of a marriage did you have?"

"Pardon me?"

"How was your relationship with Ellery?"

Searching gray eyes probed hers and seemed to pierce her soul. Just how much did this man want from her? "I don't think this is the time or the place—"

"Cut the bull, Tiffany."

"It's really none of your business—"

"Like hell! I just spent the night with you, lady, and I think that counts for something." His skin tightened over his cheekbones and his jaw hardened. An unspoken challenge flared in his intense gaze.

"Wait a minute. You didn't 'spend the night' with me. You merely sat in a chair in my room."

"Tell that to the rest of the people on the farm."

"I really don't give a rip what anyone else thinks, Zane," she replied, coloring only slightly. "What I do with my life is my own business."

He quirked a disbelieving brow.

"By the same token, I expect that you wouldn't go around to the workers and brag that you slept in the boss lady's room." Her heart was pounding wildly, but she managed to keep her voice steady.

Zane rammed fingers through his dark hair. "But I did."

"No reason to brag about it, especially since nothing happened."

"Not for any lack of wanting on my part," he admitted with a sigh of frustration. His eyes had darkened, and a tiny muscle worked furiously in the corner of his jaw. The tension that sleep had drained from his body resurfaced, and Tiffany realized for the first time just how badly this man wanted her. Her pulse jumped, and she had to force herself to stand and face him. Things were moving too rapidly, and she couldn't begin to deal with the bold desire written on Zane's rugged features.

"This conversation isn't getting us anywhere," she whispered, her voice becoming thick as her eyes lingered in the smoky depths of his. "I...I'm going to clean up and get dressed and then I'll fix you that cup of coffee. It's the least I can do since you helped out here last night...and were such a gentleman in the bargain." She motioned with a suddenly heavy hand toward the door of the room. "There's a bath down the hall, if you'd like to shave or change...."

He noticed her hesitation. "I brought a change of clothes."

"You did? Why?" Tiffany demanded. Had he intended to spend the night? Was he using her? If so, then why hadn't he tried to force himself upon her last night? Surely he had sensed her attraction to him. Zane Sheridan was a very fascinating man, and it had been a long time since she had been with a man...so very long.

"I thought I was going straight to the airport from here," he replied, abruptly bringing her back to the present.

She flushed from her wanton thoughts and smiled. "I see. Then I'll meet you downstairs later."

Without any further protests, Zane left the room. Tiffany waited until she heard him on the stairs, then she slowly closed the door to the bedroom and locked it.

A few minutes later she heard water running in the guest bathroom at the other end of the hall, and she smiled. "You're a fool," she whispered to herself as she stripped off the vibrant red robe, flung it carelessly on the foot of the bed and walked into her private bathroom. "A stranger just spent the night in your room, and if you had your way, he would be back here in a minute making furious, passion-filled love to you."

After turning on the shower, she shook her head and smiled at her unfamiliar and traitorous thoughts. "Tiffany, my friend," she warned her reflection in the steamy mirror, "this fascination with Zane Sheridan can only spell trouble."

Dropping her silvery nightgown on the floor, she stepped into the hot spray of water.

After braiding her hair into a single plait, applying just a little makeup and dressing in her favorite pair of faded jeans and a loose sweater, Tiffany headed downstairs to the kitchen. The airy room was bright with copper pots and pans suspended over the stove, plants arranged strategically on the gleaming tile counters, and oversized windows offering a view of the pasture near the broodmare barn.

The coffee was perking, muffins were baking in the oven and the previous night's dishes had been placed in the dishwasher before she heard Zane on the stairs. The inviting aromas of baking bread, coffee and cured ham wafted through the large kitchen.

"Efficient, aren't you?" he stated, offering her a lazy grin.

"I try to be." She glanced over her shoulder and felt her heart begin to pound irregularly as her eyes were caught in the silvery web of his gaze. Zane's black hair was still wet from his shower, his shadow of a beard had been shaved off to reveal the hard angle of his jaw and he was dressed casually in tan cords and a teal-blue sweater. Without his formal attire, he appeared more rakishly handsome than ever. Looking at him caused an uneasy fluttering in Tiffany's stomach.

He leaned against the counter, seemingly content to watch her work. Turning back to the coffee, she poured a cup and tried to hide the fact that her hands were unsteady.

"Cream or sugar?"

"Black is fine." He took an experimental sip, all the while observing Tiffany over the rim of the stoneware mug. "What happened to your cook?"

"She doesn't come in every day—remember? Only a couple of days a week to keep the house up, and on special occasions."

Zane observed her sure movements. God, she wasn't what he'd expected in Ellery Rhodes's wife. "You're a bit of a mystery," he thought aloud as his eyes wandered from her braid, past her slim waist to the inviting swell of her jean-clad hips.

"Ha. And what about you? Appearing on my doorstep with an offer on the farm and a wild tale about Devil's Gambit being kidnapped by Ellery...." She let her voice trail off. She couldn't think that Ellery was alive, couldn't deal with it now. Ellery wouldn't have left. He couldn't have. Not when he knew that she would think he was dead! Though their marriage had been less than ideal, certainly Ellery cared for her in his own, distant way. He wouldn't have put her through the pain of the funeral, the adjustment to widowhood, the problems of running the farm alone....

"Not to mention dead husbands," he offered, as if reading her thoughts.

Tiffany's shoulders flexed, and she held back the hot retort forming on her tongue. It wouldn't be wise to anger him, not yet. She had to find out what he wanted, what kind of game he was playing with her. With an effort, she turned her attention to the boiling water on the stove. Carefully she cracked and added the eggs.

"My husband isn't alive," Tiffany whispered, as if to convince herself.

"You're sure?"

She didn't answer him right away. She removed the muffins from the oven, and, when they were cooked, spooned the poached eggs from the pan. Only then did she say, "Ellery wouldn't let me think he was dead—he wouldn't put me through that kind of pain," she insisted, her quiet dignity steadfastly in place.

"Ellery Rhodes was a bastard." Zane's words were soft, but they seemed to thunder in the small kitchen.

"Your opinion."

"Granted; but correct nonetheless."

"And one I think you should keep to yourself!"

His bitter smile grew slowly from one side of his arrogant face to the other. He took a long swig of his coffee and noticed that Tiffany had paled. "Did you love him so much?"

"I don't understand," she began, but under his direct gaze, she changed the course of her thoughts. "Of course I loved him."

"Enough to cover up for him?"

Her simmering anger ignited, and pride took control of her tongue. "Wait a minute, Sheridan. You're way out of line."

He studied the honesty in her deep blue eyes and frowned into his mug. "My apologies," he muttered, before downing the rest of his coffee.

"If I had any brains at all, I'd throw you and your outlandish stories out of this place—"

"But you can't."

"Why not?"

He settled into the cane-backed chair he had occupied at the table the night before and flashed her a devastating smile that seemed to touch the darkest corners of her soul. "Because you believe me—" She raised her hands as if to protest and he silenced her with a knowing glare. "At least you believe a little."

Tiffany's chest was incredibly tight. She found it difficult to breathe. "I think, Mr. Sheridan, the only reasons I haven't asked you to leave are, one, because we didn't finish our discussion last night—a discussion that I have to admit piqued my curiosity about you—and two, because you helped out here last night when I was desperate." *And because I find you the most incredibly interesting man I've ever met,* she added silently to herself as she put the muffins in a basket and set them on the table next to the platter of ham and eggs. The attraction she felt to him was as crazy as the stories he spun about Devil's Gambit, and yet she couldn't fight it.

They ate in silence, neither breaking the unspoken truce while they consumed the hearty breakfast Tiffany had prepared.

After the table had been cleared, Tiffany heard Mac's footsteps on the back porch. Automatically she reached for the pot of coffee and poured a large mug of the dark liquid before adding both sugar and cream to the cup.

"Mornin'," Mac grumbled as he accepted the mug Tiffany offered. He took off his hat and placed it on top of the refrigerator. His eyes swept the interior of the kitchen and rested on Zane. The frown that began on Mac's crowlike features was quickly disguised as he took a long swallow of coffee.

So Sheridan had spent the night, Mac thought. He didn't much like the idea, didn't trust the Irishman. But Tiffany did what suited her, and if Zane Sheridan suited her, then it was none of Mac's business what went on between them. Tiffany had been alone too long as it was, and if he was uncomfortable in the Irishman's presence, Mac silently told himself it was his own problem.

"It's late for you to be getting in," Tiffany teased the ex-jockey with a warm grin.

"Not after a night that ended at three this morning."

Winking fondly at Mac, Tiffany moved toward the stove. "How about some breakfast?"

"Thanks much, but no." Mac eyed the leftover blueberry muffins but shook his head. "The missus, she made me eat before I left." He patted his lean stomach. "Couldn't hold anything else." He propped an elbow against the pantry door, finished his coffee and fidgeted. "I checked Ebony Wine this morning."

"I was about to go out there myself."

"No need; she's fine." Mac stared out the window toward the foaling shed and scowled. "She wasn't much of a mother the last time she foaled, so I don't reckon she'll miss this one much...." He shifted his weight from one foot to the other and set his empty cup on the blue tiles. "She should go into foal heat soon—next week, maybe. You plan on breeding her when she does?"

"If Vance says she's all right," Tiffany replied.

"To Moon Shadow?" Mac asked, and at the look on Tiffany's face he knew he'd made a monumental mistake saying anything in front of Zane Sheridan. He could have kicked himself for his lack of tact, but then he'd supposed that Sheridan knew what was going on. Apparently Tiffany hadn't confided in Sheridan, and Mac had let the cat out of the bag. Damn it all to hell anyway. Moving his slim shoulders in a gesture of indifference, Mac tried to undo the damage he'd caused before it was too late. "No reason to worry about it now; we've got a few days."

"I...I think I'll look in on Ebony Wine," Tiffany stated, wiping her hands on a towel hanging near the stove and steering the conversation toward safer ground. "She had a rough night."

"Didn't we all?" Mac frowned but a good-natured twinkle lighted his faded eyes. In his opinion, Tiffany Rhodes was as smart as she was pretty. "I've got to go into town—check with a guy about some alfalfa. Need anything else?"

"Just a few groceries, but I can get them later."

"Suit yourself." He nodded in Zane's direction, forced his rumpled fedora back onto his head and walked out the door.

Zane's silvery eyes rested on Tiffany's face. The near-perfect features were slightly disturbed. Obviously something the old man said bothered her. It was as if she was hiding something from him. Zane had experienced that same sensation yesterday morning when the reporter was at the house, and again last night while attending to the still-born colt. Something was bothering Tiffany Rhodes, and Zane suspected that it was more than his remarks about Devil's Gambit.

"Are you coming with me?" Tiffany asked as she walked down the short hallway to the den, slipped on her boots and pulled a worn suede jacket from the wooden hook near the French doors.

"Nothing better to do," Zane admitted, striding with her.

"Good." She scooped some envelopes from the top drawer of the desk, stuffed them into her pocket and headed outside. "I just want to drop these in the mail and pick up the paper before I go back to the foaling shed." She unlocked the French doors and stepped outside into the brisk morning air.

The world smelled fresh and new from the morning rain. Birds twittered in the trees, and the fog had begun to lift. Though the drizzle had let up, raindrops still clung tenaciously to the branches of the maple trees lining the drive. Shallow pools of water rested on the uneven surface of the asphalt.

Despite the problems with the foals and Zane's outlandish remarks about Devil's Gambit, Tiffany felt refreshed, as if the gentle morning rain had washed away the fears of the night. She noticed the dewy, crystallike web of a spider in the rhododendrons, and the woodsy scent of the earth beginning to warm from the first rays of a partially hidden sun.

It seemed the most natural thing in the world when Zane's fingers linked with hers, warming her hand. When he pulled on her hand, forcing her to stop near a thicket of oaks close to the end of the drive, she turned to face him and offered a smile. "What?"

"You don't know that you're driving me crazy, do you?" he asked gently, his gray gaze probing the vibrant blue depths of her eyes.

"And all the while I thought your wild stories and insane ideas about Devil's Gambit were genetic. Now it's my fault." Her blue eyes sparkled in the morning sunlight.

"Be serious," he suggested, his voice low and raspy. "I've wanted you from the first moment I laid eyes on you."

Tiffany laughed softly. "Now it's time for you to be serious."

"I am."

"You don't even know me—"

"I know you well enough to realize that we're good to-gether."

"In what way?"

"All ways."

"Just because you helped Ebony Wine and you...saw to it that I fell asleep last night, it isn't enough to—"

"Shh." He tugged on her arm, forcing her closer. As he looked down upon her she felt as if he were stripping her of the barriers she had so carefully placed around herself, around her heart. She smelled the clean, masculine scent of him, felt the warmth of his body, knew in a minute that he intended to kiss her and that she wouldn't do a damn thing about it.

When his lips touched hers, she closed her eyes and couldn't withhold the moan that came from her throat. Both of his hands reached upward to cup her face. Strong fingers held her cheeks while his lips moved slowly, provocatively over her mouth. He touched the underside of her jaw, gently stroking the delicate pulse in her neck. When he lifted his head, his eyes had grown dark with unspoken passion.

Tiffany swallowed with difficulty, and her blood began to throb wildly in her veins. Feminine urges, long dormant, began to heat and swirl within her, captivating her mind as well as her body.

"Tiffany," he whispered hoarsely against the shell of her ear as his hand slowly found and removed the band at the end of her braid of hair. His fingers worked the shimmery golden-brown strands until her hair tumbled free of its bond to frame her face in soft brown curls.

Her arms wound around his waist as his mouth dipped once again to the invitation of her parted lips. This time the kiss deepened, and Tiffany felt the thrill of his tongue as it sought out and mated with hers.

Liquid fire seemed to engulf her as desire flooded her veins and throbbed in her ears. *I can't want this man,* she reasoned with herself, but logic seemed to slip away. *He's using me....* But she found that she didn't care.

Beneath the still-naked branches of the towering oaks, she returned his passionate kiss and sighed in contentment when he pressed up against her and the evidence of his desire strained against the fabric of his cords.

Dear God, I don't want to love you, she thought as his arms encircled her and held her tightly to him. *I can't let myself fall for you.... I don't even know who you are or what you want from me. Is this moment just a diversion, an intricate part of your plan, or are your feelings real?*

Logic began to cool her blood, and he felt her withdrawing from him. "Let me love you," he whispered, refusing to let her go, his powerful arms holding her a willing captive.

She shook her head and tried to deny the traitorous feelings burning in her breast. "I can't...I just...can't."

"Because you still love your husband." His voice was low and damning. Dark fire smoldered in his eyes.

Her clear eyes clouded and her teeth sunk into her lower lip. When she shook her head, sunlight caught in the honeyed strands of her hair. "Because I don't know you well enough," she countered.

"You never will, unless you take a chance."

"I am. Right here. Right now. With you. Please...try to understand."

His arms dropped. "Understand what? That you don't know me?" He stepped away from her, granting a small distance between their bodies. "Or is it that you're suspicious of my motives?" His dark eyes searched her face. "Or maybe it's because you think I might be just slightly off my rocker."

She laughed despite the tension in the crisp morning air. "That just about says it all," Tiffany admitted, tossing her tangled hair away from her face. "Except that I think things are moving a little too fast for me," she said, her breathing still irregular. "Yesterday we were strangers, earlier this morning, 'friends,' and now you're suggesting that we become lovers. I'm not ready for all of this—not yet."

"Don't play games with me."

"It takes two to play," she reminded him, holding her head high, her gaze steady.

"You're a mature woman, Tiffany, not some seventeen-year-old girl. You've been married—"

"And I don't have casual affairs."

"There's nothing casual about what I feel for you." His arms encircled her waist, his warm hands splaying naturally against the small of her back.

"Give it time, Zane," she pleaded in a raspy whisper. He was so near she could feel the warmth of his breath in her hair, sense the desire heating his veins, witness the burning passion in his eyes. Her expression clouded with the indecision tormenting her mind. *How easy it would be to lie naked with him in the morning sun....*

With a sound of frustration he released her and leaned against the scaly trunk of one of the larger oaks in the thicket. Lethargic raindrops fell from the branches of the tree and glistened in his dark hair. He cocked his head to the side and forced a ragged but devastating smile. "Okay—so why not give me a chance to prove myself?"

"I am. You're still here, aren't you?"

She turned on her heel, walked the short distance to the road, extracted the envelopes from her pocket and placed them in the mailbox. Then, almost as an afterthought, she retrieved the morning paper from the yellow cylinder nailed to the fence post.

Rather than consider the implications of her mixed emotions toward Zane, she opened the paper and stared down at the headlines. Her breath froze in her throat. "Oh, dear God," she whispered as her eyes scanned the front page.

The bold headline seemed to scream its message to her in powerful black and white:

LOCAL BREEDER PLAGUED BY MYSTERIOUS DEATHS.

Chapter Six

Tiffany felt as if the wet earth were buckling beneath her feet. She stared at the two pictures on the front page of the *Clarion*. One photograph had been taken yesterday. It was a large print of Tiffany sitting at her desk. The other, slightly smaller picture was of Moon Shadow after his loss in the Kentucky Derby.

Tiffany read the scandalous article, which centered on the mysterious deaths of the foals. Not only did Rod Crawford imply that there was something genetically wrong with Moon Shadow, who had sired all of the colts, but he also suggested that Tiffany, in an effort to save her reputation as a horse breeder, had hidden the deaths from the public and the racing commission. Crawford went on to say that any horse bred to Moon Shadow was likely to produce foals with genetic heart defects.

The article reported that since Tiffany had assumed control of Rhodes Breeding Farm, she had encountered more problems than she could handle. From the time her husband and the legendary Devil's Gambit had died, and Tiffany had been in charge of the farm, she had experienced nothing but trouble. It appeared that either Tiffany Rhodes was the victim of fate or her own gross incompetence.

"No!" Tiffany whispered, forcing the hot tears of indignation backward. She crumpled the damning newspaper in her fist. No mention had been made of Journey's End or any other of Moon Shadow's living, healthy progeny. Rod Crawford had twisted and butchered her words in a piece of cheap sensational journalism. Nausea began to roil in her stomach. "Damn it, nothing is wrong with him! Nothing!"

Her words sounded fragile into the late morning air, as if she were trying to convince herself.

Zane had watched as Tiffany read the article. She had paled slightly before anger settled on her elegant features. Now she was clenching the newspaper in her small fist and trembling with rage.

"What happened?" he demanded.

"Rod Crawford wrote his article," Tiffany explained.

"The reporter who was here just yesterday?"

Tiffany let out a furious sigh and looked upward to the interlaced branches of the oak and fir trees. Shafts of sunlight passed through the lacy barrier to dapple the wet ground. "I didn't think the article would be printed this soon," she replied, somehow stilling her seething rage, "but I guess in the case of a scandal, even the *Clarion* holds the presses."

She expelled an angry breath and coiled her fist. "Damn it all, anyway!" She had trusted Rod Crawford and the *Clarion*'s reputation, and her trust had backfired in her face. The slant of the article was vicious, a personal attack intended to maim Tiffany's reputation. It was the last thing she had expected from a paper with the reputation of the *Santa Rosa Clarion*.

Zane touched her lightly on the shoulder in an attempt to calm her. "What are you talking about?"

"This." Her breasts rose and fell with the effort as she handed him the newspaper.

As Zane quickly scanned the article, his dark brows drew together in a savage scowl and his skin tightened over his cheekbones. A small muscle worked furiously in the corner of his jaw, and his lips thinned dangerously.

After reading the story and looking over the photographs, he smoothed the rumpled paper and tucked it under his arm. Every muscle had tensed in his whip-lean body. He was like a coiled snake, ready to strike. "Is there any truth in the article?"

"Enough to make it appear genuine."

"Great." He frowned and pinched the bridge of his nose with his thumb and forefinger, as if attempting to ward off a threatening headache. "Why didn't you tell me about this?"

Tiffany clenched her impotent fists. "I had enough to worry about with you and your crazy theories about Devil's Gambit. I didn't want to cloud the issue with the problem with Moon Shadow's foals."

"Even after last night, when I was with Ebony Wine?"

"There wasn't time." Even to her own ears, the excuse sounded feeble.

"And that's why you didn't want me near Rod Crawford. You were afraid I'd tell him what I knew about Devil's Gambit, he would report it and something like this—" he held up the newspaper and waved it in her face angrily "—might happen."

"Only it would be much worse."

He shook his head in disbelief. "I wouldn't have, you know." He could read the doubts still lingering in her eyes and silently damned himself for caring about her.

As if physically restraining his anger at her lack of trust in him, he handed the paper back to Tiffany. "I guess I can't blame you—I did come storming in here yesterday." He managed a stiff smile and pushed his hands into the back pockets of his cords. After taking a few steps, as if to increase the distance between them, he turned and faced her. Thoughtful lines etched his brow, but the intense anger seemed to dissolve. "So tell me—the colt that was born last night—he was sired by Moon Shadow. Right?"

"Yes."

Zane raked frustrated fingers through his hair. "Then the death last night will only support the allegations in Crawford's newspaper column."

Tiffany felt as if everything she had worked for was slowly slipping through her fingers. "I suppose so," she admitted with a heavy sigh. Dear God, what was happening to her life? Suddenly everything seemed to be turning upside down. Zane Sheridan, a man whom she barely knew, whom she desired as a man but knew to be an enemy, was clouding her usually clear thinking at a time when she desperately needed all of her senses to prove true. He was voicing her worst fears, and she had trouble keeping the worried tears at bay.

"You should have told me."

"I couldn't."

"Because you didn't trust me and you thought that I might use the information on Moon Shadow against you," he said flatly, as if reading her thoughts.

So close to the truth! Was she so transparent to this man she had met only yesterday? Or was it because he knew more about her than he was willing to admit? "Something like that," she allowed, raising one suddenly heavy shoulder. "It really doesn't matter now."

"Look, woman," he said, barely able to contain his simmering anger. "You'd better start trusting me, because it looks like you're going to need all the friends you can get."

Her eyes took on a suspicious light. "But that's the problem, isn't it? I'm not quite sure whether you're on my side or not—friend or foe."

"Wait a minute—" He looked at her incredulously, as if she'd lost her mind. "Didn't I just tell you that I'm attracted to you? Wasn't I the man trying to make love to you just a few minutes ago?"

Tiffany elevated her chin fractionally. Now was the time to see exactly where Zane stood. Her dark brows arched suspiciously. "Sleeping with the enemy isn't something new, you know. It's been documented throughout history."

"Oh, give me a break!" he spit, his palms lifting upwards as if he were begging divine interference. "Did Ellery scar you so badly that you can't trust any man?"

"Ellery has nothing to do with this."

"The hell he hasn't!" Zane thundered, shaking his head in disbelief. His arms fell to his sides in useless defeat. "You're not an easy woman to like sometimes," he said softly as he approached her. He was close enough to touch. He was offering his strength, his comfort, if only she were brave enough to trust him.

"I haven't asked you to like me—"

He reached out and grabbed her arm. "Oh, yes, you have. Every time you look at me with those wide, soul-searching eyes, you beg me to like you. Every time you smile at me, you're inviting me to care about you. Every time you touch me, you're pleading with me to love you."

Tiffany listened in astonishment, her heart beginning to pound furiously at his suggestive words. She closed her eyes in embarrassment. How close to the truth he was! His fingers wrapped more tightly over her upper arms, leaving warm impressions on her flesh.

"Look at me, dammit," he insisted, giving her a shake. When she obeyed, Zane's flinty eyes drilled into hers. "Now, lady, it looks as if you've got one hell of a problem on your hands. There's a good chance that I won't be able to help you at all, but I don't think you're in much of a position to pick and choose your friends.''

She tossed her hair away from her face and proudly returned his intense stare. "Maybe not."

"So let's try to figure out why those foals are dying, right now."

"How?"

"First I want to take a look at Moon Shadow."

Tiffany hesitated only slightly. Zane was right. She needed all the allies she could find. She checked her watch and discovered that it was nearly noon. No doubt the telephone was already ringing off the hook because of the article in the morning paper. There was no time to waste. Straightening her shoulders, Tiffany cocked her head in the direction of the stallion barns.

"Mac usually takes him outside about this time. He's probably getting some exercise right now."

Moon Shadow was in a far corner of the field. His sleek black coat shimmered in the noonday sun and he tossed his arrogant ebony head upward, shaking his glossy mane and stamping one forefoot warily.

Zane studied the nervous stallion. As a three-year-old, Moon Shadow had been impressive. He boasted a short, strong back, powerful hindquarters and long legs that could propel him forward in an explosion of speed at the starting gate that had been unmatched by any of his peers. He'd won a good percentage of his starts including two jewels of the Triple Crown. His most poignant loss was the Kentucky Derby, in which he had been jostled and boxed in near the starting gate and hadn't been able to run "his race," which had always been to start in front, set the pace and stay in the lead.

Zane blamed Moon Shadow's Derby disaster on several factors, the most obvious being that of a bad jockey. Moon Shadow's regular rider had been injured the day of the race, and his replacement, Bill Wade, was a green, uncaring man who had later lost his license to ride.

Mac was leaning over the fence, a piece of straw tucked into a corner of his mouth. Suddenly the black horse snorted, flattened his ears to his head, lifted his tail and ran the length of the long paddock. His smooth strides made the short dash appear effortless.

"He knows he's got an audience," Mac said as Tiffany approached. Wolverine was resting at the trainer's feet. At the sight of Tiffany, he thumped his tail on the moist ground. She reached down and scratched the collie's ears before propping her foot on the lowest board of the fence and resting her arms over the top rail.

"He's going to have more," Tiffany said with a sigh.

Mac's eyes narrowed. "More what?"

"More of an audience."

"What d'ya mean?" Instantly Mac was concerned. He read the worry in Tiffany's eyes.

"I'm afraid Moon Shadow is going to get more than his share of attention in the next couple of weeks. Take a look at page one." Tiffany handed Mac the paper before shading her eyes with her hand.

"Son of a bitch," Mac cursed after reading the article. He pushed his hat back to the crown of his head. "A pack of lies—nothing but a goddamn pack of lies." His eyes flickered from Zane to Tiffany before returning to Moon Shadow. "Damn reporters never have learned to sort fact from fiction." After smoothing the thin red hair over his scalp, he forced the frumpy fedora back onto his head. "A good thing you and Vance already told the Jockey Club about the dead colts."

"Yeah, right," Tiffany agreed without much enthusiasm. "But wait until the owners who have broodmares pregnant with Moon Shadow's foals get wind of this."

Mac frowned and rubbed the toe of his boot in the mud. "You'll just have to set them straight, Missy. Moon Shadow's a good stud. He's got the colts to prove it. Why the hell didn't that bastard of a reporter write about Journey's End or Devil's Gambit?''

Tiffany's eyes moved from Mac to Zane and finally back to the stallion in question. "I don't know," she answered. "Probably because he needed a story to sell papers." And he'd get one, too, if Zane decided to publicize his conjectures about Ellery and Devil's Gambit.

"How many foals were affected?" Zane asked.

"Three—no, Ebony Wine's colt makes four," Tiffany replied softly. "Three colts and a filly. Two died shortly after birth, the colt last night was stillborn and Charlatan...well, he lived longer, a couple of days, but..." Her voice faded on the soft afternoon breeze.

The silence of the afternoon was interrupted only by the wind rustling through the fir needles and the sound of Moon Shadow's impatient snorts.

"And they all died from heart failure?" Zane asked, staring at the proud stallion as if he hoped to see the reasons for the tragic deaths in the shining black horse.

Tiffany nodded, and Mac shifted the piece of straw from one corner of his mouth to the other.

"Seems that way," Mac muttered.

"Unless Vance discovers something different in the autopsy of the colt born last night," Tiffany added and then shook her head. "But I doubt that he'll find anything else."

"What about other horses bred to Moon Shadow?"

"Fortunately, none of the foals of mares from other owners have been affected—at least not yet. I've corresponded with all of the owners. So far, each mare has delivered a strong, healthy foal."

"Thank God for small favors," Mac mumbled ungraciously.

"Some owners even want to rebreed to Moon Shadow," Tiffany said, almost as an afterthought.

"But you're not breeding him?"

"Not until we find out what's going on."

"I don't blame you." Zane's gaze returned to the imperious stallion, who was tossing his head menacingly toward the spectators.

"He knows we're talkin' about him," Mac said fondly. "Always did like a show, that one." He rubbed the back of his weathered neck. "Should've won the Triple Crown, ya know. My fault for letting that son of a bitch ride him."

"Mac's been blaming himself ever since."

"I should've known the boy was no good."

"Quit second-guessing yourself. Ellery thought Bill was a decent jockey. Moon Shadow didn't win and that's that."

Mac frowned as he stared at the horse. "The closest I've come to a Triple Crown. Moon Shadow and Devil's Gambit were the finest horses I've ever seen race."

Tiffany stiffened at the mention of Devil's Gambit. "Mac's prejudiced, of course. The owners of Secretariat, Seattle Slew and a few others would have different opinions. But Moon Shadow sure used to be a crowd-pleaser," Tiffany remarked thoughtfully as she stared at the fiery black stallion.

"Aye. That he did," the old trainer agreed sadly as he rubbed the stubble on his chin. "That he did."

Tiffany spent the rest of the day showing Zane the farm. As Mac had stated, Ebony Wine seemed none the worse from her trauma the night before, and if Vance Geddes gave his okay, Tiffany wanted to breed her as soon as the mare was in heat.

As much as it broke her heart, Tiffany decided that Moon Shadow couldn't be allowed to sire any more foals until it was proved beyond a doubt that the cause of his foals' deaths wasn't genetic.

By the time she and Zane headed back to the house, it was late afternoon. The March sun was warm against Tiffany's back. As they walked toward the back porch, she slung her jacket over her shoulder. Zane had been with her all day, and it seemed natural that he was on the farm, helping with the chores, offering her his keen advice and flashing his devastating smile.

"So you've already had him tested," Zane remarked as he held open the screen door to the broad back porch.

"Yes. And so far the semen samples have shown nothing out of the ordinary. I've asked for additional tests, but Vance Geddes seems to think that nothing will be discovered."

"What about the mares?"

She frowned and sighed. "Each horse has been examined by several vets. Blood samples, urine samples...every test available. The mares seem perfectly healthy.

"So all of the evidence points to Moon Shadow."

Tiffany nodded as she wedged the toe of one boot behind the heel of the other and kicked it off. She placed the scarred boots in the corner of the porch near the kitchen door. "It looks that way," she admitted.

"But you don't believe it."

"A good stud just doesn't go bad overnight." She pursed her lips together and ran weary fingers through her unruly hair. "Something has to have happened to him—I just don't know what."

"All the mares were bred to him around the same time?"

"Within a few weeks—I think. However, there are still mares who haven't dropped their foals."

"And you think they may have problems?"

Her blue eyes clouded with worry. "I hope to God they don't," she whispered as she started toward the door to the house. Zane's hand on her arm restrained her.

"I need to ask you something," he said quietly. The tone of his voice sent a prickle of fear down her spine.

"What?"

"Do you have any enemies, anyone who would want to hurt you?" His eyes had darkened as they searched her face.

"None that I can think of."

"What about this Crawford, the guy who wrote the article? Why would he want to distort the truth?"

"I couldn't begin to hazard a guess." She looked at the paper Zane was still carrying under his arm. "I guess the *Clarion* is into sensationalism these days."

"No personal reasons?"

"No."

His eyes drove into hers. "How about someone else who might want to see you exposed as incompetent?"

Tiffany stiffened, and cold dread settled between her shoulder blades. "Like whom?"

"I don't know—a competitor maybe?" When she shook her head in disbelief, her hair tumbled over her shoulders. He tightened his fingers around her arms. "A spurned lover?"

"Of course not!"

His grip relaxed a little. "You can't think of anyone who would want to hurt you? Someone with a big enough grudge against you or this farm to want to see your dirty laundry in black and white?" He was staring at her boldly, daring her to reply. "It would have to be someone with inside information."

Tiffany's eyes grew cold, and she felt a painful constricting of her heart. "The only person who remotely fits that description is you."

Zane stiffened. Tiffany saw the anger flash in his eyes, but he didn't bother to refute her accusation. His lips thinned until they showed white near the corners. "You know there was no love lost between myself and your husband. If Ellery were alive today, I'd probably do what I could to ruin him." He looked away from her and for a moment, pain was evident in the rugged planes of his face. "I despised the man, Tiffany, but you have to believe that I would never intentionally hurt you."

"Even if Ellery is still alive?" she whispered.

He closed his eyes against the possibility. The craving for vengeance that had festered in his blood still poisoned him, but as he gazed down upon Tiffany's face, Zane knew that he was lost to her. His hatred for Ellery couldn't begin to match the intensity of his feelings for this proud, beautiful woman. "If Ellery Rhodes walked through the door tonight, I would still detest him. But—" he reached out and gently stroked her chin "—because of you, I would leave."

Tiffany swallowed the uncomfortable lump forming in her throat and ignored the hot sting of tears against her eyelids. How desperately she longed to believe him. "Even if I asked you to stay?"

"What are you saying, Tiffany?" he asked, his face close to hers. "If Ellery is alive, would you leave him for me?"

"I...I don't know," she admitted, confused at the emotions warring within her. She ached to say yes and fall into Zane's arms, never to look back. If only she could love him for now, this moment, and cast away any thought to the future, or the past.

Slowly he pulled her to him, and Tiffany felt his larger body press urgently against hers. She leaned on him, and he kissed her forehead. "I can't make things different between us," he said, gently smoothing her hair away from her face.

"Would you, if you could?"

"Yes," he replied quickly as he had a vision of her lying naked in Ellery Rhodes's bed. "I wish I'd known you long ago."

In the privacy of the screened porch, with the fragrance of cherry blossoms scenting the air, nothing seemed to matter. It was a private world filled with only this one strong, passionate man. Tears pooled in Tiffany's eyes and clung to her lashes. "I think that it's better not to dwell on the past...or wish for things that could never be."

He tilted her face upward with his hands, and his lips claimed hers in a kiss that was filled with the desperation of the moment, and the need to purge all thoughts of her husband from her mind.

Her lips parted willingly for him, and his tongue touched the edges of her teeth before slipping into her mouth and plundering the moist cavern she so willingly offered.

A raw groan of frustrated longing escaped from his lips as he molded his hungry body to hers. She wound her arms around him, held him close, clinging to him as if afraid he would leave her empty and bereft.

"Tiffany," he whispered into her hair and let out a ragged breath. "Oh, Tiffany, what am I going to do with you?"

Whatever you want, she thought, returning his kiss with a bursting passion that had no earthly bounds.

His hands found the hem of her sweater and slipped underneath the soft fabric to press against the silken texture of her skin. Her breath constricted in her throat, and when his fingers cupped the underside of her breast she felt as if she were melting into him. A soft moan came from her throat as his fingers softly traced the lacy edge of her bra. She felt the bud of her nipple blossom willingly to his touch as his fingers slid slowly upward.

Zane's breathing became labored, a sweet rush of air against her ear that caused tantalizing sparks of yearning to fire her blood. "Let me love you, sweet lady," he pleaded, fanning her hair with his breath.

If only I could! Her desire throbbed in her ears, burned in her soul, but the doubts of the night filtered into her passion-drugged mind, and before she lost all sense of reason, she pulled away from him, regret evidenced in her slumberous blue eyes. "I...I think it would be best if we went inside," she said raggedly, hoping to quell the raging storm of passion in her blood.

The tense lines along the edge of his mouth deepened. "You want me," he said, holding her close, pressing the muscles of her body to his. "Admit it."

Her heart was an imprisoned bird throwing itself mercilessly against her rib cage. She lost her sense of time and reason. "I want you more than I've ever wanted a man," she whispered, trying to pull free of his protective embrace. "But wanting isn't enough."

"What is?"

Love, her mind screamed, but the word wouldn't form on her lips. How often before had she felt love only to see it wither and die? The love of Tiffany's mother had been so fragile that Marie had left her only daughter in the care of a drunken father. Edward's love hadn't been strong enough to conquer the drink that eventually killed him, and Ellery...Ellery probably didn't know the meaning of the word.

"I...I'm not sure," she admitted, her voice quavering unexpectedly.

"Oh, hell," Zane swore in disgust, releasing her. "Neither am I." He looked thoroughly disgusted with himself, and he rammed his hands into his pockets, trying to quiet the fury of desire straining within him. The heat in his loins seemed to sear his mind. Never had he wanted a woman so painfully. He felt as if his every nerve were raw, charged with lust.

Tiffany stared at Zane until her breathing had silenced and her racing pulse had slowed to a more normal rate. She entered the house, and the smells of roast and cinnamon filled her nostrils. "Louise?" she called as she went into the kitchen. The plump woman with graying hair and a ready smile was extracting a deep-dish apple pie from one of the ovens. "I thought you were going out of town for the weekend."

"Not until tomorrow." Louise set the hot pie on the tile counter and turned to face Tiffany. "I thought maybe you could use a little help around here today."

"You read the article in the *Clarion.*"

Louise's full mouth pursed into an angry pout. "Yep. I read it this morning and canceled my subscription before noon. That was the trashiest piece of journalism I've ever read. Rod Crawford should be strung up by his—'' her eyes moved from Tiffany to Zane ''—hamstrings.''

Tiffany smiled at the angry housekeeper. "You shouldn't have canceled your subscription."

"Hmmph. What I should have done was write a letter to the editor, but I suppose that would only make the situation worse, what with the publicity and all."

At that moment the phone rang, and Tiffany reached to answer it.

"It's been ringing off the hook all afternoon." When Tiffany hesitated, Louise continued. "Reporters mostly. A couple of other breeders, too. The messages are on your desk."

"I'll take the call in the den," Tiffany decided, straightening her shoulders.

"Vultures," Louise muttered as she opened the oven and checked the roast.

Tiffany answered the phone in the den on the sixth ring.

"Tiffany, is that you?" an agitated male voice inquired.

"Yes."

"This is Hal Reece." Tiffany's heart sank. Reece had bred one of his mares to Moon Shadow. Was he calling to tell her that the foal was dead? Her palms began to sweat and her pulse jumped nervously.

"What can I do for you, Mr. Reece?"

The stuffy sixty-year-old paused before getting to the point. "I read an article about your farm in the *Clarion*. No one told me there was any genetic problem with Moon Shadow."

"There isn't."

"But the article stated—"

"What the article stated was only half the story." Tiffany's eyes clashed with Zane's as he entered the den.

"Then you're saying that those foals didn't die?" he questioned, relief audible in his voice.

"No," Tiffany replied, bracing herself by leaning on the desk. "It's true we've lost a few foals—"

"Moon Shadow's foals," he clarified.

"Yes. But there is no reason to think that the problem is genetic. I've had Moon Shadow tested by several veterinarians. You're familiar with Vance Geddes, aren't you?"

"Why, yes. Good man, Geddes."

"He's been involved with the problem from day one. He's concluded that there's no evidence that the deaths were genetically related."

"But certainly they were linked."

"It appears that way."

"And the natural assumption is that it was the sire, as all the foals were his."

Tiffany heard the hopeful note in Hal's voice. She hated to discourage him. Forcing herself to remain calmly professional, she held her voice steady as she clutched the receiver in a deathlike grip. "Moon Shadow has proved himself a good stud. Journey's End and Devil's Gambit are proof enough of that. Most of the foals that he sired this year had no problems."

"No other owner has complained?" Reece asked, sounding dubious.

"None, and I've been in contact with each of them. So far, Moon Shadow has sired twenty-three perfectly healthy foals—something Mr. Crawford neglected to print."

"But three have died."

There was no use in hiding the truth from Reece or any of the other owners who had bred their expensive mares to Moon Shadow. It would only look worse later. Tiffany gritted her teeth and closed her eyes. "Four. We lost another colt last night."

"Oh, God!" His voice sounded weak.

Zane was standing near the fireplace, one shoeless stockinged foot propped against the stone hearth.

"When is your mare due to foal?" Tiffany asked.

"Any day now."

"I'm sure you'll find that you have a healthy Thorough-bred on your hands."

"I'd better, Tiffany," Hal said softly. "I'm not a rich man; I can't afford a loss like this. I'm sure the insurance company wouldn't cover the cost of my stud fee—"

"Mr. Reece, if you do happen to lose the colt and we discover that the problem stemmed from breeding your mare to Moon Shadow, I'll refund the stud fee."

"And then what? My mare's lost nearly a year of prime breeding time."

Tiffany's face became rigid. "I won't be able to do anything about that, Mr. Reece. It's the chance we take as breeders." She heard herself repeating Zane's advice of the night before. "When your mare does foal, I'd appreciate a call from you."

"You can count on it. Good day," he replied frostily, and Tiffany replaced the receiver. As soon as she set it down the phone rang again.

"Don't answer it," Zane advised, seeing the way she had paled during her lengthy conversation.

"I have to."

"The calls can wait."

"I don't think so. I have ten or twelve owners who are probably in a state of panic."

The phone rang again.

"It could be the press," Zane argued.

"Then I'll have to deal with them as well. I can't just hide my head in the sand. This was bound to happen sooner or later." She reached for the phone and answered it. A male voice demanded to speak to Tiffany Rhodes.

"This is she," Tiffany replied. The man identified himself as a reporter for a San Francisco paper. The telephone call was a short interview, and by the time it was over, Tiffany felt drained.

Zane sat on the edge of the desk, his worried gaze studying her as she turned around, clicked on a small computer in the bookcase and started typing onto the keyboard when luminous green letters appeared on the screen.

"What're you doing?"

"Getting a printout of all the owners who still have broodmares pregnant with Moon Shadow's foals. I think it would be best if I called them, rather than having them read a story like the one in the *Santa Rosa Clarion.*"

"This can wait until morning."

Tiffany shook her head and refused to be deterred. "I'd just as soon get it over with. The sooner the better." The printer began rattling out the list of owners as Tiffany checked the phone messages Louise had stacked on her desk. "Great," she mumbled. She held up one of the messages and handed it to him. "A reporter for a television station in San Francisco wants an interview." She smiled grimly. "What do you bet that it's not to talk about Journey's End's career?"

Zane frowned. "No wager from me, lady. I learned a long time ago not to bet money unless it was a sure thing—and then only when the man you're betting against is honest." His voice was low, and edged in anger. From the look on Zane's face, she knew that he was somehow referring to Ellery.

The printer stopped spewing out information, and the silence in the small room seemed deafening.

At that moment, Louise appeared, balancing a tray in her plump hands. "I thought you two could use a cup of coffee," she explained. Noticing the tension in the room and the silent challenge in Tiffany's eyes, Louise pursed her lips together thoughtfully and amended her offer. "Or I could get you something stronger—"

"Coffee's fine," Zane replied, turning to watch her and sending a charming grin in her direction.

"Yes, thank you," Tiffany said, once Zane's gaze had released her.

"Dinner will be in about an hour."

Tiffany managed a frail smile. "Louise, you're a life-saver."

The large woman chuckled. "I'm afraid you'll need more than a hot meal before the evening's done."

"Don't be so optimistic," Tiffany remarked cynically.

"Just my nature," Louise replied before leaving the room.

"What else have you got on that computer?" Zane asked, studying the list of owners.

"Everything."

"Like what?"

"Health records on the horses, the price of feed, the stud fees we charged, equipment. Everything."

"Including a profile of your Thoroughbreds?"

"Every horse that's been a part of the farm."

"Can you get me a printout on Moon Shadow?"

She managed a tight smile. "Sure."

"How about the mares he was bred to, especially the four that lost their foals?"

Tiffany sat down at the keyboard. "This has already been done, you know."

"Humor me. I need something to do while you're tied up with the phone. I may as well be doing something constructive since I canceled my flight."

"Can't argue with that." Tiffany requested the information from the computer, and when the printer started spewing out profiles of the horses in question, Tiffany started with the first of what promised to be several uncomfortable telephone calls to the owners of mares bred to Moon Shadow.

Chapter Seven

Here, drink some of this," Zane suggested. He handed Tiffany a glass of white wine. "Maybe it will improve your appetite."

"And my disposition?" She accepted the glass and took a sip of the white Burgundy. The cool liquid slid easily down her throat, and she eyed her plate of forgotten food with a sigh.

"They really got to you, didn't they?" Zane asked as he leaned back in his chair and frowned into his glass. He had finished Louise's dinner of roast beef, parslied potatoes and steamed broccoli before noticing Tiffany's neglected plate.

"Let's just say I'm glad it's over," she replied and then amended her statement, "or I hope to God it is."

What if any of the unborn foals were to die shortly after birth? What would happen to her and the farm? The telephone conversations with the owners who had mares bred to Moon Shadow hadn't gone well at all. By the time she had contacted or left messages with all the owners, Tiffany had felt as if every nerve in her body had been stretched as tightly as a piano wire. During two of the more difficult calls, she had been threatened with lawsuits, should the foals be born with life-threatening heart problems.

She couldn't begin to do justice to Louise's delicious meal. With a weary shake of her head, she pushed her plate aside, leaned back in the chair and ran tense fingers through her hair.

Zane offered her a sad, understanding smile. "Come on, the dishes will wait. Let's finish this—" he held up the opened bottle of wine "—and relax in the study."

"I don't think that's possible."

"Come on, buck up." He got up from the table and placed a comforting hand on her shoulder. "Things are bound to get better."

"That's a strange statement, coming from you," she stated. He shrugged his broad shoulders and his smile faded. "But I guess you're right," she continued, slapping the table with new resolve. "Things can't get much worse." *Unless another foal dies.*

The den seemed warm and intimate. The glowing embers of the fire and the muted illumination from a single brass lamp with an emerald-colored shade softened the corners of the room and reflected on the finish of the cherry-wood walls. The thick Oriental carpet in hues of green and ivory, the etchings of sleek horses adorning the walls and the massive stone fireplace offered a sense of privacy to the room.

Zane stoked the smoldering coals in the fireplace. *As if he'd done it a hundred times. Here. In her home.* His actions seemed so natural, as if he were an integral part of the farm. As he knelt before the fire, he lifted a chunk of oak from the large basket sitting on the warm stones of the hearth. "This should do it," he mumbled to himself as he placed the mossy log on the scarlet embers. Eager flames began to lick the new fuel and reflect in golden shadows on

Zane's angular face. His shirt was stretched over his back, and Tiffany watched his fluid movements as he worked. When the fire was to his satisfaction, he dusted his hands together and studied the ravenous flames.

As she sipped her wine and observed him, Tiffany felt the long dormant stirring of feminine desire. Urges that were better denied began to burn in her mind. *I won't let myself fall for him,* she promised but knew that her efforts would prove futile. He was already an integral part of her life. Ever since last night, when he had bent over the lifeless foal and tried to force air into the still lungs, Zane Sheridan had become a part of Rhodes Breeding Farm. Whether she liked it or not.

She dragged her eyes away from his strong physique and concentrated on the clear liquid in her wineglass. "Don't you have some place you have to be?" she asked.

The lean frame stiffened. He hesitated for just a moment before turning to face her. "Later."

"Tonight?" she asked in attempted nonchalance. Her tongue caught on the solitary word.

He nodded curtly. "I've got some early appointments in San Francisco tomorrow." He noticed the slight tensing in her shoulders. *Damn her, that strong will and pride will be her downfall...or mine.* "Things I can't put off any longer." He finished his wine and stared at her. "Is that a hint?"

"No.... I mean, I just think it's strange that you've been here—" she made a big show of checking her watch "—over twenty-four hours and still haven't gotten down to the reason you came."

"The time of reckoning—right?" His eyes met her gaze boldly before glancing at the portrait of the horse.

She took a seat on the edge of the gray corduroy couch. "Close enough. But first I want to thank you for helping last night. I really appreciate everything you did...."

"You're sure about that?"

She remembered waking up and finding him sleeping in the uncomfortable chair with his feet propped on her bed. "Yes," she whispered. "For everything."

"And now you want to know about Devil's Gambit," Zane thought aloud as he stood and stretched his arms over his head. It was an unconscious and erotic gesture. His sweater rose, displaying all too clearly his lean abdomen. His belted cords were slung low over his hips and Tiffany glimpsed the rock-hard muscles near his navel. She imagined the ripple of the corded muscles of his chest, his muscular thighs and lean flanks.... She had to look away from him and force her mind from the sexual fantasy she was envisioning. What was wrong with her? She'd never reacted this way to a man, not even Ellery. Until Zane Sheridan had walked into her life, she had considered herself nearly uninterested in the opposite sex.

One look from Zane's steely gray eyes had drastically altered her entire perception of her own sexuality. Her new feelings were at once exciting and frightening. Zane was the one man she couldn't begin to trust...not with her body or her soul. He had already admitted that he was waging a vendetta of sorts, and she didn't doubt for a minute that he was the kind of man who would use and destroy her because of his hatred of Ellery.

Zane took a final sip of his wine and then set the empty goblet on the mantel. "I meant to tell you about Devil's Gambit last night," he explained, "but Ebony Wine had other things on her mind."

Tiffany nodded and clutched the stem of her crystal glass more tightly as she remembered the agonizing scene in the foaling shed and the innocent stillborn colt. Had it been only last night? So many things had changed, including her respect and feelings for Zane. "So what about now?"

Zane angled his head to the side and studied the wariness in her eyes. She was sitting on the edge of the gray cushions, waiting for him to explain his reasons for being there.

"No time like the present, I suppose." He walked over to the bar and splashed three fingers of Scotch into an empty glass. "I think your horse—"

"You mean Devil's Gambit?"

"Right. I think he's in Ireland, using an alias."

"Now I know you're crazy." What did he mean about Devil's Gambit being in Ireland? His story was getting more far fetched by the minute.

If she had any guts at all, she would tell him to get out of her house...her life, take his wild stories and shove them. Instead she twirled the stem of the wineglass in her fingers and stared up at him.

"Just hear me out. Have you ever heard of a horse named King's Ransom?"

"Yes," she admitted, recalling the Irish Thoroughbred. "But I really don't keep up on the European horses, not as much as I should, I suppose. There just isn't enough time. Dustin handles that end of the business."

"I'm not surprised," Zane replied with obvious distaste.

"What does that mean?"

"Only that sometimes it's hard to tell Ellery and Dustin apart." He paced across the room before sitting on the warm stones of the hearth.

"So you know Dustin?" That knowledge came as a shock to her and she felt a new wariness steal over her heart. *Hadn't Dustin mentioned King's Ransom to her—something about the horse's fame as a stud?* Tiffany couldn't recall the conversation....

"We've met." Zane leaned his elbows on his knees and cradled his drink with both of his hands.

"And you don't like him any more than you liked Ellery."

"As I said, they're too much alike to suit my taste."

Tiffany was stunned. Dustin had his faults, of course, but she'd come to rely on her brother-in-law and his savvy for horses. It seemed as if Zane were determined to destroy anything and anyone who was solid in her life.

"Not much does, does it?" she countered.

"What?"

"Suit your taste."

He hesitated. His eyes darkened and for a moment she imagined that he might suggest that she suited him. Instead he lifted an appreciative dark brow. "You're right—not much."

Tiffany's throat constricted, and she sipped her wine to clear the tight lump that made it difficult to breathe.

If he noticed her discomfort, Zane chose to ignore it and get to the point. "Anyway, this horse, King's Ransom, was a disappointment when he raced. He had all the qualities to perform on the track—great bloodlines, perfect conformation and a long, easy stride. He had the look of a winner about him, but he just didn't seem to have the grit...or heart to be a champion. He never finished better than fifth, and consequently he was retired about seven years ago and put out to stud.

"The first of his offspring began running about four years ago, and even though they inherited all his physical characteristics, none of the colts and fillies were anything to write home about. It seemed as if they all ended up with his lack of drive."

"So what does this have to do with Devil's Gambit?" Tiffany asked. Her blue eyes mirrored her worry. Despite her arguments to the contrary, she was beginning to understand what Zane was hinting at.

"I'm getting to that. All of a sudden, less than two years ago, when that year's two-year-olds and three-year-olds hit the track, look out! Overnight, King's Ransom was producing some of the fastest horses in Europe."

"That's not impossible," Tiffany said uneasily. She felt a sudden chill and shivered before getting up and walking closer to the fire...to Zane.

"But highly improbable. It's the same principle as what's happening here with Moon Shadow, in reverse. Just as a good stud won't go bad overnight, the reverse is true. A mediocre stallion doesn't become the greatest stud in Ireland by a fluke." Zane was looking up at her with his magnetic gray eyes. He knew that he had Tiffany's full attention. Her glass of wine was nearly untouched, her troubled blue eyes reached into the blackest corners of his soul. *God, she was beautiful.* He swirled his drink and stared into the amber liquor, trying to still the male urges overcoming him.

"I own a mare that I had bred about five years ago to King's Ransom," Zane continued. "The colt that was born from that union was just what I expected—a solid horse, a plodder, but nothing that would compare to his recent foals. I rebred that same mare to King's Ransom three years ago, and the resulting filly has already won two races and come in second in another. This horse is a full sister to the first."

Tiffany's dark honey-colored brows drew together pensively as she tried to remember what it was about King's Ransom...Vaguely she recalled a conversation with Dustin. Dustin had been going on and on about King's Ransom and his ability as a sire. At the time, it hadn't seemed all that important. Dustin was always raving about one horse or another—comparing his current favorite to the horses he and Tiffany owned.

"It might be worth it to breed one of the mares, say Felicity, to King's Ransom," Dustin had insisted.

"But the cost of shipping her would be prohibitive," Tiffany had replied. "The insurance alone—"

"I tell you, that stud's got what it takes!" Dustin had been adamant. "He could sire the next Devil's Gambit!"

Now, as Dustin's words came back to her, Tiffany paled. If what Zane was suggesting was true, then Dustin must have been involved! "I...I don't believe it," Tiffany said, taking a sip of her wine and trying to ignore the chilling implications running through her mind.

This was absurd. Ludicrous. Her relationship with Dustin had always been solid, and after Ellery's accident it had been Dustin who had helped her over the rough spots, given her his ear, offered a strong shoulder to cry on.

"Believe it. Devil's Gambit is siring foals and King's Ransom is getting all the credit. Your horse is being used, Tiffany!"

She squared her shoulders and trained disbelieving eyes on Zane. "I don't know why you came here," she said. "If it was to trick me into selling the farm, then you may as well leave now. All of this—" she moved both arms in a sweeping gesture meant to encompass everything that had transpired between them "—has been a very entertaining show, but I don't believe any of it. You're wasting your breath."

Zane pursed his lips together in frustration. With a frown he got up, crossed the room and picked up his briefcase.

"God, Tiffany, you don't make it easy," he muttered as he set the leather case on the wooden desk and silently wondered why it bothered him so much that he had to prove himself to this woman. He could hardly expect that she would believe his story without proof. After snapping the case open and extracting a white envelope, he handed the slim packet to her.

With trembling fingers Tiffany opened the envelope and extracted a faded photograph of a black stallion.

"This," he said angrily while pointing at the horse in the photo, "is a picture of King's Ransom. He looks a lot like Devil's Gambit, don't you think?"

The resemblance was eerie. Tiffany couldn't deny what was patently obvious. Even though the photograph was old and faded, it was glaringly evident that the stallion's size and conformation were incredibly like that of the dead horse.

Zane reached inside his briefcase again. This time he took out the manila envelope he had given her the night before. It still contained the photographs he had insisted were those of Devil's Gambit. Tiffany might have believed him last night except for the fact that the white stocking on the horse's foreleg was missing.

"Are those two horses the same?" he demanded. His jaw was rigid, his gaze blistering as he searched her face.

She studied the photographs closely. A cold chill of dread skittered down her spine. The horses were nearly identical, but definitely not one and the same. Only by placing the photographs side by side was Tiffany able to discern the subtle differences between the two horses. The slope of the withers was different, as was the shape of the forehead. Only a professional would notice the small dissimilarities.

Tiffany closed her eyes against Zane's damning truth.

"Are they the same horse?" he repeated, his voice low.

Slowly, she shook her head.

Zane set the pictures on the desk and expelled a heavy sigh. Finally, he had gotten through to her! He poked a long finger at the more recent photograph. "This," he said, "is the stallion that's supposed to be King's Ransom. I say he's Devil's Gambit."

Tiffany swallowed against the dryness settling in her throat. Here was the proof that her husband had lied to her, that her proud stallion was still alive, that everything she had believed for four years was nothing more than an illusion created by her husband. *Devil's Gambit and Ellery were alive!* "How did you know?" she finally asked in a forced whisper.

He rubbed his hand over his chin and closed his eyes. "I didn't really know, not for a long time. I guess I became suspicious when the second foal, the filly, exhibited such a different temperament from her brother.

"When she started racing as a two-year-old, I was certain she was the fastest horse on the farm, though her bloodlines weren't nearly as good as several other horses."

He walked over to the fire and looked into the golden flames, as if searching for easy answers to his life. "I didn't think too much about it until I got to talking to several other owners who had noticed the same phenomenon on their farms: all of King's Ransom's latest offspring were markedly different from his first foals." Zane smiled to himself, amused by a private irony. "No one was really asking questions—all the owners were thrilled with their luck, and of course, King's Ransom's stud fees have become astronomical since the latest colts and fillies have begun racing."

Tiffany lifted her hands and shook her head in silent protest. "It still could be a coincidence," she whispered. Her suggestion was a desperate attempt to right her crazily spinning world, to hold on to what she had believed to be true for four long years, and both she and Zane knew it.

"Look at the pictures, Tiffany," Zane quietly insisted. "You're knowledgeable enough to realize those two stallions are different. Something isn't right at Emerald Enterprises."

"Pardon?"

"Emerald Enterprises owns the farm."

"And therefore King's Ransom."

"If that's what you want to call him."

Still the connection to her horse wasn't completely clear. "And you think Devil's Gambit is somehow involved?"

"I know he is."

"Because...someone switched horses, planned the accident, thereby killing the replacement horse and Ellery? Then what about Dustin? How did he manage to escape with his life?"

"Maybe he planned it."

The words settled like lead in the room. Only the occasional crackle and hiss of the fire disturbed the thick, condemning silence. "Dustin wouldn't..." she said, violently shaking her head. "He couldn't kill Ellery...they were brothers...very close...."

"Maybe it wasn't intentional. I told you that I think Ellery was in on the swindle."

Her frigid blue eyes held Zane's gaze. "That doesn't make a hell of a lot of sense, you know," she rasped, her body beginning to shake from the ordeal of the past two days. "Ellery owned the horse. Devil's Gambit was worth a lot more alive than he was dead!" She raised a trembling hand in the air to add emphasis to her words, but Zane reached for her wrist and clutched it in a deathlike grip.

"Just hear me out. Then you can draw your own conclusions."

"I already—"

He broke off her protests by tightening his fingers over her arm. "Please listen." His grip relaxed but his stormy eyes continued to hold her prisoner.

"All right, Zane. I'll listen. But in the end, if I don't believe you, you'll have to accept that."

"Fair enough." He released her and took a seat on the corner of the desk. His stormy eyes never left the tense contours of her elegant face. "When I requested a third breeding to King's Ransom, at the high stud fee, I was granted it. But because of the stallion's 'temperamental state' I wasn't allowed to witness my horse being bred."

"And you didn't buy that excuse?" Tiffany guessed.

"It sounded like bull to me. It just didn't make a lot of sense. I'd witnessed the first breeding but was out of the country when the second foal was conceived."

"So what happened?"

"I began asking a lot of questions. Too many to suit the manager of the farm. All of a sudden I was told that King's Ransom's services were, after all, unavailable. He was booked to cover far too many mares as it was, and I was asked to pick up my mare and leave."

"Before she was bred?"

"Right."

Tiffany began to get a glimmer of the truth, and it was as cold as a winter midnight.

Zane walked over to the hearth. As he sat on the warm stones he studied the amber liquor in his glass. "I picked up the mare, and the manager didn't bother to hide his relief to be rid of me. As I was leaving I saw a horse I recognized as King's Ransom running in a distant field. I thought it odd, since the manager had told me not five minutes before that King's Ransom was supposedly in the breeding shed."

"So you took these pictures!" she said breathlessly, the scenario becoming vivid in her confused mind.

"I'm a camera buff and happened to have my camera and telephoto lens with me. I grabbed what I needed from the glove box and photographed the horse. I took several shots and noticed that the stallion was running with a slight misstep. I hadn't heard about any injury to King's Ransom, and that's when I began to suspect that there might be two horses using the same name."

Tiffany's eyes were wide and questioning. "And from that you just deduced that one of the horses was Devil's Gambit?"

"It wasn't that difficult, really," Zane stated, his silvery eyes delving into hers. "Black Thoroughbreds are fairly uncommon, much rarer than bay or chestnut."

Tiffany nodded, her heart freezing with the fear that he was telling the truth. Dear God, what had Ellery done?

"Because of King's Ransom's age and coloring, it was relatively easy to discover what horse was being used in place of him to cover his mares. I did some research, and once I saw the pictures of Devil's Gambit again, I knew that he was the sire responsible for the faster offspring in the past few years."

"This is all still conjecture, you know," she said, trying to find any way possible to refute what he was saying. Even as she did so, she knew that she was grasping at straws.

"You're right. Except for one fact."

Tiffany steeled herself. "Which is?"

"That six years ago the ownership of the breeding farm where King's Ransom is standing at stud changed hands. A corporation now owns the farm. It took a lot of digging, but I finally found out that the primary stockholder in Emerald Enterprises is none other than your brother-in-law."

"Dustin?" Tiffany gasped, hoping with all her heart that Zane would come up with another name, any other name.

"One and the same."

Tiffany felt weak but outraged. Her knees buckled and she leaned against the desk for support. Even if everything Zane told her was the truth, she had to settle it herself with Dustin and Ellery...*if* Ellery was alive. *If* she could. Two very big "ifs." For a moment her voice failed her. When at last she could speak, all she could manage was a hoarse whisper. "I think, Mr. Sheridan," she suggested, "that you'd better leave."

"Are you so afraid of the truth?"

Tiffany closed her eyes, and her finely arched brows drew together. *Yes, Zane,* she thought, *I am afraid. I'm afraid that what you're telling me is reality. I'm afraid the man I trusted as a brother-in-law lied to me, I'm afraid that my husband has betrayed me and I'm afraid, so afraid of you—and what you do to me!*

She reached for her wineglass with shaking fingers. Her voice was husky. "You seem to have done your homework," she admitted. "But just because Dustin owns part of the farm in Ireland—"

"Did you know about it?" he demanded.

She managed to shake her head, and the golden light from the fire caught in the soft brown silk of her hair. Zane fought against the sudden tightness in his chest.

"Don't you think that's odd—since you're still business partners here in the States?"

Odd as hell, she thought to herself as she pushed the hair from her face and stared at the ceiling. Her brother-in-law had been the one solid thing in her life when her world had shattered in pain and desperation on the night that Ellery and Devil's Gambit were killed. Becoming a widow had been a new and frightening experience, and the scandal about Ellery and his tragic horse had only made facing widowhood worse. Reporters hadn't left her alone for over two weeks. If it hadn't been for Dustin and his strength…"I don't know everything about Dustin's business. He's just my brother-in-law, not my…"

"Husband?"

Her throat was parched, and the words forming in her mind were difficult to say. "Have you…did you…see any evidence to indicate that Ellery might still be alive?" she asked, her fingers tightening over the edge of the desk fiercely enough that her knuckles showed white.

"No."

A lump formed in her throat. "But you can't be sure?" she insisted in a breathless whisper.

Zane frowned darkly. "Oh, lady, I wish I could answer that one for you," he said fervently.

She felt the sting of tears and forced them back. "If Ellery was alive, he wouldn't have let me believe that he was dead," she said as much to convince herself as Zane. Her small hands balled into fists, and she pounded them against the varnished surface of the desk she had used for four years…Ellery's desk. "You know that you're destroying everything I've worked for, don't you? In two days, everything I've believed in is slowly being torn apart…and I don't understand why."

"Don't you want to know if your husband is alive?"

"Yes!"

"And if he is?"

"Oh, God." She clasped her hand over her mouth before she managed to steady herself. "I…I don't know."

"Would you divorce him?"

She shook her head and pressed back the tears threatening her eyes. "No. Not until I heard his side of the story."

"And when you did?" Zane asked, his features becoming harsh.

Tiffany let out a ragged breath. "I don't know. It's all so unbelievable—I don't have all the answers."

Zane's eyes bored into her as if searching for her soul. *Damn Ellery Rhodes and what he had done to his beautiful wife!* Despite the desire for revenge seeping through his blood, Zane knew as he watched Tiffany battle against tears that he could never hurt her. It would be easy to make love to Rhodes's wife, but Zane knew instinctively that she would never forgive him if he took advantage of her vulnerable state and she later found out that her husband was alive.

She managed to slowly get hold of herself. "Why does all this matter to you, and why on earth would you want to buy this farm?" she questioned, her voice a whisper. "You have your choice of every breeding farm on the market—so why this one?"

"I'm not interested in just any farm. I already have one in Ireland."

"And that's what you do—breed horses, when you're not bothering widows?"

His lips thinned in disgust. Against his better judgment, Zane crossed the room and stood near the desk, near the attractive woman leaning against the polished surface. Her head was thrown back, her white throat exposed, her silken hair falling in a reckless tumble of honey-brown that touched the desk.

"Have I bothered you so much?"

"More than you'll ever guess," she admitted, straightening. She rubbed her arms, hoping to warm the inner chill of dread settling between her shoulders. After glancing up at the portrait of Devil's Gambit, she turned cold, suspicious eyes on Zane.

"You really believe everything you've told me, don't you?"

"It's the truth."

"And is that why you want the farm? Do you want to buy me out, and then blow this whole thing wide open about Devil's Gambit? That way there would be an investigation and you would have a chance, as owner of Rhodes Breeding Farm, of recovering him?"

"I don't think it would work that way," Zane said stiffly. "You would still own the horse. That's not the reason I want this farm."

"Then what is, Zane? Why did you come here in the first place?" He was much too close, but she didn't give in an inch. Proudly she faced him, her soft lips pressed into a frown, her skin stretched tightly over the gentle curve of her cheek.

Zane's dark eyes drove into her very soul. "Ellery Rhodes stole from me."

"What are you talking about?"

Deciding to distance himself from her, Zane walked over to the bar and splashed another drink into his glass. *How much could he confide to Ellery Rhodes's widow without blowing everything?* "It's not a subject I like to discuss," Zane admitted after taking a long swallow of the warm Scotch. "But about six years ago Ellery won a large amount of cash from me."

"And you hate him for that?" Tiffany was incredulous. What kind of a man was Zane?

"Not until I found out that the game was rigged. Oh, by the way, your brother-in-law, Dustin, was in on it, too."

"I don't believe it."

"Believe it. Your husband was little more than a thief."

Tiffany was numb from the tattered state of her emotions. "And you've waited all this time, just to get even with him," she guessed, her voice without inflection. "It didn't matter that he was dead—you just had to do something, *anything* to get even."

Zane saw the disbelief and silent accusations in Tiffany's eyes. He wanted to purge himself, tell all of the story, but couldn't. Stasia's betrayal had been long ago, but it was still an open wound that continued to bleed. He'd accused himself of still loving his ex-wife, even after she'd run off with Ellery Rhodes. But Zane knew better. He doubted if he ever had loved Stasia, but his battered pride was still raw from her deceit.

"I want this farm," he said as thoughts about Stasia gave him renewed conviction. The look on his face was intense, slightly threatening.

"I'm sorry, Zane. I told you yesterday that if I ever decided to sell, the first option would be Dustin's."

"Even when you know that he deliberately lied to you?"

"If he did, you mean. I can't believe—"

Zane cut her off by slicing the air with his hand. He strode over to the desk, reached inside his briefcase and handed her a thick packet of legal documents.

"What are these?" she asked, slowly scanning the complicated pages.

"Corporate documents, ownership papers."

"How did you get them?"

"It doesn't matter. Just read." He hated to put the damning evidence in front of her, but she'd been so bullheaded about Ellery and Dustin, he'd had no choice. Tiffany didn't strike him as the kind of woman who would live in a fantasy world, but maybe when a woman loved a man as passionately as Tiffany loved Rhodes... He frowned darkly and finished his drink in one swallow. His inner vision of Tiffany entwined in Ellery Rhodes's arms turned his thoughts black, and a senseless anger took hold of his mind.

Tiffany sifted through the documents, and as she did her heart contracted painfully. Dustin's signature was scrawled all over the legal papers concerning Emerald Enterprises and the purchase of the farm in question. Without a doubt, some of Zane's story was true. Just how much, she would have to determine on her own, when issues such as the dead foals and her feelings for Zane didn't clutter her mind.

Pursing her lips together she handed the papers back to Zane.

"They're yours," he said.

"I don't want them."

"I have extra copies, and I think you might want to go over these more carefully while I'm gone."

"You're leaving?" *Oh, God, not now. Not when I need your arms to protect me...*

"Have to," he admitted with obvious reluctance.

"I see," she replied stunned. How long did she expect him to stay? He'd already mentioned that he had business back in San Francisco. It was only a matter of time until they went their separate ways.

She stared sightlessly down at the documents she still held in her hands. Since Zane had been with her, she had avoided thinking about the time he would leave. *This is crazy, let him go, before you do something you'll regret later....*

His hands molded over her upper arms. The warmth of his touch made her knees weaken, and she had to fight the urge to fall against him for support.

"While I'm gone, I want you to consider selling the farm to me," he said sharply, his gentle fingers in stark contrast to his harsh words.

He was a man of contradictions, ruthless one moment, kind the next; sensitive to her desires as a woman, yet insensitive to her needs as a person. She told herself she couldn't possibly fall in love with him and yet she knew that fate had already cast the die. She was falling desperately and hopelessly in love with the stranger from Ireland.

"It's just not that easy, Zane. Dustin still owns twenty-five percent—I can't make a decision without him."

"Then consider selling out your portion. I'll deal with Dustin later." The tone of his voice was harsh, his jaw hard.

"It's just not possible."

"Anything's possible, Tiffany. Don't you know that?"

As possible as falling in love with you? Dear Lord, what has happened to my common sense?

As if reading her unspoken question, Zane smiled gently. The tense line of his jaw relaxed as slumberous eyes embraced hers. One long finger traced the elegant curve of her neck. "I'll be back in a few days," he promised.

Her lips trembled beguilingly. "There's no need. You know my position on selling the farm—"

"And what about Devil's Gambit?"

She frowned and pushed an errant lock of golden hair over her shoulder. "I...I don't know," she admitted, eyeing the portrait of the proud stallion. She needed time alone, time to think and sort out everything Zane had stated. How much of his story was fact and how much was pure fiction?

"You'll need a contact in Ireland."

The thought that Zane might be leaving the country shocked her. For this short time she'd had with him, she felt as if they'd grown incredibly close.

"I'll have to think about that—"

"Tiffany?"

"Yes?" She looked up and found him staring at her. For most of the evening he had forced himself to stay away from her physically. But standing next to her with the warmth of the fire against his back, smelling the scent of her perfume, seeing the honest regret in her blue eyes, was too much to bear. The restraint he had placed upon himself began to dissolve into the shadowy room.

He touched the seductive contour of her jaw, and she closed her eyes. His hands were gentle as they lingered near her throat. "Come with me to San Francisco," he suggested impulsively as his blood began to heat and he forgot his earlier promise to himself. He wanted Tiffany Rhodes as he'd never wanted a woman.

"Oh, Zane, I can't."

"Why not?" His fingers had wrapped around her nape, under the curtain of her hair. She had trouble thinking clearly as his hands drew her near to him, and his lips touched her eyelids.

"I have...too many things to do...too much to think about...."

"Think about me—"

"That, I can assure you, I will," she promised fervently, her words the barest of whispers.

When his lips touched hers, he tasted more than the flavor of rich Burgundy. His tongue skimmed the soft surface of her mouth, gently prying her lips apart. Tiffany had no desire to stop him. She felt reckless, daring. Her raw emotions had pushed rational thought aside. Though she barely knew him, her body trembled at his touch, thrilled at his gentle caress.

His fingers slid down her arms to wrap securely over her waist, pulling her willing body to his. He moaned when he felt her hands, which had been gently touching his shoulders, grip the corded muscles more tightly. She was warm, pliable, yielding....

Silently cursing the doubts in his mind, he crushed her body to his. He felt the heat in her blood, tasted her need when her mouth opened willingly to him, smelled the heady scent of perfume mingling with burning pitch. The ache in his loins began to pound with the need of this woman—Ellery Rhodes's wife.

Tiffany let her arms hold him close. She knew he would be leaving soon, and she had to savor each sweet second she had with him. When she felt the weight of his body gently push her to the floor, she didn't resist. Her hands linked behind his head, and she let herself fall until the soft cushion of the carpet broke her fall and was pressed against her back.

"I want you," he whispered, his face taut with desire. "God forgive me, but I want you."

Her blue eyes reflected the golden flames of the fire, and her hair was splayed in tangled curls on the deep, green carpet. Passion darkened her gaze and lingered in her eyes. "There's no need for forgiveness," she murmured, her fingers stroking the back of his neck, his tensed shoulder muscles.

Her blood was pulsing violently through her veins, heating the most intimate parts of her. Her heart felt as if it would burst with need, want. It continued to beat an irregular rhythm in her ears, making her oblivious of anything but the desire of this man...this stranger. As she gazed into his silvery eyes, she wondered if what she was feeling was love or lust and found she didn't care.

"Tiffany," he whispered against her hair. He was lying over her, his chest crushing her breasts as if he were afraid she would escape, his long legs entangled with hers. "I didn't want this to happen." His ragged breathing was filled with reluctance.

"I know," she whispered.

He kissed the curve of her neck and tingling sensations raced wildly down her body. Dear Lord, she couldn't think when he was touching her, couldn't reason.... Before she could try to explain her feelings, his rugged face loomed over hers. He gazed down upon her and passion darkened his eyes. *Think of Ellery,* she told herself, *there is a slim chance that he might be alive. Though he betrayed you, he is still your husband.*

Zane's lips captured hers, and despite the arguments in her mind she wrapped her arms around his neck and let her fingers wander in his thick, obsidian hair. His touch was electric, and all the nerves in her body screamed to be soothed by him.

I can't do this, she thought wildly, when his hands rimmed the boat neck of the sweater and teased the delicate skin near her collarbone. He lowered his head and pressed his moist tongue to the hollow of her throat, extracting a sweet torment that forced her pulse to quiver.

He kissed her again, more savagely this time, and she responded with a throaty moan. When he lifted his head, he gazed into her eyes, then pulled the sweater over her head, baring her breasts to the intimate room. A primitive groan slid past his lips as he looked down at her. The lacy bra, the sheerest of barriers to him, displayed the ripeness of her breasts and their pink tips. Already the nipples were rigid, thrusting proudly against the silky fabric and offering the comfort to soothe him if he would only suckle from them. "God, you're beautiful," he said, running first his eyes and then his tongue over the delicious mounds of white and feeling the silken texture of her skin beneath the sheer lace. She trembled with the want of him.

The wet impression of his tongue left a dewy path from one rose-tipped peak to the next. Tiffany struggled beneath him, arching up from the carpet and pulling him to her with anxious fingers digging into the thick muscles of his shoulders.

In a swift movement he removed his sweater and tossed it beside Tiffany's on the floor. She stared at him with love-drugged eyes. His chest was lean and firm; dark skin was covered with still darker hair. His abdominal muscles rippled when she lifted a hand to stroke him, and his nipples grew taut as she stared at him.

He lowered himself over her and covered her mouth with his. His tongue tasted of her, dipping seductively into her mouth only to withdraw again. The heat within her began to ache for all of him. She wanted him to touch her, fill her, make long, passionate love to her until the first shafts of morning light filtered through the windows.

When his mouth moved slowly down her neck to pause at the shadowy valley between her breasts, she cried out his name. "Zane, please," she whispered, begging for his touch. Thoughts of a distant past with Ellery infiltrated her mind. *I couldn't feel this way with Zane if Ellery were still alive.... I couldn't!*

In response to her plea, he unclasped the bra and removed it from her, staring at the blushing beauty of her breasts.

"What do you want, sweet Tiffany?" he asked, his slumberous gray eyes searching hers.

Her throat tightened and she closed her eyes. Her dark lashes swept invitingly downward. "I want you—all of you."

He dipped his head and ran his tongue over one proud nipple. "Do you want me to love you?"

"Please...Zane...yes!" *Didn't he know? Couldn't he see the love in her eyes as she opened them to search his face?*

"All of you?" He kissed the other nipple, but his eyes locked with hers for an electrifying instant. His teeth gently teased the dark point, and she quivered from the deepest reaches of her soul.

"All of me," she replied and groaned when he began to suckle hungrily at one delicious peak. His large hands held her close, pressing against her naked back and warming her exposed skin. Tiffany felt waves of heat move over her as he kissed her, caressed her, stroked her with his tongue. She cradled his head, holding him close, afraid he would leave her bereft and longing. As his mouth and tongue tasted her, drew out the love she felt, the hot void within her began to throb with desire.

"Make love to me, Zane," she whispered when the exquisite torment was more than she could bear. "Make love to me and never let me go...."

It was the desperate cry of a woman in the throes of passion. Zane knew that Tiffany had unwittingly let her control slip. He positioned himself above her and his fingers toyed with the waistband of her jeans, slipping deliciously on her warm abdomen. She contracted her muscles, offering more of herself, wanting his touch. Her body arched upward eagerly, her physical desire overcoming rational thought.

Her fingers strayed to the button on his cords and he felt it slide easily through the buttonhole. Her hands did delightful things to him as she slid the zipper lower. He squeezed his eyes shut against his rising passion. His need of her was all-consuming, his desire throbbing wildly against his cords. His fingers dipped lower to feel the smooth skin over her buttocks, and he had to grit his teeth when she began to touch him.

"Tiffany," he whispered raggedly, forcing himself to think straight. He remembered all too vividly that Ellery Rhodes could very well be alive. If Zane took her now, and Ellery was alive, Tiffany would never forgive him. "Wait." His voice was hoarse. With gentle hands he restrained her fingers. She stared up at him with hungry, disappointed blue eyes.

God, what he wouldn't give to forget all his earlier vows to himself. If he made love to her now, before the mystery surrounding Devil's Gambit was resolved, before he had meted out his revenge on Ellery Rhodes, before he had purchased the farm, she would end up hating him.

"I...had no intention..." *Of what? Making love to Ellery Rhodes's woman? As just revenge for what he did to you?* "...of letting things get so out of hand."

She read the doubts on his face and closed her eyes. "Forgive me if I don't believe you," she murmured, trying to roll away from him. "But I seem to recall a man who, this very morning, matter-of-factly insisted that we become lovers." Tears of embarrassment flooded her eyes.

"It's not for lack of any wanting on my part," he replied.

That much she didn't doubt. She'd felt the intensity of his desire, witnessed the passion in his eyes, felt the doubts that had tormented him. "Then what?" she asked, reaching for her sweater. "Are you teasing me, trying to find a way to convince me to sell the farm to you?" she accused.

He flinched as if she had physically struck him, and his entire body tensed. "You know better than that."

"I don't think I know you at all. I think I let my feelings get in the way of my thinking."

His fist balled impotently at his side and his face hardened. "Would you feel better about it, if we resumed what we started and I took you right here...even though Ellery might still be alive?"

"Of course not," she gasped. Her blood had cooled and reason returned.

He reached out and tenderly pushed her hair from her eyes. "Then wait for me," he asked, his voice low. "I just want to make sure that you won't regret anything that might happen."

"Are you sure you're concerned for my feelings, or your own?"

"Oh, lady," he whispered, forcing a sad smile. His fingers trembled slightly when he brushed a solitary tear from her eye. "Maybe a little of both." He reached for her and his fingers wrapped possessively around her neck. Closing his eyes against the passion lingering in his blood, he kissed her sensuously on the lips. "I'll be back...."

Chapter Eight

"This isn't the smartest thing you've ever done, Missy," Mac warned as he finished his coffee and pushed his hat onto his head. He scraped his chair back from the table and placed the empty cup on the tile counter, not far from the area where Louise was rolling dough.

"The least you could do is show a little support," Tiffany teased. She smoothed the hem of her cream-colored linen suit and smiled at Mac's obvious concern.

"After that newspaper article in the *Clarion*, I'd think you'd have more sense than agree to another interview."

"Can't argue with that," Louise chimed in as she placed a batch of cinnamon rolls in the oven.

"Okay, so the interview with Rod Crawford was a mistake. This one will be different." Tiffany leaned against the counter and attempted to look confident.

"How's that?" Mac's reddish brows rose skeptically on his weathered face.

"The reporter from the *Times* is Nancy Emerson, a roommate of mine from college."

"Hmmph." Louise was busily making the second batch of rolls and didn't look up as she spread the cinnamon and sugar over the dough. "How do you know she won't do the same thing that Crawford did? In my book a reporter's a reporter. Period."

"Nancy's a professional."

"So was Crawford."

"I talked about the interview. I told her I would only do it if it didn't turn out to be a hatchet job."

"I bet she liked that," Louise remarked sarcastically as she began furiously rolling the dough into a long cylinder. "It's none of my business, mind you, but didn't you bank on the reputation of the *Clarion*?"

"Yes," Tiffany said with a sigh.

Mac noted Tiffany's distress. "Well, if you think you can trust her—"

"I just know that she won't print lies," Tiffany insisted. "She's been with the *Times* for over six years and written dozens of articles on horse racing in America and abroad. She's extremely knowledgeable and I figured she'd give an unbiased, honest report." Tiffany lifted her palms in her own defense. "Look, I had to grant an interview with someone. I've had over a dozen calls from reporters in the past three days."

"I can vouch for that," Louise agreed as she sliced the rolls and arranged them in a pan.

Louise had insisted on working at the farm every day since Zane had left and Tiffany was grateful for the housekeeper's support. Life on the farm had been hectic in the past few—had it only been four?—days. It seemed like a lifetime since she'd been with Zane.

"Well, I guess you had no choice," Mac allowed.

"None. The longer I stall, the more it seems as if we're hiding something here."

"Aye. I suppose it does," Mac mumbled as he sauntered to the back door. "I'll be in the broodmare barn if you need me." He paused as his fingers gripped the doorknob, glanced back at Tiffany and shifted uncomfortably from one foot to the other. "It looks like Alexander's Lady's time has come."

Tiffany felt her heart fall to the floor. Alexander's Lady was pregnant with Moon Shadow's foal. Tiffany closed her eyes and gripped the edge of the table. Louise stopped working at the counter.

"Oh, Lord," the large cook muttered, quickly making a sign of the cross over her ample bosom. Then, with a knowing eye in Tiffany's direction, she smiled kindly. "This one will be all right, honey...I feel it in my bones."

"I hope to God you're right," Tiffany whispered.

"It's in His hands now, you know. Not much you can do 'bout it," Mac advised with a scowl. "Worryin' ain't gonna help."

Tiffany studied Mac's wrinkled brow. "Then maybe you should take your own advice."

"Naw—I'm too old and set in my ways to stop now. Anyway, worryin's what I do best." The trainer raised his hand in the air as a salute of goodbye and opened the door to the back porch, just as the doorbell chimed. Mac's frown deepened. "Looks like your friend is here."

Tiffany managed a thin smile. "Good. We may as well get this over with."

"Good luck," Louise muttered, once again hastily making the sign of the cross with her flour-dusted hands as Tiffany walked out of the kitchen.

"Tiffany! You look great," Nancy said with heartfelt enthusiasm as Tiffany opened the door.

The slim, dark-haired woman with the bright hazel eyes appeared no different than she had six years ago. Dressed in navy-blue slacks and a crisp red blouse and white jacket,

Nancy looked the picture of efficiency. Short dark-brown curls framed a pixielike face filled with freckles and smiles.

"It's good to see you, Nance. Come in." Tiffany's grin was genuine as she hugged her friend. It had been years since she'd seen Nancy. Too many years. The two women had parted ways right after college. Tiffany's father had died, and Nancy had moved to Oregon to marry her high school boyfriend.

"And what a beautiful house," Nancy continued, her expressive hazel eyes roving over the sweeping green hills surrounding the white-clapboard and brick home. "This is something right out of *Gone with the Wind*!"

"Not quite, I don't think."

"All you need is a couple of mint juleps, a porch swing and—"

"Rhett Butler."

Nancy laughed. "I suppose you're right. But, God, Tiff, this is *fabulous!*"

"The house was Ellery's idea," Tiffany admitted as Nancy's eager eyes traveled up the polished oak banister and marble stairs to linger on the crystal chandelier. "He thought the farm would appear more genuine if it had a Southern atmosphere."

"This is beyond atmosphere, Tiffany, this is flair!"

Tiffany blushed a little under Nancy's heartfelt praise. She'd forgotten what it was like to be around the exuberant woman. Though Nancy had to be thirty, she didn't look a day over twenty-five, and part of her youthful appearance was due to her enthusiasm for life.

Tiffany showed Nancy the house and grounds of the farm. "This is heaven," Nancy insisted as she leaned against a redwood tree and watched the foals romp in the late-morning sun.

"I like it."

"Who wouldn't? Let me tell you, I'd give an arm and a leg to live in a place like this."

Tiffany laughed. "And what would you do? You're a city girl by nature, Nance."

Nancy nodded in agreement. "I suppose you're right."

"You'd miss San Francisco within the week."

"Maybe so, but sometimes sharing a two-bedroom apartment with two kids and a cat can drive me up the wall. The girls are five and four, and you wouldn't believe how much energy they have."

"They probably get it from their mother. Genetics, you know."

"Right. Genetics. The reason I'm here."

Tiffany ignored the comment for now. "So why don't you bring the kids out here for a weekend sometime?"

Nancy's bright eyes softened. "You mean it?"

"Of course."

"They're a handful," the sprightly reporter warned.

"But they'd love it here, and I adore kids."

Nancy was thoughtful as she stared at the horses frolicking in the lush grass of the paddock. "So why didn't you have any?"

Tiffany shrugged. "Too busy, I guess. Ellery wasn't all that keen on being a father."

"And you?"

"It takes two."

Nancy sighed and lit a cigarette. A small puff of blue smoke filtered toward the cloudless sky. "Boy, does it. Raising the kids alone is no picnic. Ralph has them every other weekend, of course, but sometimes... Oh, well. Look, I'm here for an interview, right? Tell me what you've been doing since you took over the farm."

Nancy took a tape recorder from her purse and switched it on. For the next hour and half Tiffany answered Nancy's questions about the farm—the problems and the joys.

"So what's all this ruckus over Moon Shadow?" Nancy asked, her hazel eyes questioning.

"Hype."

"What's that supposed to mean?"

"Come on, I'll show you." Tiffany led Nancy to the stallion barn and Moon Shadow's stall. Moon Shadow poked his ebony head out of the stall, held it regally high and flattened his ears backward at the sight of the stranger. "Here he is, in the flesh, the stallion who's been getting a lot of bad press."

"What you referred to as 'hype'?"

"Yes. He's fathered over a hundred Thoroughbreds in the past eight years, several who have become champions."

"Like Devil's Gambit?"

Tiffany's heart seemed to miss a beat. She didn't want to discuss Devil's Gambit with anyone, including Nancy. "Yes, as well as Journey's End."

"Rhodes Breeding Farm's latest contender. He promises to be the next Devil's Gambit," Nancy observed.

"We hope so."

Moon Shadow's large brown eyes wandered from Tiffany to the reporter and back again. Tiffany reached into the pocket of her skirt and withdrew a piece of carrot. The proud stallion nickered softly and took the carrot from Tiffany's hand.

"He's been a good stud," Tiffany emphasized while rubbing the velvet-soft black muzzle.

Tiffany continued to talk about Moon Shadow's qualities and the unfortunate incidents with the dead foals. Whenever Nancy posed a particularly pointed question, Tiffany was able to defend herself and her stallion by pointing to his winning sons and daughters.

Nancy had snapped off her tape recorder and stayed through lunch. Tiffany felt more relaxed than she had in days when she and Nancy reminisced about college.

"So what happened between you and Ralph?" Tiffany asked, as they drank a cup of coffee after the meal.

Nancy shrugged. "I don't really know—it just seemed that we grew in different directions. I thought that the kids would make a difference, but I was wrong." When she saw the horrified look in Tiffany's eyes, she held up her hand. "Oh, don't get me wrong, Tiff. It wasn't that Ralph wasn't a good father—" she shrugged her shoulders slightly "—he just wasn't comfortable in the role of breadwinner. Too much responsibility, I suppose. Anyway, it's worked out for the best. He's remarried, and I'm dating a wonderful man."

"And the girls?"

Nancy sighed and lit a cigarette. "It was rough on them at first, but they seem to be handling it okay now."

"I'm glad to hear it."

"It's hard to explain," Nancy said softly. "It just seemed that the longer we lived together, the less we knew each other or cared...."

"That happens," Tiffany said. Hadn't she felt the same doubts when Ellery was alive? Hadn't there always been a distance she was unable to bridge?

"Yeah, well..." Nancy stubbed out her cigarette. "As I said, I think it's for the best. Oh, God, look at the time! I've got to get out of here."

Tiffany watched as Nancy gathered her things, and then she walked her friend to the car. "I was serious when I told you to bring the kids out for a weekend. Just give me a call."

"You don't know what you're asking for."

Tiffany laughed. "Sure I do. It'll be fun. Come on, Nance, those girls could use a little fresh country air, and they'd love being around the horses."

Nancy eyed the rolling hills of the farm wistfully. "Be careful, Tiff, or I just might take you up on your offer."

"I'm counting on it."

Nancy's car was parked in the shade of a tall maple tree near the back of the house. When they reached the car, Nancy turned and faced Tiffany. "This has been great," she said. "The best interview I've done in years."

"Do you do many stories about Thoroughbreds?" Tiffany asked.

"Some—mainly from the woman's angle," Nancy replied. "Most of the time I write human interest stories—again, from the woman's perspective. The reason I got this assignment is that I read the article in the *Clarion* and stormed into my editor's office, insisting that since I knew you, I would be the logical person to write a more in-depth article for the *Times*. He really couldn't argue too much, since I used to cover all the local and national races." Her hazel eyes saddened a little. "I think you, and not your horse, were the victim of bad press, my friend."

Tiffany shrugged, but smiled. "Maybe." A question formed in her mind and she had to ask. "When you were working on the races, did you ever hear of a stallion named King's Ransom?"

"Sure. But he wasn't much of a champion, not until recently. From what I understand his services as a stud are the most sought-after in Ireland."

"Who owns him?"

Nancy smiled. "That's the interesting part. It's kind of a mystery. He's syndicated of course, but the largest percentage of the stallion is owned by Emerald Enterprises." Tiffany's heart felt as if it had turned to stone. *Zane had been telling the truth!*

"Which is?"

"A holding company of sorts," Nancy replied.

"I see," Tiffany said, her heartbeat quickening. "What about a man by the name of Zane Sheridan?" she asked.

Nancy was about to get into the car but paused. "Now there's an interesting man."

"Oh?" Tiffany cocked her head to the side and the smile on her lips slowly faded. "Do you think he's somehow involved with Emerald Enterprises?"

"I don't really know, but I doubt it. He owns a farm near the one owned by Emerald Enterprises. Why are you so interested?"

"I'm not...not really." Tiffany lied in ineffectual non-chalance. "He was here a couple of days ago, looking at some horses."

"He's a bit of a mystery," Nancy said. She leaned against the car door and stared up at the blue sky as she tried to remember everything she could about the breeder from Ireland. "He's a tough guy, from what I hear. Ruthless in business. He grew up on the streets of Dublin. Had several scrapes with the law and ended up working as a stable boy at an Irish Thoroughbred farm in the country. The owner of that particular farm took a liking to him, sent him to school, and once educated, Sheridan made a small fortune breeding horses." She sighed as she tried to remember the fuzzy details of a scandal that had occurred in the past.

"And then, well, it's kind of foggy, but from what I remember, he was in some sort of trouble again. A scandal, and he lost his fortune and his wife. I can't remember all the details right now."

The news hit Tiffany like a bolt of lightning. Though stunned, she managed somehow to ask, "His wife is dead?"

"No—she ran off with this guy named...God, what was it? Rivers, I think. Ethan Rivers, an American.... Like I said, it's kind of a mystery. No one really knows what happened to this Rivers character or Sheridan's wife."

The thought of Zane being married did strange things to Tiffany. "How long ago was this?" she asked.

"Geez, what was it? Five years, maybe more like seven, I'm really not sure." She pursed her lips as she thought and then, when she checked her watch, nearly jumped out of her skin. "Look, I've got to go. Deadlines, you know. I'll call you soon."

"Good. I'd like that."

Nancy got into her car and settled behind the wheel. The engine started, and Nancy rolled down the window. "The article on the farm should be in the paper no later than

Thursday. I'll send you a copy." With a brilliant smile, she fingered a wave at Tiffany and forced the little car into gear.

Tiffany watched the car disappear down the tree-lined drive, but her mind was miles away. Nancy's visit had only increased her restlessness. Where was Zane and why hadn't he called?

Hours later, Tiffany was walking back from the half-mile track near the old barn when she heard a familiar voice.

"Tiffany!"

A tall man wearing a Stetson was running toward her. Tiffany shielded her eyes from the ever-lowering sun and smiled when she recognized her brother-in-law.

"Dustin!" She hadn't expected him back for another week.

"Hello, stranger," he said as he reached her and gathered her into his arms to twirl her off the ground. How had she ever doubted him? "What's this I hear about you getting some bad press, little lady?"

"Some?" Tiffany repeated with a shake of her head. "How about truckloads of it."

"You can't be serious." He flashed her a brilliant smile.

"Four of Moon Shadow's foals have died—all from heart failure."

Dustin lifted his hat, pushed a lock of brown hair out of his eyes and squinted into the setting sun toward the exercise track, where Mac was still working with a yearling. "So I read."

"You and the rest of the world." Tiffany pushed her hands into the pockets of her jeans. Her conversation with Zane came hauntingly back to her, and she wondered just how much she could confide in Dustin. He did own twenty-five percent of the farm and was entitled to know everything that was going on...well, almost everything. "I have owners who are threatening me with lawsuits if the mares they bred to Moon Shadow drop foals that die."

"How many mares are involved?" Dustin's hand reached out and took hold of her arm. They had been walking toward the old barn where Tiffany had been headed. Near the building, Dustin stopped her.

"About twelve," she said. "Some of them took the news fairly well. The others, well...they weren't so understanding."

"In other words they're ready to rip your throat out."

"Close enough."

"Damn!" Dustin let out an angry blast. "This is the last thing we need right now. Okay, so what about the mares that have already foaled?"

"The foals that eventually died were from our mares. So far, every mare bred to Moon Shadow from another farm has dropped a healthy colt or filly."

"So much for small favors."

"I guess we should consider ourselves lucky that this isn't a contagious virus," she said.

"You're sure?" Dustin didn't sound convinced.

"Um-hm. Vance checked everything carefully. At first he thought it might be sleepy foal disease, but fortunately it wasn't."

"Yeah, fortunately," Dustin muttered sarcastically.

Tiffany pushed open the door to the old barn and checked the supply of grain stacked in sacks in the bins. The interior was musty and dark, the only light filtering through the small window on the south side of the building and the open door. Dustin leaned against a post supporting the hayloft and watched her make notes in a small notebook.

Once she had finished counting and was satisfied that the inventory of feed was about what it should be, she started back toward the door.

Dustin's hand on her arm stopped her. His topaz-colored eyes pierced into hers. "So what happened to those foals?"

Tiffany shook her head and her honey-brown tresses glowed in the shadowy light from the windows. "Your guess is as good as mine."

"What does Vance say?"

"Nothing good, at least not yet."

He leaned against the post, shoved the hat back on his head so he could see her more clearly and drew Tiffany into the circle of his arms. His voice was low with concern, his gold eyes trained on her lips. The intimate embrace made Tiffany uncomfortable. All Zane's accusations concerning Dustin began to haunt her. Maybe she should ask him flat out about the circumstances surrounding Devil's Gambit's death, but she hesitated. There was just enough of the truth woven into Zane's story to give her pause.

Dustin read the worry on her features. "Do you think there's a possibility that Moon Shadow's to blame for the deaths?"

Tiffany frowned and tried to pull away from him. "No."

"But all the evidence—"

"Is circumstantial."

"I see." Dustin released her reluctantly and cleared his throat. "So what are you doing with him?"

"Nothing. I can't breed him. Not until I know for certain that the problem isn't genetic."

"Then you do have reservations?"

Tiffany bristled slightly. "None, but what I don't have is proof. Unfortunately, Moon Shadow has already been tried and convicted by the press. He's as good as guilty until proved innocent."

"Bitter words..."

"You haven't been here trying to talk some sense into the reporters, the owners, the television people."

"No," he conceded with obvious regret. "But I bet you handled them."

Tiffany lifted a shoulder. "As well as I could. I had an interview with Nancy Emerson from the *Times* this morning."

Dustin smiled. "Your old roommate?"

"Uh-huh."

He breathed deeply. "Good. It never hurts to know someone in the press."

Tiffany decided to set her brother-in-law straight. "I didn't buy her off, you know."

"I know, I know, but at least she's on our side. She should be objective; thank God for small favors."

Something in Dustin's attitude made Tiffany uneasy. *You're overreacting,* she told herself, all because of Zane Sheridan and his wild accusations.

Dustin smoothed back his wavy hair. "I've got to hand it to you, Tiff. You've come a long way," he said appreciatively. "There was a time when I didn't think you would be able to pull yourself together."

"I have you to thank for getting me back on my feet," she replied, uncomfortable with the personal tone of the conversation. She was reminded of Zane and the accusations he had made about Dustin. Today, in the fading sunlight, those allegations seemed positively absurd. Dustin was her brother-in-law, her friend, her partner. The man who had pulled her out of the depths of despair when Ellery and Devil's Gambit had been killed.

Then what about the farm in Ireland, the one owned by Emerald Enterprises? What about Dustin's signature on the ownership papers? What about King's Ransom?

She decided to broach the difficult subjects later, once she had learned the reason for Dustin's unexpected visit. Was it possible that he knew Zane had been here? Had someone tipped Dustin off, possibly Zane himself?

Tiffany felt a growing resentment and anger at Zane. Single-handedly he had destroyed her trust in the only family she had ever known.

"Come on," she suggested, pushing her worrisome thoughts aside as she walked through the open door of the barn. "I'm starved. Louise made some cinnamon rolls this morning, and I bet we can con her out of a couple."

Dustin looked as if he had something he wanted to say but held his tongue. Instead he walked with Tiffany to the house and waited patiently while she kicked off her boots and placed them on the back porch.

"Are you staying long?" she asked, once they were in the kitchen and seated at the table.

Dustin hedged slightly. "Just a couple of days."

"And then?"

"Back to Florida."

"To check on Journey's End?"

"Right." He took a long swallow of his coffee, and his golden eyes impaled her. "You think you could spare the time to come with me?" he asked, his voice uncommonly low.

Tiffany ignored the hidden innuendos in his tone. They'd covered this territory before, and Dustin obviously hadn't taken the hint. The scene in the old barn emphasized the fact. Dustin had never hidden the fact that he would like to pursue a more intimate relationship with her, but Tiffany just wasn't interested. Dustin seemed to assume that her lack of interest was due in part to loyalty to Ellery, and Tiffany didn't argue the point. He just couldn't seem to get it through his thick skull that she wasn't interested in a relationship with a man—any man.

Except Zane Sheridan, her mind taunted. Would she ever be able to get him out of her mind? In four days, he hadn't phoned or stopped by the farm. All of his concern for her while he was here must have been an act, a very convincing act. Still, she couldn't forget him.

"Tiff!"

"Pardon?"

Dustin was frowning at her. He'd finished his coffee, and the cup was sitting on the table. His empty plate showed only a few crumbs and a pool of melted butter where his cinnamon rolls had sat. "You haven't heard a word I said," he accused.

"You're right."

"So where were you?"

"What?"

"You looked as if you were a million miles away."

"Oh, I guess I was thinking about Moon Shadow," she lied easily, too easily. "Mac thinks another one of his foals will be born tonight."

Dustin leaned back in his chair and let out a low whistle. "No wonder you're worried. If this one dies, the press will be crawling all over this farm again. Maybe I'd better stay a few extra days."

Waving off his offer, she shook her head. "No reason. You know you're welcome to stay as long as you like, but if you have things to do, go ahead and do them. I can handle everything here."

He walked around the table, stood behind her and placed his hands on her shoulders. "You're sure?"

Tiffany tensed. "Of course I am."

As if receiving her unspoken message, he dropped his hands to his sides. "You know that's one of the qualities I admire about you, Tiff, your strength."

"I guess I should be flattered."

Dustin stepped away from her and rested his hips against the counter. All the while his eyes rested on her worried face. "Is something else bothering you?" he asked.

"Isn't that enough?"

"I suppose so." He shrugged his broad shoulders and folded his arms over his chest. Silent reproach lingered in his eyes. The air in the kitchen became thick with tension.

Tiffany heard the screen door bang shut. Within minutes Mac was in the kitchen.

"Don't tell me, you smelled the coffee," Tiffany guessed, reaching for a cup and feeling relieved that the inquisition with Dustin was over for the moment.

"Aye, that I did."

"Well, pull up a chair, sit yourself down and help yourself to a roll, while I get you a mug."

Mac's faded eyes rested on Dustin. Not bothering to hide a frown, he cocked his head toward the younger man. "'Evenin', Dustin. Didn't expect you back for a while."

Tiffany handed Mac the cup.

Dustin managed a tight grin as he offered the older man his hand. "I read an article about the foals dying and thought I should come back—" his gold eyes moved to Tiffany "—since no one bothered to tell me what was going on."

"I thought I'd wait until Vance had something concrete to go on," Tiffany stated.

"And how long would you have waited?"

"Not much longer."

"It was a hell of a way to find out, you know," Dustin said, his anger surfacing, "by reading about it in the paper." He rammed his fingers through his hair in frustration. For a moment he appeared haunted.

"You're right. I should have called, but I didn't because there wasn't a damned thing you or I or anyone else could do."

"I suppose you're right about that," Dustin conceded with a frown and then turned his attention to Mac. "I was just trying to convince Tiffany here that she ought to come to Florida and see for herself how Journey's End is doing."

"Not a bad idea," Mac agreed, though there were reservations in his eyes. He removed his hat and took a chair at the table. "That way she could check up on Bob Prescott, see that he's doing a good job of training the colt."

Prescott was a young trainer who traveled with the horses while they were racing. He was a damned good man around a horse, but there was something shifty about him that Mac didn't like. The missus called it jealousy. Mac wasn't so sure, but he couldn't put his finger on the problem, and Bob Prescott had molded Journey's End into a fine racing machine.

Dustin's smile froze. "See, Tiffany, even Mac agrees that you could use a vacation. A little Florida sun might do you a world of good."

Tiffany managed a thin smile for both men and finished her coffee. "It'll have to wait until we're over this crisis." She leaned back in the chair and held up a finger. "However, you can bet I'll be at the Derby this year."

"You think Journey's End will make a good show of it?" Dustin asked as he placed his empty cup in the sink and wiped an accumulation of sweat from his brow.

"Not a show nor a place, but a win," the crusty old trainer predicted.

"High praise coming from you," Dustin observed.

"Journey's End is a fine colt. He's got the heart, the look of eagles if you will, but his temperament's got to be controlled...guided." He lifted his wise old eyes to Dustin's face. "I just hope that Bob Prescott knows what he's doing."

"He does."

"Then Journey's End should win the Derby," Mac stated without qualification. "He's the best horse I've seen since Devil's Gambit or Moon Shadow."

Dustin nearly choked on his final swallow of coffee and turned the subject away from Devil's Gambit. "We all know why Moon Shadow lost the Derby, don't we?" Dustin asked pointedly.

Mac's faded eyes narrowed. "Aye, that we do. I haven't made any excuses about it, either. I should never have let that jockey ride him."

"He was Ellery's choice," Tiffany intervened, sensing an argument brewing between the two men.

"And I shouldn't have allowed it." Mac straightened his wiry frame from the chair, and his fedora dangled from his fingers as he turned to Tiffany. "I called Vance. I'm sure we'll have another foal before morning."

Tiffany took in a ragged breath. "Let me know when the time comes."

"Aye. That I will." With his final remarks, Mac walked out of the room and the screen door banged behind him.

Tiffany whirled on Dustin. "That was uncalled for, you know," she spit out.

"What?"

"Those remarks about Moon Shadow and the Derby."

"Serves the old man right. I never have figured why you keep that old relic around, anyway."

Tiffany was furious and shaking with rage. "Mac's not old, nor a relic, and he's the best damned horseman in this state, maybe the country. He knows more about Thoroughbreds than you or I could hope to know in a lifetime. Let's just hope, brother-in-law, that he doesn't take your remarks to heart and quit on us. We'll be in a world of hurt, then, let me tell you!"

Dustin had visibly paled but scoffed at Tiffany's remarks. "You're giving him too much credit," he said with a shrug as he stared out the window. "You're genuinely fond of the old goat, aren't you?"

"Mac's been good to me, good to this farm, good to Ellery and good to you. Why you continue to ridicule him is beyond me. Unless you'd secretly like to see him leave."

"It wouldn't affect me one way or the other."

"Like hell, Dustin. We had an agreement, remember?" she reminded him. "I run the operations of the farm, you handle the PR. Right now, because of all the adverse publicity with Moon Shadow's foals, it seems to me that you've got more than your share of work cut out for you!"

With her final remark Tiffany stormed out of the kitchen, tugged on her boots and went off to make amends with

Mac. Why did Dustin have to provoke the trainer now when she needed Mac's expertise the most?

Mac was already at his pickup when Tiffany caught up with him. "I'm sorry," she apologized. She was out of breath from her sprint across the back lawn and parking lot.

"No need for that, Missy," Mac said with a kindly smile as he reached for the door handle on the old Dodge. "What Dustin said was the truth."

"No, it wasn't. Even with his regular jockey, there was no assurance that Moon Shadow would win."

"He was the odds-on favorite."

"And we all know how many long shots have won when it counted. Besides, it's all water under the bridge now," she assured him. "We'll just pin our hopes on Journey's End. And maybe this time, we'll win the Derby."

"I hope so," Mac said, pursing his lips together thoughtfully as he studied the lush Northern California countryside that made up the pastures of Rhodes Breeding Farm. "It's time you got a break." He opened the door to the truck. "I'll be back after dinner to check on Alexander's Lady. My guess is she'll foal around midnight."

"See you then." Tiffany stepped away from the old truck and Mac started the engine before shoving it into gear. Tiffany felt her teeth sink into her lower lip as she watched the battered old pickup rumble down the long driveway.

Three hours later Tiffany was in the foaling shed, watching, praying while the glistening chestnut mare labored. The air was heavy with the smell of sweat mingled with ammonia and antiseptic.

Vance and Mac were inside the stall with the horse while Tiffany and Dustin stood on the other side of the gate. Alexander's Lady was lying on her side in the thick mat of straw, her swollen sides heaving with her efforts.

"Here we go," Vance said as the mare's abdomen contracted and the foal's head and shoulders emerged. A few minutes later, the rest of the tiny body was lying beside the mare.

Vance worked quickly over the newborn, clearing the foal's nose. As Tiffany watched she noticed the small ribs begin to move.

Tiffany reached for the switch that turned on the white heat lamps to keep the precious animal from catching cold.

"Let's leave the lamps on for two or three days," Vance suggested, his round face filled with relief as the filly tested her new legs and attempted to stand. "I don't want to take any chances."

"Neither do I," Tiffany agreed, her heart warming at the sight of the struggling filly. She was a perfect dark bay, with only the hint of a white star on her forehead.

Tiffany slipped into the stall and began to rub the wet filly with a thick towel, to promote the filly's circulation. At that moment, the mare snorted.

"I think it's time for Mom to take over," Vance suggested, as he carefully moved the foal to the mare's head. Alexander's Lady, while still lying on the straw, began to nuzzle and lick her new offspring.

"Atta girl," Mac said with the hint of a smile. "'Bout time you showed some interest in the young-un." He stepped out of the stall to let mother and daughter get acquainted.

Vance stayed in the stall, watching the foal with concerned eyes. He leaned against the wall, removed his glasses and began cleaning them with the tail of his coat, but his thoughtful gaze remained on the horses, and deep furrows lined his brow.

"Is she all right?" Tiffany asked, her heart beating irregularly. Such a beautiful filly. She couldn't die!

"So far so good." But his lips remained pressed together in an uneasy scowl as he attended to the mare. Alexander's Lady groaned and stood up. She nickered softly to the filly.

As if on cue, the little newborn horse opened her eyes and tried futilely to stand.

"Come on, girl. You can do it," Tiffany whispered in encouragement. The filly managed to stand on her spindly, unsteady legs before she it fell back into the straw. "Come on..."

"Good lookin' filly," Mac decided as the little horse finally forced herself upright and managed the few steps to the mare's side. "Nice straight front legs...good bone, like her dad." Mac rubbed his hand over the stubble on his chin.

Tiffany's heart swelled with pride.

"She looks fine," Vance agreed as he watched the filly nuzzle the mare's flanks and search for her first meal.

"So did Charlatan," Tiffany reminded him, trying her best not to get her hopes up. The filly looked strong, but so had Felicity's colt. And he had died. A lump formed in Tiffany's throat. She couldn't imagine that the beautiful little filly might not live through the night.

"Keep watch on her," Vance stated, his lips thinning.

"Round the clock," Tiffany agreed. "We're not going to lose this one," she vowed, oblivious to the worried glances being exchanged between the veterinarian and the trainer.

"What have you decided to name her?" Dustin asked, seemingly entranced by the healthy young horse.

"How about Survivor?" Tiffany replied. "Better yet, how about Shadow's Survivor?"

"As in Moon Shadow?" Dustin inquired.

"Yes." Tiffany glanced at the suckling baby horse. The fluffy stub of a tail twitched happily. "I like it."

"Isn't it a little premature for a name like that?"

"I hope not," Tiffany whispered. "I hope to God, it's not."

"Missy," Mac said gently, touching her sleeve.

"Don't say it, Mac," Tiffany said, holding up her hand. "This little filly is going to make it. She's got to!" Tiffany's lips pressed together in determination, as if she could will her strength into the little horse.

"I just don't want you to be too disappointed."

"I won't be." Tiffany's jaw tensed, and her blue eyes took on the hue of newly forged steel. "This horse is going to live."

"I'll stay overnight in the sitting-up room, watching the monitor. If anything goes wrong, I'll call," Mac volunteered.

"Good." Vance washed his hands and removed his bloodied white jacket. "I want this filly babied. I want her to stay inside for a full three days, under the lamps. We're not out of the woods yet, not by a long shot. And as for the mare, make sure she gets bran mash for three days."

"You got it," Mac agreed, casting one last worried glance at the filly. "Now, Missy, why don't you go up to the house and get some sleep? You can take over in the morning."

Tiffany glanced at the two horses. "Gladly," she whispered.

As she walked out of the foaling shed and into the windy night, Tiffany felt the sting of grateful tears in her eyes. Large crystalline drops began to run down her cheeks and catch the moon glow. *Everything would be perfect,* she thought to herself as she shoved her hands into the pockets of her jacket and started walking on the path to the house, *if only Zane were here to see for himself the strong little daughter of Moon Shadow.*

Chapter Nine

Zane cradled his drink in his hands as he stared at the two other men in the office. His attorney, John Morris, sat behind the oiled teak desk. The other fellow, a great bear of a man, had been introduced by John as Walt Griffith. He was staring out the window at the black San Francisco night.

Walt Griffith wasn't what Zane had expected. When Zane had asked John to hire the best private investigator in California, he'd expected to meet a slick L.A. detective, a man who was street smart as well as college educated. Instead, John had come up with Griffith, a semiretired investigator nearly seventy years old, with thick, gray hair, rotund waistline, clean-shaven jowls and an eye-catching diamond ring on his right hand.

Griffith made Zane slightly uneasy, but he managed to hide his restlessness by quietly sipping his bourbon and water.

"So you want to locate your ex-wife," Griffith said at last while frowning at the city lights illuminating that particular section of Jackson Square.

"That's right." Zane shifted uncomfortably in his chair, and his lips tightened at the corners.

"Maybe she doesn't want you to know where she is."

"She probably doesn't." Zane cocked his head and studied the large man. What was he getting at?

Griffith clasped his hands behind his back. "I wouldn't do this for anyone, you know, but John and I—" he looked at the worried attorney "—we go way back. He says you're straight."

"Straight?" Zane repeated, turning his eyes to the attorney. John took off his reading glasses and frowned.

"I assume that John knows you well enough," Griffith continued. "He told me you weren't a wife-beater or some other kind of psycho."

Zane cocked a dubious dark brow at his friend. "Thanks," he said with a trace of sarcasm.

Griffith turned and leaned against a bookcase filled with leather-bound law books. He withdrew an imported cigar from the inside pocket of his suit coat and studied the tip. "Let me tell you, boy," he said, pointing the cigar in Zane's direction. "I've seen it all, and I'm not about to do anything that smacks of brutality." His small, brown eyes glittered from deep in their sockets, and Zane had the distinct impression that Griffith had gotten himself into trouble more than once from something "smacking of brutality." "If I didn't owe John a favor, I wouldn't have bothered to take your case at all. You seem to have somewhat of a checkered past yourself."

Zane forced a severe smile and his gray eyes met Griffith's intense stare. "I wouldn't physically abuse a woman, any woman. Including Stasia."

"Abuse doesn't have to be physical."

Zane's anger got the better of him, and his fingers tightened around his drink. "There's no love lost between Stasia and me," he admitted, his eyes sparking furiously. "But I have no intention of hurting her. Actually, the less I have to do with her, the better. The only reason I want to locate her is because I think she'll be able to help me with some answers I need." Zane smiled at the irony of it all. "Believe me, Griffith, if there was another way to deal with this problem, I'd be glad to hear it. I don't relish the thought of confronting my ex-wife any more than you want this assignment."

Griffith struck a match and lit his cigar. As he puffed, a thick cloud of pungent smoke rose to the ceiling. "Answers?" he asked, rolling Zane's words over in his mind. "About the other woman?"

Zane nodded.

Griffith's thick gray brows rose questioningly as he became interested in the Irishman's case. "Does she know you're checking up on her?"

Zane was cautious. He had to be with this man. "Tiffany?"

"Right."

Zane shook his head and scowled into his drink. "No."

"Hmmph." Griffith drew in on the cigar until the tip glowed red. "This other woman—this Rhodes lady, what's she to you?" he demanded.

"A friend."

Griffith shook his great head, and his eyes moved from Zane to John. "I thought you said he'd put all his cards on the table."

"He will." John glared severely at Zane. "You wanted the man." He motioned to indicate the investigator. "So help him."

At that moment, Zane realized he'd run out of options. He hesitated only slightly, and the smile that curved his lips appeared more dangerous than friendly. "All right, coun-

selor, I'll level with Griffith, *if* he promises that everything
I tell him will be kept in the strictest confidence."

"Goes without saying," Griffith grumbled, lowering
himself into the chair next to Zane and folding his hands
over his round abdomen. "Now, Mr. Sheridan, kindly explain why you're so interested in these two women, your
wife and your...'friend.'"

As she came downstairs the morning after Alexander's
Lady had foaled, Tiffany felt as if a great weight had been
lifted from her shoulders. She had slept soundly, and only
once, at about four, had she woken up. After turning on the
monitor in the den and assuring herself that both the mare
and the filly were alive and resting as well as could be expected, she trudged back up the stairs and fell into her bed.
She had gone to sleep again instantly and had awakened refreshed.

"Good morning," Tiffany said with a cheery smile as
Louise entered the kitchen and placed her purse on the table.

Louise's eyes sparkled. "It must be, from the looks of
you," she decided. "Don't tell me—that Sheridan fella is
back again."

"No," Tiffany quickly replied. She avoided the housekeeper's stare by pulling a thermos out of the cupboard near
the pantry, and managed to hide the disappointment she felt
whenever she thought about Zane. "Alexander's Lady is
now the mother of a healthy filly," Tiffany stated, forcing
a smile.

"Thank God!" Louise removed her coat and hung it in
the closet. "This calls for a celebration!"

"Champagne brunch maybe?" Tiffany suggested.

Louise thought for a moment and then nodded. "Why
not? It's about time we had some good news around here."
She pulled her favorite apron out of the closet, tied it loosely
around her waist and began rummaging through the draw-

ers looking for the utensils she needed. After grabbing a wooden spoon, she tapped it thoughtfully against her chin and said, "I can fix something for when? Say around noon?"

"That would be perfect," Tiffany agreed. "Vance should be back by then and maybe we can persuade him to stay."

At that moment the telephone rang, and without thinking Tiffany reached for the receiver and settled it against her ear. "Hello?" she said into the phone, hoping for a fleeting second that the caller would be Zane.

"Tiffany? Hal Reece, here."

Tiffany's heart fell to the floor, and her stomach tightened painfully. Obviously his mare had foaled. Her fingers tightened around the receiver. "Yes?"

"I just wanted to report that Mile High delivered."

Tiffany braced herself for the worst. She was already imagining how she would deal with the press, the lawsuit, the other owners.... "When?"

"Three nights ago."

"And?" Tiffany's heart was thudding so loudly she was sure Hal could hear it.

Louise stopped rattling in the cupboards; the serious tone of Tiffany's voice warned her of impending doom. Usually she wouldn't eavesdrop, but this time, under the circumstances, the kindly housekeeper couldn't hide her interest in the strained conversation.

"And, I'm glad to say, we have three-day-old colts—healthy ones," Hal announced.

"Colts? Plural?"

"That's right, Tiffany," Hal said, his voice nearly bursting with pride. "Can you believe it? After everything we worried about, I end up with twins—and beauties at that."

"Wonderful," Tiffany replied as she sagged against the pantry doors and tried desperately to keep her voice professional. Louise's worried face broke into a wide grin.

"I knew it all along, you know," the proud owner went on, "but we did have a few tense moments during the labor. From the look on the trainer's face while Mile High was delivering, I thought the colt was stillborn, but that wasn't his concern at all! He just hadn't expected number two." Hal went on to describe in minute detail all the physical characteristics of each of his new horses and ended by saying, "Look, Tiffany, I would have called you a couple of days ago, but, well, I wanted to be sure that...you know, we didn't have any problems."

"I understand," Tiffany replied, remembering Charlatan's short life. "I'm just pleased that it turned out so well."

"Yes, yes. And, uh, look, I'm sorry about the things I said the other night. I was...well, there's just no excuse for my behavior."

"It's okay," Tiffany said with a sigh.

"Have you heard from any of the other owners?" Hal asked.

"You're the first."

"Well, good luck. And mind you, if anyone tries to give you any trouble, let me know. Maybe I'll be able to help."

"Thank you."

He was about to ring off, but changed his mind. "One other thing, Tiffany."

"Yes?"

"As soon as all this...ballyhoo over Moon Shadow passes, I'd like to breed a couple of mares to him again."

Tiffany smiled. Hal Reece's words were the final olive branch offered to bridge the rift between them. "Thank you," she said gratefully, "I'll be in touch."

Tiffany hung up the phone and grinned at Louise.

"Good news?" Louise guessed with a knowing smile.

"The best. Hal Reece's mare gave birth to twins. *Healthy* twin colts. Three nights ago. They've been examined by a vet, given a clean bill of health and even insured by the insurance company."

"That does it," Louise said with a toss of her head. "We'll have that celebration brunch after all."

"Hal is only one owner," Tiffany murmured as if to herself, "but at least it's a start." After pouring herself a hot cup of coffee, she filled the thermos, pushed open the door with her shoulder and started down the steps of the back porch. Wolverine, who had been lying beneath a favorite juniper bush near the brick stairs, trotted over to greet her.

"How's it going, boy?" Tiffany asked, checking to see that he had food and fresh water in the appropriate dishes. The collie tilted his head to the side, and his tail wagged slowly as she spoke. Tiffany set the thermos on the top step, took a sip from her coffee and scratched the old dog behind the ears. "Haven't you been getting enough attention lately?" she asked in an understanding voice. "All those horses are kind of stealing the show right now, aren't they?"

Wolverine whined and placed a furry paw on her bent knee.

Tiffany laughed and shook her head. "You're still the boss, though, aren't you?" As she picked up her things and turned toward the foaling shed, Wolverine trotted behind her, content with the little bit of attention he'd received.

The hinges on the door creaked as Tiffany entered the whitewashed building. Mac was standing at Alexander's Lady's stall and writing on a white card that Tiffany recognized as the foaling record.

"Good morning, Missy," the trainer said, without bothering to look up. When his job was finished, he placed the foaling record back on the post near the stall. Once the card was complete, Tiffany would enter the appopriate information into the farm's computer.

"That it is," she said, mimicking Mac's speech pattern.

Mac's brown eyes twinkled. "What's got you in such good spirits?" Forcing a tired smile, he leaned over the railing of the foaling box. "Could it be this little lady, here?"

"She's got a lot to do with it," Tiffany admitted. The little filly hid behind the protection of her mother's flank. At the filly's skittish behavior, Alexander's Lady's ears flattened to her reddish head, and she positioned herself between the intruders and her foal.

"Mama's takin' her job seriously," Mac decided.

"Good."

The newborn poked her inquisitive nose around the mare's body and stared at the strangers through intelligent brown eyes.

"I told you she'd make it," Tiffany said. The precocious little bay looked so healthy. *The filly couldn't die. Not now.*

Mac's knowing eyes traveled over the mare and foal, but he didn't offer his thoughts to Tiffany. She read the hesitation in his gaze. It's still too early to tell, he was saying without uttering a word.

As Tiffany watched the two horses, she realized that the stall had already been cleaned. The smell of fresh straw and warm horses filled the small rooms attached to the broodmare barn which were used for the express purpose of foaling.

"You didn't have to stay in the sitting-up room," Tiffany remarked, knowing that she was wasting her breath. Mac was from the old school of horse training. "There's a monitor in the den."

"Aye, and what good does it do ya?"

"I used it last night."

Mac laughed. "As if you don't trust me." She was about to protest, but he stilled her with a wave of his arm. "I like to be close, especially since we've had so much trouble. If anything goes wrong, I'm right next door." He cocked his head in the direction of the sitting-up room positioned between the two foaling boxes. "It's what I'm used to."

Tiffany didn't argue. Mac had been around horses long before the introduction of video cameras and closed-circuit television. "There's fresh coffee up at the house, and Louise is in the process of whipping up a special brunch, if you can stick around."

"The missus—"

"Is invited, too."

Mac rubbed a hand over the stubble on his chin and cracked a wide smile. "She might like that, ya know. She's always grumblin' 'bout cookin' for me," he teased.

"I'll bet." Tiffany laughed in reply. Emma McDougal positively doted on her husband of over forty years, but Mac was none the worse for his wife's spoiling. "Why don't you grab a cup of coffee, or take this thermos and then go home for a while? Bring Emma back with you around eleven."

"And what about you?"

"I'll stay here until Vance arrives." Tiffany checked her watch. "And then, if Vance approves, we'll let John watch the horses."

"If you think you can trust him—"

Tiffany waved Mac off. "John's only nineteen, I grant you, but he's been around horses all his life, and he's the best stable boy since—"

"You?" Mac asked, his eyes saddening.

Tiffany pushed aside the unpleasant memories. When she had been a stable boy to her father, Mac had been with the horses on the racing circuit, but he had learned of her duties through Ellery. "Maybe," she acknowledged. "Now, go on, get out of here."

Mac took his cue and left Tiffany to watch over the new mother and filly. The little bay foal scampered around her mother on legs that had grown stronger with the passing of the night. "You're going to make it, aren't you?" Tiffany asked, before glancing at the foaling record and noting that everything had been recorded perfectly. The time that the mare's water broke, when the foal was born, when it stood, and when it first suckled were duly noted along with the foal's sex and color. Everything looked normal.

Tiffany looked at the impish bay horse and let out a long sigh. "Let her live," she prayed in a soft whisper that seemed to echo through the rafters in the high ceiling.

She was just straightening up the sitting-up room when she heard the door to the foaling shed creak open.

"Tiffany?" Dustin called softly.

"In here." She peeked around the corner and was surprised to find Dustin dressed in a business suit. "What's going on?" she asked, pointing a moving finger at his neatly pressed clothes.

"I'm going back to Florida."

"Today?" She stepped back into the corridor to meet him. His face was set in hard determination, and a small frown pulled at the corners of his mouth.

"Have to."

Tiffany held her palms up in the air. "Wait a minute! You just got here yesterday."

Dustin's gold eyes held hers. "Do you want me to stay?" he asked, his voice much too familiar in the well-lit building. The only other sound was the whisper of hay being moved by the horses' feet.

"Yes...no..." She shook her head in bewilderment. "If you want to. What's the rush?"

He looked genuinely disappointed and refused to smile. "I only came back to make sure that you were all right," he admitted, his frown deepening. "And from the looks of it, you're fine." His eyes slid down her slim form. She was clad only in worn jeans and a pink pullover, but with her hair wound over her head and the sparkle back in her intense blue eyes, she appeared both elegant and dignified, a no-nonsense lady who had her act together.

"Did you expect to find me in a crumpled heap—falling apart at the seams?"

Dustin shook his head but didn't smile at her attempt to lighten the mood. "I guess not. But it happened once before," he reminded her.

"That was different. Ellery was killed." She watched the smooth skin over Dustin's even features but saw no trace of any emotion that would betray his inner thoughts. Dustin acted as if he believed his brother dead.

"Right," he agreed.

"As well as Devil's Gambit."

Dustin looked up sharply, and in that split second Tiffany knew that he was lying to her. For the past four years, Dustin had been lying through his even white teeth. Without considering the consequences of her actions, she turned toward the stall and forced herself to appear calm, though her heart was pounding irregularly in her chest. It was time to find out how much of Zane's story was fact and how much was fiction, and she had to do it now, before Dustin left.

"I was thinking," she remarked, sliding a furtive glance in Dustin's direction.

"About?"

"Well, I still don't want to use Moon Shadow as a stud. Not until I understand what happened to those four foals, and I hear from the other owners."

Dustin nodded. Tiffany saw the movement from the corner of her eye. She propped her elbows on the rail and continued to watch the filly.

"So I was hoping to send some of our mares to other stallions, if it's not too late to nominate them."

"Sounds good to me." Dustin checked his watch and shifted from one foot to the other.

"You have any ideas on whom I should call?" she asked, her throat dry with dread.

"What?"

She shrugged. "Well, you're always high on one horse or the other. You know, a few years ago you thought we should breed Felicity to King's Ransom."

Dustin stiffened. The movement was slight, nearly imperceptible, but Tiffany caught it. "He's a good sire. Proof enough of that on the European tracks recently."

"Do you still think it's a good idea to send Felicity to him?"

"An impossible one, I'd say. King's Ransom's got to be booked solid."

Tiffany lifted one shoulder. "I just thought that maybe you knew the owner—could pull a few strings."

Dustin's eyes narrowed in suspicion. He came over to the stall and stood next to her. "You want favors? That's not like you, Tiff. You're the one who always plays by the rules."

"This is an unusual case—"

Dustin's arms reached for her, drew her close. "What is it with you?" he whispered against her hair. "What's going on here?" His finger traced the line of her jaw before lingering on the pout of her lips.

Her mind racing fast, Tiffany slid out of the circle of his arms and clasped her arms behind her back. She cocked her head upward to meet his gaze. "I just feel pushed against a wall sometimes," she said, knowing she was treading on thin ice with the turn in the conversation. She forced her hands into the pockets of her jeans and hoped to God that she wasn't betraying her inner feelings.

"And how would breeding one of our horses to King's Ransom change that?"

"It wouldn't, I suppose. There are plenty of good studs, here in the States." Lord, she hoped that she was a better actress than she had ever given herself credit for. "But we need a winner—a real winner."

"We've got Journey's End," he volunteered, intrigued with the change in her. His brother's widow was a mystifying creature; wild one minute, sedate the next. Intelligent, proud and sexy as hell. Dustin decided then and there that

he would gladly give half his fortune for the chance to tame
her fiery spirit.

"I know," Tiffany replied. "But what we really need is
another horse like Devil's Gambit."

Dustin paled slightly, his hands dropped to his sides, but
for the most part, he managed to keep his composure intact. "He's gone, Tiff. So is Ellery. You've got to face it.
You're never going to have another horse just like Devil's
Gambit, and you've got to forget this unreasonable loyalty
to a dead man."

He captured her arm with his fingers and tugged her
gently to him. "You need to live again, Tiffany. Without the
ghosts of the past surrounding you. Ellery is gone.... Think
about letting another man into your life." He paused dra-
matically, and his gilded eyes darkened with passion.

Tiffany wanted to recoil from him and shout that another man was already in her life, that she had committed
her heart to a man she barely knew, and she was dying inside without him. Instead, she pulled away before the embrace became more heated.

"Think about me," he suggested, his eyes raking over her
in lusty appraisal.

"I...I have too much on my mind to think about starting
new relationships," she said, knowing the excuse was as
feeble as it sounded. If she wasn't careful, Dustin would see
through her act. "The foals—" she angled her head in the
direction of the newborn filly "—Journey's End's career...a lot of things."

Dustin tugged at his stiff collar, but his golden eyes never
left her face. "You said you felt pushed against the wall."

"I do." She lifted her shoulders in a nonchalant gesture
and gambled with what she hoped was her trump card.
"Someone's offered to buy me out."

Dustin froze. "What?"

It was too late to back down now. "A man was here last
week."

"*What* man?"

"An Irishman. Zane Sheridan."

Dustin looked as if he would sink right through the floor. All of his well-practiced composure seemed to slide through the concrete.

"Ever heard of him?"

"Yeah. I know him." Dustin shook his head. "What does he want with this farm? He already breeds horses in Europe."

"Maybe he wants to break into the American market," Tiffany suggested, her fingers tightening over the railing of the stall. God, she was a terrible liar.

Dustin began to pace the length of the short corridor. "Maybe," he said as if he didn't believe a word of it. His mouth tightened and he ran a hand over his brow to catch the droplets of cold sweat that had begun to bead on his forehead. "I suppose he told you all sorts of wild stories."

"Like?" Tiffany coaxed.

"Like—hell, I don't know." He held up a hand in exasperation and looked up at the cross beams of the shed. "I may as well be honest with you, Tiff."

Here it comes. Dustin is about to confess, Tiffany thought, suddenly cold with dread.

"There wasn't much love lost between Sheridan and Ellery," Dustin announced. His topaz eyes softened, as if he wished he could save her some of the pain he was about to inflict. For the first time Tiffany realized that Dustin did, in his own way, truly love her. "They were involved in a poker game—for high stakes. Sheridan lost. I don't think the man likes to lose, and he took it none too well, let me tell you. He even went so far as to claim that Ellery had been cheating. God, I was there. I don't know how Ellery could have cheated. From where I sat, Ellery won fair and square."

"How—how much money was involved?"

"Somewhere around two hundred thousand dollars, I think. Supposedly it wiped Sheridan out. But apparently he's back on his feet again."

Tiffany's mouth was dry with tension. "You haven't seen him since?"

"No, but I know he breeds horses in Ireland. I've seen a few of them race. He's got a two-year-old filly who's ripping up the tracks."

"The filly sired by King's Ransom?"

Dustin cast her a worried glance and nodded curtly. "I wouldn't trust that man, Tiffany. He's got a reputation in Europe for being ruthless." Dustin began stalking back and forth in front of the stall. "I don't understand why he wants to buy you out. What did you say to his offer?"

"That I wasn't interested, and if I ever did want to sell out my part of the operation, you had first option."

Some of the tension in his shoulders dissipated. "Good." He raked his fingers through his hair. "Did he say anything else?"

"Not much," Tiffany lied with a twinge of regret. "But I think he'll be back with a concrete offer."

"Great," Dustin muttered, his gold eyes impaling her. "Whatever you do, Tiff, don't sell out to that bastard."

"Are you still interested in owning all the farm?" she asked. Several years before, Dustin had offered to buy her out, but she had steadfastly refused.

"Of course I am. I just never thought you'd want to sell."

"I'm not sure that I do."

"Then you will give me first option?"

"When the time comes...."

Dustin appeared relieved, but there was something else that he was hiding from her; she could read it in the shadows of his eyes.

"Dustin." She touched his sleeve lightly. "Is there something you're not telling me?"

Dustin walked away from her and pushed his hands into the back pockets of his slacks. His shoulders slumped in defeat. "Well, maybe I shouldn't be telling you this," he grumbled, condemning himself. "It's all water under the bridge now."

Tiffany's heart nearly stopped. Was Dustin going to admit that Devil's Gambit was alive and siring foals as part of an incredible charade that would rock the Thoroughbred racing world on two continents? She felt almost physically ill with dread.

"Ellery was involved with a woman back then."

"Oh, God," she whispered, rocked to the very core of her soul as she began to understand what Dustin was saying. She felt cold all over; her heart was heavy in her chest. "A woman that Zane was in love with?" she guessed, praying that she had misunderstood her brother-in-law.

Dustin's brows quirked at Tiffany's familiar use of Sheridan's name. He let out an angry oath. "More than that, I'm afraid. She was Zane Sheridan's *wife, Stasia.*"

Tiffany sucked in her breath and her throat began to ache painfully. Truth and fiction began to entangle in her confused thoughts. What was Dustin saying? "Wait a minute..." Dustin was giving her too much information and it made her head swim. She had thought he was going to confess about Devil's Gambit, but instead he had brought up Zane's ex-wife...and *Ellery*. Dear God, was that why Zane had come to the farm, his gray eyes filled with revenge? Had he pretended interest in her only to throw her off guard? "Nancy Emerson said something about Zane's wife running out on him, but not with Ellery. The man's name was—"

"Ethan Rivers."

Tiffany swallowed against the dread flowing in her blood. "No." She had to deny what Dustin was suggesting and her shoulders slumped.

"Tiffany, listen!"

She shook her head and fought against hot tears. "Are you trying to tell me that Ellery used an alias?" She clamped her fingers over the top rail of the stall for support.

"Sometimes."

Pained blue eyes delved into Dustin's murky gaze. "But why?" Alexander's Lady sensed the tension and snorted.

Dustin waved off Tiffany's question as if it were insignificant. "Sometimes it was just easier...if people didn't know we, Ellery and I, were brothers."

"I don't understand." *And I don't think I want to. It would be easier not to think that Ellery used me in the past and that Zane is using me still....*

"You don't have to," Dustin said harshly and then softened a little when he saw her stricken face. "Tiffany, it really doesn't matter, not now. When Ellery and I were first getting started, we had to do a lot of...maneuvering to get established. Sometimes, when we were in Europe trying to sell some of our stock, it was just easier for Ellery to pose as a rival bidder to drive up the price of one of our own horses. Once in a while it backfired and no one bought the horse in question, but other times, well, we came out of it a few dollars richer. We didn't really hurt anyone by it."

Tiffany's eyes grew round with horror. "Oh, no?" she rasped as anger replaced despair. She leaned against a post for support, but her blue eyes blazed with rage. "You can justify it any way you want, even give it such fancy terms as 'maneuvering to get established,' Dustin, but I think what you and Ellery did was manipulate people and the system to pad your wallet." Tiffany felt sick inside, empty. "That's illegal—"

"Probably not," Dustin denied. "Immoral, maybe, and probably unethical—"

"And crooked." She saw the fury spark in his eyes and she forced control on her own anger. "Oh, Dustin. Why didn't Ellery tell me?" she asked in a broken whisper. Her knees threatened to give way. She had been married to Ellery, loved him in her own way, and he had betrayed her trust.

"Hey, don't get down on Ellery," Dustin said as if reading her thoughts. "This all happened before he knew you, and he did a hell of a lot for you and your bum of a father. Where would you have been if Ellery hadn't supported you, paid your way through college and then married you?"

"I don't know," she admitted. "But the lies—"

He touched her chin and lifted it, forcing her to look into his eyes. He felt her tremble with rage. "Look, it's over and done with," Dustin said, his eyes searching hers. "Ellery's dead...." He lowered his head and would have kissed her if it hadn't been for the question she had to ask.

"Is he, Dustin?" she demanded, pulling away from him and wrapping her arms protectively over her breasts.

Dustin was visibly stunned. "What kind of a question is that?"

"A legitimate worry, wouldn't you say?"

"Tiffany, listen to what you're saying!"

"How do I know that he isn't alive and using that alias...Ethan Rivers...or another one for that matter, in Europe somewhere?" Her hands were shaking at her sides. "For all I know, he could be living in France or England or Ireland, racing horses, married to someone else." She was rambling and she knew it, and she had to get hold of herself before she tipped her hand and gave her act away.

"I was there, Tiffany, at the accident. I saw Ellery...." His face went ashen and in that single moment of honesty, Tiffany believed her brother-in-law. "As hard as it is for you to accept, Ellery's gone."

Tiffany managed to square her shoulders, but tears pooled in her eyes before trickling down her face in a broken silvery path. "I didn't really doubt it," she admitted, brushing the unwanted tears aside. "But you've just told me some things that are a little hard to accept."

Dustin glanced at his watch again and cursed. "Damn! I've got to go if I'm going to catch that plane." He looked at her longingly once again, silently offering himself.

Tiffany shook her head and lifted it with renewed determination. Her eyes, when they met Dustin's direct gaze, were cold.

"If you need me—"

"No. Journey's End needs you," she said. "The Florida Derby is next week."

"You could come down," he suggested without much hope.

"Not until I make sure that this little one—" Tiffany cocked her head in the direction of the inquisitive filly "—and her brothers and sisters are okay."

With a reluctant sigh, he turned away. "I'll call," Dustin promised, wondering why the hell he cared. He had lots of women who would do anything he wanted, so why was he hung up on his brother's wife?

"Good."

With only a moment's indecision, Dustin walked crisply out of the foaling shed, and Tiffany slumped against the wall in relief. *Ellery* was Ethan Rivers? *Ellery* had run off with Zane's wife, Stasia? The woman who had been Ellery's mistress when Tiffany was in college?

Tiffany's head was throbbing with unanswered questions. "Oh, Zane," she whispered brokenly. "What are you involved in?"

She was still going over the conversation with Dustin in her mind when Vance Geddes arrived to check the mare and foal. His brow knitted with worry as he started the examination, but the furrows slowly eased as he studied the frisky filly.

"It looks like she's going to make it," he said, relief audible in his voice. "By the time Charlatan was this old, there were already signs of distress."

"Thank God," Tiffany murmured, her mind only half on the conversation. Where was Zane? Why did he want the farm? Why hadn't he explained about Stasia and Ellery?

"Tiffany?" Vance asked for the second time.

"Oh, what?"

Vance shook his head and offered a small smile. "I said it looks as if we can take her out in a few days. I think you've got yourself a racehorse here."

"Wonderful." Tiffany eyed the little filly fondly. "Now we really do have a reason to celebrate."

"Pardon?"

"I was hoping that you could join the rest of us for lunch...brunch—" she lifted her shoulders "—whatever you want to call it."

"I'd be glad to. Just let me get cleaned up."

"I'll meet you at the house," she said, leaving the foaling shed and instructing the stable boy to look after the mare and filly. She headed toward the house and didn't notice the warm spring sunshine, the gentle breeze lifting the branches of the fir trees near the drive or the crocuses sprouting purple, gold, and white near the back porch.

All of her thoughts were centered on Zane and what, if anything, he wanted from her.

By the time Tiffany got back to the house, Louise was working furiously. The smell of honey-glazed ham, homemade apple muffins, black coffee and steamed vegetables filled the room. Louise was humming as she carefully arranged a rainbow of fresh fruit in a crystal bowl.

"It smells great in here," Tiffany said as she walked into the kitchen and tried to shake off the feeling of impending dread that had settled on her shoulders during her discussion with Dustin. "What can I do to help?"

Louise smiled. "Nothing. All the work's about done. Just go change your clothes. We're eating on the sun porch."

"Ummm. Fancy."

"It's a celebration, isn't it?"

"That it is. Let me set the table—"

"Already done."

"You are efficient, aren't you?"

"I don't get much of a chance to show off anymore. It feels good," Louise admitted, holding up the clear bowl of fruit for Tiffany's inspection. The cut crystal sparkled in the late morning light.

"Beautiful," she murmured, and the housekeeper beamed. "If you're sure there's nothing I can do..."

"Scat! Will ya?" Louise instructed with a severe frown that broke down completely as she laughed.

Tiffany chuckled. "All right. I'll be down in about twenty minutes."

She walked toward the stairs and remembered the times she and Ellery had entertained. It had been often and grand. Louise had always enjoyed "putting out a spread" as she had called it. Ellery had insisted that entertaining potential buyers was all part of the business, and he had been at his best when dressed in a black tuxedo and contrasting burgundy cummerbund while balancing a glass of champagne between his long, well-manicured fingers.

It seemed like aeons ago. And all that time, while Tiffany was married to Ellery, he was probably leading a double life as a stranger named Ethan Rivers, and having an affair with Zane Sheridan's ex-wife, Stasia.

Tiffany's heart twisted painfully and she balled small fists in frustration. How could she have been so blind?

It would be easy to blame it on youth or naiveté, but the truth of the matter was that she had been so anxious to love someone and have him love her in return, she had closed her eyes to the possibility that her husband had been anything but what she had wanted to see.

Stop punishing yourself, she warned, as she slipped out of her clothes, rewound her hair onto her head and stepped into the shower. *It's over and done!*

Or was it? Was Dustin telling the truth when he said that Ellery was dead, or was it just part of a complex cover-up to hide the fact that Devil's Gambit was alive and that another horse and *another man* died in the fire? Oh, dear God, would Ellery have been involved in anything so vile as murder? The thought turned her blood to ice water and she had to steady herself against the wet tiles. A cold wave of nausea flooded over her, and Tiffany felt for a minute as if she were going to vomit.

"Oh, God," she cried softly, forcing herself to stand.

No matter what else, she couldn't—wouldn't—believe that Ellery would take part in the death of another human being.

She turned off the shower and wrapped herself in a bath sheet without really thinking about what she was doing. With trembling fingers, while her head was still pounding with the cold truth of the past, she dressed in a bright dress of indigo polished silk, and pinned her hair in a tousled chignon. After touching up her makeup and forcing her morbid thoughts to a dark corner of her mind where she could examine them later, she started down the stairs. As she did, the doorbell chimed loudly.

"I'll get it," she called to Louise and hurred down the remaining three steps to the foyer and walked to the door, her heels echoing sharply against the imported tile.

Squaring her shoulders, she opened the door, expecting to find Mac's wife, Emma McDougal. Instead, her eyes met the silvery gaze of the only man who had ever touched her soul.

"Zane," Tiffany whispered, and felt the need to lean against the door for support. It had been more than a week since she had seen him, and in that time so many truths had been uncovered.

Now, as she looked at the man she loved, Tiffany felt as if she were staring into the eyes of a total stranger.

Chapter Ten

Zane leaned against one of the white columns supporting the roof of the porch and stared at Tiffany. His hands were thrust into the pockets of his jeans, and his slumped posture was meant to be casual, but his shoulder muscles were tight, so tense they ached.

God, she was beautiful, more beautiful than he remembered. Dressed in shimmering blue silk, with her golden brown hair pinned loosely to her crown, Tiffany looked almost regal. A single strand of gold encircled her throat, and thin layers of silk brushed against her knees.

After what seemed like a lifetime, Zane finally spoke. "Are you going out?" he asked, his gray eyes delving into hers. One look at Ellery Rhodes's widow had destroyed all of Zane's earlier promises to himself. After the meeting with Griffith just three days ago, he had silently vowed that he would stay away from Ellery Rhodes's widow. Now, as he gazed into her intriguing blue eyes, he knew that keeping away from her would be impossible. Despite all the excuses he'd made to himself to the contrary, seeing Tiffany again was the single reason he had returned to Rhodes Breeding Farm.

Tiffany, recovering from the shock of seeing him again, managed to square her shoulders and proudly hold his gaze. Though her heartbeat had quickened at the sight of him, she forced herself to remember Dustin's condemning words. *Sheridan's got a reputation for being ruthless.... Ellery was involved with Zane Sheridan's wife.*

"No," she finally replied, "I'm not going out.... We're having a special lunch, sort of a celebration."

Zane detected new doubts in her exotic blue eyes, doubts that hadn't clouded her gaze when he had last seen her. The small hairs on the back of his neck prickled in warning. Something was wrong here, and he intended to find out what it was. Silently he cursed himself for staying away so long. In the course of the past week, someone had destroyed all the trust Tiffany had previously felt for him. It didn't take long to figure out who was to blame, and his fists balled at the thought of Dustin Rhodes.

Zane straightened and walked closer to her. "Tiffany, what's wrong?" he asked, gently placing his fingers on her shoulders and pulling her close.

"Don't," she whispered, knowing that her battle was already lost. She wanted to melt into him. Just seeing him again had been enough to make her heartbeat race in anticipation. Maybe Dustin had been wrong about Zane, maybe he had lied.

She leaned heavily on Zane, letting his strong arms wrap around her. Her face was pressed to his chest, and she could feel the warmth of his breath on her hair, hear the even rhythm of his pounding heart.

Don't fall under his spell again, a small voice inside her cautioned. *Remember what Dustin said about Ellery and*

Zane's wife. He's probably here just to get information about Stasia. He's been using you all along.

"Tiffany?" Zane urged, his voice low, husky. She closed her eyes and let his earthy scent fill her nostrils. It felt so right to have his arms around her. Without examining her motives, she clung to him as if she expected him to vanish as quickly as he had appeared.

"I...I didn't think you were coming back," she whispered, ignoring the doubts filling her mind. He was here, now, with her. Nothing else mattered.

"I said I would."

"But it's been—"

"Too long." The corded arms tightened around her, and his warm hands splayed against the small of her back, pressing her body to his and heating her skin through the thin material of her dress. "I should have called," he admitted, feeling his body beginning to respond to the soft, yielding contour of hers, "but I've been in and out of airports for the better part of a week."

She lifted her head and studied the weariness in his face. Wherever he'd been, the trip had taken its toll on him. The brackets near the corners of his mouth had deepened, and there was a general look of fatigue in his eyes. His clothes, a pair of jeans and a plaid shirt, were clean but slightly rumpled, and his chin was just beginning to darken from the day's growth of beard.

"Have you been out of the country?" she asked.

"Part of the time."

Because of Devil's Gambit, or your wife?

Tiffany knew that she should pull away from him, now, before she was lost to him forever. She shouldn't let him into her house or her life. Not again. Too many events in his past were entangled with Ellery's life and left unexplained. There were too many questions that demanded answers....

For a passing moment she considered confronting him with what she had learned from Dustin, just to gauge his reaction, but she couldn't. The sight of his drawn face, windblown black hair and slightly wrinkled clothing did strange things to her heart. Despite all of Dustin's accusations, despite the lies, she still loved this rugged man from Ireland with every fiber of her soul.

"Come inside," she invited, managing, despite her doubts, the trace of a smile. "Louise is making a special brunch."

"Why?" Zane's dark brows cocked expressively. He was getting mixed signals from Tiffany; one moment she seemed to have a wonderful secret she wanted to share with him, and her indigo eyes sparkled; the next second her smile would fade and her lips would compress into a determined line of defiance.

"Alexander's Lady had a filly—a healthy filly," Tiffany said, pushing her dark thoughts aside.

Zane relaxed a little, and he gently touched her cheek. She had to concentrate to keep her mind on the conversation. "I assume from your expression that she had been bred to Moon Shadow."

"Yes." Tiffany attempted to extract herself from his embrace, to put some mind-clearing distance between his body and hers, but his strong arms refused to release her.

"When was the filly born?"

"Just last night."

"Isn't the celebration a little premature?" he asked softly, remembering the other colt, the one that had lived a day or so before collapsing from heart failure and dying.

"Maybe, but I doubt it. Vance thinks the filly will live," Tiffany said with conviction. She recognized the unspoken question in Zane's eyes and knew that he was thinking about Charlatan's short life. "Vance wasn't so sure last night," she admitted, "but this morning the filly's been scampering around her stall like a champion. Even Vance has taken her off the critical list.''

Zane hazarded a charming half-smile that touched Tiffany's heart. ''That is good news.'' He kissed her lightly on the forehead, and Tiffany's heart seemed to miss a beat. *How could she react this way, love this man, when he had lied to her?*

''And there's more,'' she managed to say. ''Hal Reece called and told me that his mare, Mile High, gave birth to twin colts—healthy colts, about three days ago. He's even been able to insure them.''

Zane's grin spread slowly over his rugged features. He squeezed her for a minute and laughed. God, when was the last time he'd laughed? It had to have been years ago.... It was so easy with Tiffany, so natural. ''You're right, you should celebrate.''

Tiffany's eyes warmed. ''Louise would love it if you joined us.''

''Us?''

''Mac and his wife Emma, Vance, Louise and myself.'' She read the hesitation in his gaze and realized that he felt like an outsider. Her elegant features sobered. ''It's not a private party, Zane,'' she said softly with a seductive smile, ''and you're very much a part of it. After all, you were here the night Ebony Wine delivered. Besides, Louise would skin me alive if she knew you were here and wouldn't have brunch with us after all the work she's gone to.''

''Then how can I refuse?''

''You can't.''

She pulled away from him, but his fingers caught her wrist. ''Tiffany?''

''What?''

When she turned to face him, he tugged on her arm again and pulled her close against his body. ''Just one more thing.''

"Which is?" she asked breathlessly.

In answer, he lowered his head and his lips brushed seductively over hers. His breath was warm and inviting, his silvery eyes dark with sudden passion. "I missed you," he whispered against her mouth, then his lips claimed hers in a kiss that was as savage as it was gentle. The warmth of his lips coupled with the feel of his slightly beard-roughened face made her warm with desire.

Tiffany moaned and leaned against him, letting her body feel the hard texture of his. His tongue gently parted her lips and flickered erotically against hers. Heat began to coil within her before he pulled his head away and gazed at her through stormy gray eyes.

"God, I missed you," he repeated, shaking his head as if in wonder at the conflicting emotions warring within his soul.

Tiffany had to clear her throat. "Come on. Louise will have my head if her meal gets cold." Still holding his hand, she led him toward the back of the house and tried to forget that Zane had once been married to Ellery's mistress.

"I haven't eaten like this since the last time I was here," Zane remarked to Louise, who colored slightly under the compliment. Everyone was seated at the oval table in the sun room, which was really an extension of the back porch. The corner of the porch nearest the kitchen had been glassed in, affording a view of the broodmare barn and the pasture surrounding the foaling shed. Green plants, suspended from the ceiling in wicker baskets or sitting on the floor in large brass pots, surrounded the oak table, and a slow-moving paddle fan circulated the warm air.

"We should do this more often," Tiffany decided as she finished her meal and took a sip of the champagne.

"Used to be," Mac mused while buttering a hot muffin, "that we'd have parties all the time. But that was a long time ago, when Ellery was still alive."

Tiffany felt her back stiffen slightly at the mention of Ellery's name. When she looked away from Mac she found Zane's gray eyes boring into hers. An uncomfortable silence followed.

"Hasn't been any reason to celebrate until now," Louise said, as much to diffuse the tension settling in the room as to make conversation. Her worried eyes moved from Tiffany to Zane and back again.

"What about Journey's End's career?" Vance volunteered, while declining champagne. He shook his head at Mac, who was tipping a bottle over his glass. "I've got two more farms to visit today." When Mac poured the remainder of the champagne into his own glass, Vance continued with his line of thinking. "If you ask me, Journey's End is reason enough to celebrate."

"Maybe we'd better wait on that," Tiffany thought aloud. "Let's see how he does in the Florida Derby."

"That race shouldn't be too much of a problem if Prescott handles him right," Mac said.

"What then?" Zane asked the trainer.

"Up to Kentucky for the Lexington Stakes."

"And then the Kentucky Derby?"

"That's the game plan," Mac said, finishing his drink and placing his napkin on the table. He rubbed one thumb over his forefinger nervously before extending his lower lip and shrugging. "I just hope Prescott can pull it off."

"He's a good trainer," Emma McDougal stated. She was a petite woman of sixty with beautiful gray hair and a warm smile. She patted her husband affectionately on the knee in an effort to smooth what she saw as Mac's ruffled feathers. She knew that as much as he might argue the point, Mac missed the excitement of the racetrack.

"When he keeps his mind on his horses," Mac grumbled.

"Don't you think he will?" Zane asked.

Mac's faded eyes narrowed thoughtfully. "He'd better," he said with a frown. "We've come too close to the Derby before to let this one slip through our fingers."

Tiffany pushed her plate aside. "Delicious," she said to Louise before turning her attention back to the trainer. "Would you like to work with Journey's End in Lexington? You could help Bob Prescott get him ready."

"Oh, there's no doubt I'd like to, Missy," Mac replied, ignoring the reproachful look from his wife. "But it wouldn't do a lick of good. Journey's End, he's used to Prescott. We can't be throwin' him any loops, not now. Me going to Kentucky would probably do more harm than good."

"So the die is cast?" Tiffany asked, feeling a cold premonition of doom as she looked through the windows and noticed the thick bank of clouds rolling over the mountains from the west.

"Aye, Missy. That it is...that it is."

Tiffany spent the rest of the afternoon with Zane, and for the first time in more than a week she began to relax. She had planned to drive into town in the afternoon but decided that she'd rather spend the time on the farm.

In the early evening, she took Zane into the foaling shed and proudly displayed Shadow's Survivor. Within the confines of the large stall, the inquisitive filly cavorted beneath the warm heat lamps.

"Vance says she'd be able to go outside in a couple of days," Tiffany said.

"I'll bet you're relieved." Zane's eyes moved from the mare and foal to Tiffany.

"I'll be more relieved when I hear from the rest of the owners," she responded as she led Zane out of the foaling shed. "Until I know that no more foals will die, I can't really relax."

Dusk was just beginning to settle on the hills surrounding the farm. Lavender shadows lengthened as the hazy sun settled behind the ridge of sloping mountains to the west. Clouds began to fill the darkened sky. "This is my favorite time of day," she admitted, watching as the stable boys rounded up the horses for the evening. The soft nickering of mares to their foals was interspersed with the distant whistle of a lonely stallion. Tiffany chuckled. "That's Moon Shadow," she explained. "He always objects to being locked up for the night."

"Do you blame him?" Zane asked.

"Oh, no. That's what makes him a winner, I suppose."

"His defiance?"

She frowned into the gathering darkness and linked her arm through his. A cool breeze pushed her dress against her legs as they walked. "I prefer to think of it as his fire, his lack of docility. He's always had to have his way, even as a foal. He was the boss, had to be in the lead."

"The heart of a champion."

Tiffany pursed her lips thoughtfully and her elegant brows drew together. "That's why I hate what's been happening to him—all this conjecture that there's something wrong with him."

"Have you found an answer to what happened to the dead foals?"

After expelling a ragged sigh, Tiffany shook her head. "Nothing so far. Vance has gone to independent laboratories, asked for help from the Jockey Club and the racing commission, and still can't get any answers."

"Not even enough information to clear Moon Shadow's name?"

"No." She placed a restraining hand on her hair as the wind began to loosen her chignon. "The new foals—the healthy ones—should prove that the problem isn't genetic."

"Unless another one dies."

She shuddered inside at the thought.

Zane noticed the pain in her eyes and placed a comforting arm over her shoulders. "You really love it here, don't you?"

"What?"

He rotated the palm of his free hand and moved his arm in a sweeping gesture meant to include the cluster of buildings near the center of the farm, the sweeping green pastures enclosed by painted white fences, the horses grazing in the field and the gentle green hills guarding the valley. "All of it."

She couldn't deny the attachment she felt for this farm. It was the only home she'd known. She felt as much a part of it as if it had been in her family for generations. It was, and would always be, the only thing she could call her heritage. "Yes," she answered. "I love it. I love the horses, the land, the excitement, the boredom, *everything*."

"And is that what I felt when I came back here this morning?"

"What do you mean?"

"When I arrived here, you looked at me as if I were a thief trying to steal it all away from you."

"Did I?"

He didn't answer, but she saw the determination in the angle of his jaw. He wouldn't let up until he found out what was bothering her. She had no recourse but to lie or to confront him with what she'd learned from Dustin.

The day with Zane had been so wonderful, and she knew that it was about to end. "It had nothing to do with selling the farm to you, Zane. You, or anyone else, can't force me to sell."

The arm around her tightened. She felt the unleashed tension coiling his body. "Then what?"

"While you were gone, a few things happened," she admitted. They had been walking down a wide, well-worn path, past the old barn and through a thicket of maple trees surrounding a small pond. The water in the small lake had taken on an inky hue, reflecting the turbulent purple of the sky.

"What things?"

"Dustin came home."

All of the muscles in Zane's body tightened. The thought of Dustin Rhodes, here, alone with Tiffany, made his stomach knot with dread. It was insane to feel this...jealousy. Dustin owned part of the farm; he could come and go as he pleased. Zane's jaw hardened, and his back teeth ground together in frustration.

"You weren't expecting him?"

"No."

"Then why did he return?"

"He said it was because of all the bad press surrounding Moon Shadow. He wanted to make sure that I was all right."

"He could have called."

"I suppose," she admitted, taking a seat on a boulder near the pond. "But I think he wanted to see me face to face."

"Why?" Zane demanded, his eyes glittering in the dark night.

"Dustin helped me pick up the pieces when Ellery was killed," she whispered. "I was pretty shook up."

"Because you loved your husband so much?" he asked, reaching for a flat stone and thrusting it toward the water.

He watched as it skipped across the pond creating ever-widening ripples on the water's smooth surface.

"Because my whole world was turned upside down." The wind picked up and clouds shadowed the moon.

"And if he walked back into your life right now?" Zane asked, bracing himself against the truth.

"It would be upside down all over again."

"And who would you lean on?"

Tiffany breathed deeply. "I hope that I'm strong enough to stand by myself—no matter what happens," she said softly.

The air was thick was the promise of rain, and the clouds covering the moon became more dense. High above, the branches of the fir trees danced with the naked maples.

Zane turned to face her and his broad shoulders slumped in resignation. Gray eyes drove into hers. "You know that I'm falling in love with you, don't you?"

Tiffany's heart nearly stopped. *If only I could believe you, Zane. If only you hadn't lied to me. If only I could tell what was true and what was false.*

She wrapped her arms around her knees and shook her head. "I don't think love can enter into our relationship," she said, staring at the dark water and refusing to face him.

"It's nothing I wanted," he admitted and pushed his hands into his back pockets. "But it happened."

"Zane—" her protest was cut short when he strode purposely over to the rock and scooped her into his arms. "Please don't..." she breathed, but it was the cry of a woman lost. When his lips crushed against hers, she responded willingly, eagerly to him, mindless of the wind billowing her dress or the heavy scent of rain in the air.

He gently laid her on the grass near a stand of firs, and his fingers caught in the golden strands of her hair. Slowly he withdrew the pins and twined his fingers in the silken braid as he pulled it loose. The golden hair fell to her shoulders, framing her face in tangled honey-brown curls.

"I've wanted to make love to you from the first moment I saw you," he whispered. His body was levered over hers, and his silvery eyes caught the reflection of the shadowy moon. She trembled when his hands lingered on her exposed throat to gently stroke the sensitive skin near her shoulders.

"That's not the same as loving someone," she replied, her voice breathless as his hand slowly, enticingly, slid down the silky fabric of her dress and softly caressed her breast.

A spasm of desire shot through her. "Oh, my God," she whispered while he looked at her, touching her with only one hand. Her breathing became rapid and shallow as slowly he caressed the silk-encased peak, rubbing the sheer fabric against her. Tiffany began to ache for the feel of his hands against her skin.

The fingers slid lower, down her thigh, to the hem of her dress. She felt the warm impression of his fingertips as they stroked her leg through her sheer stocking.

I shouldn't be doing this, she thought wildly. *I don't even really understand what he wants of me....*

"Tell me you want me to make love to you," he rasped against her hair. His tongue traced the gentle shell of her ear, and his breath fanned seductively against her skin.

"Oh, Zane...I..." Her blood was pounding in her temples. She trembled with desire.

"Tell me!"

"Oh, God, yes." She closed her eyes against the truth and felt the hot tears moisten her lashes. *I don't want to love you,* she thought for a fleeting moment. *Dear Lord, I don't want to love you.* He lowered his head and kissed her eyelids, first one and then the other, tasting the salt of her tears and knowing that he couldn't deny himself any longer.

"I love you, Tiffany," he whispered, while his fingers strayed to the pearl buttons holding the bodice of her dress together, and his lips touched her neck, moving over the smooth skin and the rope of gold. His tongue pressed against the flickering pulse in the hollow of her throat.

"No." *If only she could trust him.*

"I've loved every minute I've spent with you...."

Each solitary button was slowly unbound, and the shimmery blue fabric of her dress parted in the night. Her straining breasts, covered only by a lacy, cream-colored camisole and the golden curtain of her hair, pressed upward. The dark points seductively invited him to conquer her, and Zane felt hot desire swelling uncomfortably in his loins at the dark impressions on the silky fabric.

He groaned at the sight of her. He slowly lowered his head to taste one of the ripe buds encased in silk. His tongue toyed with the favored nipple until Tiffany's heart was pounding so loudly it seemed to echo in the darkness. His hands caressed her, fired her blood, promised that their joining would be one of souls as well as flesh.

Somewhere in the distance, over the sound of Zane's labored breathing, she heard the sound of lapping water and the cry of a night bird, but everything she felt was because of Zane. Liquid fire ignited from deep within her and swirled upward through her pulsing veins.

His warm tongue moistened the lace and left it wet, to dry in the chill breeze. She shuddered, more from the want of him than the cold. When his hands lifted the dress over her head, she didn't protest.

Tenderly at first, and then more wildly, he stroked her breasts until she writhed beneath him, trying to get closer to the source of her exquisite torment. He removed the camisole slowly and then let his lips and teeth toy with one sweet, aching breast. Tiffany moaned throatily, from somewhere deep in her soul.

His tongue moistened the dark nipple until it hardened beautifully, and then he began to suckle ravenously, all the while touching the other breast softly, making it ready. Just when Tiffany thought she could stand no more of the sweet torment, he turned to the neglected breast and he feasted again.

"Oh, Zane," Tiffany cried, her fever for his love making demands upon her. She was empty, void, and only he could make her whole again.

His hands continued to stroke her while he slowly removed the remaining scanty pieces of her clothing. She felt her lace panties slide over her hips. Warm fingers traced the ridge of her spine and lingered at the swell of her hips.

He touched all of her, making her ready, while she slowly undressed him and ran her fingers hungrily over his naked chest. His muscles rippled beneath her touch, and she was in awe at the power her touch commanded.

He kicked off his jeans almost angrily and was only satisfied when he was finally lying atop her; hard male muscles pressed heatedly against their softer feminine counterparts.

The need in him was evident; his eyes were dark with desire, his breathing labored, his heartbeat thudding savaging against her flattened breasts. A thin sheen of sweat glistened over his supple muscles. His lips pressed hungrily, eagerly over hers.

"Let me love you, sweet lady," he coaxed, rubbing against her seductively, setting her skin aflame with his touch.

Her blood pulsed wildly in her veins. All thoughts of denial had fled long ago. The ache within her, burning with the need for fulfillment, throbbed with the want of him.

"Please," she whispered, closing her eyes against the glorious torment of his fingers kneading her buttocks.

Her fingers stroked him, and he cried out her name. He could withhold himself no longer.

With only a fleeting thought that this woman was the widow of Ellery Rhodes, he gently parted her legs and delved into the warmth of the woman he loved. His body joined with hers and he became one with the wife of the man he had vowed to destroy. He whispered her name, over and over again, as if his secret incantation could purge her from his soul.

He watched in fascination as she threw back her head and exposed the white column of her throat. Her fingernails dug into the muscles of his back before she shuddered in complete surrender. His explosion within her sent a series of shock waves through his body until he collapsed over her.

"I love you, Tiffany," he whispered, his breathing as raspy as the furious wind. He twined his fingers in her hair and let his head fall to the inviting hollow between her breasts. *Oh, but to die with this beautiful woman.*

Tiffany's entire body began to relax. The warmth within her seemed to spread into the night. Zane touched her chin with one long finger and kissed her lips.

Lying naked in the dark grass, with only the sounds of the night and the gentle whisper of Zane's breath, she felt whole. Large drops of rain began to fall from the black sky, but Tiffany didn't notice. She was only aware of Zane and his incredible touch. His fingers traced the curve of her cheek. "I meant it, you know," he whispered, smiling down at her.

"What?"

"That I love you."

Tiffany released a tormented sigh and pulled herself into a sitting position. "You don't have to say—"

His fingers wrapped possessively around her wrist and his eyes bored into hers. "I only say what I mean."

"Do you, Zane?" she asked, her face contorted in pain as the doubts of the morning and her conversation with Dustin invaded her mind. God, how desperately she wanted to believe him.

"What is it, Tiffany?" he asked, suddenly releasing her. "Ever since I arrived, I've gotten the feeling that something isn't right. What happened?"

Tiffany decided there was no better time for the truth than now. Before she became more hopelessly in love with him, she had to settle the past. She reached for her dress, but Zane restrained her. "I want answers, Tiffany."

"Not nearly as badly as I do." She pulled away from him and grabbed her clothes. As she quickly dressed, she began to talk. "I told Dustin that you had been here and expressed interest in buying the farm." The rain began in earnest, running down her face and neck in cold rivulets.

Zane's expression grew grim. "He wasn't too pleased about it, I'd guess."

"That's putting it mildly. He nearly fell through the floor."

"And what did he suggest?"

"That I shouldn't even consider selling to you. In fact, he seemed to think that I shouldn't have anything to do with you."

"He's afraid, Tiffany."

She began working on the buttons of her dress while Zane slipped on his jeans. "That's what I thought, too. At one point I was certain that Dustin was going to confess about switching horses and admit that Devil's Gambit is alive."

Zane was reaching for his shirt but stopped. "Did he?"

"No."

He slipped his arms through the sleeves but didn't bother with the buttons. His shirttails fluttered in the wind. "Then what, Tiffany? Just what the hell did he tell you that upset you so?"

Tiffany wrapped her arms around her breasts and stared at Zane. The wind caught her hair and lifted it off her face which was glistening with raindrops. "Dustin said that not only did you lose most of your money to Ellery in an honest poker game—"

"Honest my ass!"

"—but that Ellery also ran off with your wife."

Zane gritted his teeth together and rose. "Damn!" he spit out as he stood and stared at the pond, legs spread apart, hands planted on his hips.

Tiffany's heart ached as she watched him. *Deny it, Zane,* she thought. *Tell me Dustin lied...anything...tell me again that you love me.*

"He told you only part of the story," Zane said. He walked over to the boulder and propped one foot on it as he stared across the small lake. "It's true, Stasia ran off with Ellery, and at the time I felt like killing them both."

He still loves her, Tiffany realized, and fresh tears slid down her cheek to mingle with the drops of rain.

"So did you come here looking for her?" she asked, her voice thick and raw.

"No."

"Then why?"

"I can't lie to you, Tiffany."

"You already have."

"No—"

"I asked you if you were married," she whispered.

"And I'm not."

"You just conveniently forgot that you had been?" She looked up at the cloudy sky. "You never even mentioned her."

"She's not something I like to think about," he confessed.

"But your feelings were strong enough to bring you here. You can't expect me to believe that you're not looking for her."

He walked over to the grassy knoll on which she was sitting, knelt down and placed his fingers over her shoulders. She quivered betrayingly at his familiar touch. "I knew she wouldn't be here, but yes, I need to find her."

Tiffany closed her eyes against the truth. "Why?"

"Because she's the only one who can clear up what happened to Devil's Gambit...and Ellery."

"Ellery is dead," Tiffany murmured, hugging her knees to her and setting her chin on them.

"How do you know?"

"I asked Dustin."

"He wouldn't tell you the truth—"

"Dustin cares about me, Zane. He admitted some pretty horrible things, such as conning other owners at the yearling sales in Europe. He said that Ellery would pose as another person, someone named Ethan Rivers."

"Did he explain about Devil's Gambit?"

"No."

"But?" he coaxed.

"From his reaction, I'd have to guess that your assumption about Devil's Gambit is correct. He wouldn't admit that Devil's Gambit was alive, but it was fairly obvious when I mentioned King's Ransom and Devil's Gambit in the same breath that something wasn't right."

"You should be more careful around him," Zane warned. "He's dangerous, and he has a lot to lose if he's uncovered."

"I'm not sure that he's the man in charge."

"What do you mean?"

"I don't know, just a feeling I got that there was someone else pulling his strings."

"I don't know who it would be."

"Neither do I."

"That's why I have to find Stasia," Zane said. "She might be able to help us."

"I doubt it."

Zane lifted his head and his sharp eyes bored into Tiffany. "You knew her?" he guessed incredulously.

Tiffany nodded, remembering Stasia's long, dark hair, even features and seductive dark eyes. Stasia's sultry beauty was enough to capture any man, including Zane. "She was here on the farm with Ellery when I was in college. Later, once I had returned, my father died and Ellery asked me to marry him."

"What happened to Stasia?"

"I don't know. Ellery wouldn't talk about it. The day after he asked me to marry him, she moved out. I never saw her again, but I'm sure that she despises me."

"Probably," he said with a snort. "Stasia knows how to carry a grudge." He saw the unasked questions in Tiffany's wide eyes and began to explain about a time in his life he would rather have forgotten.

"When I met Stasia, she was barely eighteen. She was beautiful and anxious to get out of a bad home situation. I thought at the time that I was in love with her, and we got married. I was just starting then, trying to set up a successful farm of my own. Fortunately, I had a few decent breaks. I was lucky and after a few years, I...we, Stasia and I, owned a small farm about thirty miles from Dublin. It was a beautiful place," he said, smiling slightly at the fond memories, "thick green grass, stone fences twined with bracken, the rolling Irish countryside...a perfect place for breeding Thoroughbreds. That's when I started breeding successfully. And how I met Ethan Rivers."

"Ellery," Tiffany whispered.

Zane's smile had left his face and his rugged features pulled into a dark scowl. "One and the same. It happened about six years ago. Ethan was looking for some yearlings and came out to the farm. Later that night we began drinking and playing poker with another man from America who was supposedly interested in some of my horses."

"Dustin," Tiffany guessed, not daring to breathe.

"Right again. Anyway, on that night, Dustin folded early, claimed the stakes were too high for him. But I kept on drinking and playing, urged on by my lovely wife."

"Oh, no—"

"That's right. Stasia was already involved with Ethan Rivers, and when I lost it cost me two hundred thousand dollars. I had to sell the farm to pay Rivers off."

"But if you thought the game was crooked—"

"I didn't. Not then. Only much later, when I went back to that pub and got to talking to one of the regulars, I learned that the old man, who was named O'Brien, had watched the game and thought it might be rigged. A few days later, he'd overheard Dustin and his brother talking— about the game and Stasia."

"Why didn't he talk to you sooner?" she asked. "There must have been plenty of time before you sold the farm."

"O'Brien was caught eavesdropping by Ellery. Ellery was furious that he might be found out, and he threatened the old man with his life. O'Brien didn't doubt for a minute that Ellery would make good his threats to kill both him and his wife. By the time his conscience got the better of him and he found me, I'd managed to sell the farm."

"Who would buy it so quickly?"

Zane's jaw became rigid and his eyes turned deadly. "A corporation."

Tiffany finally understood, and her throat went dry with dread. "Emerald Enterprises."

"That's right. The farm I used to own now belongs to Dustin and Ellery, if he's still alive."

"Oh, God, Zane," she murmured, covering her face with her hands. *Had she been so young and foolish that she had never seen Ellery for what he really was?* She lifted her eyes and felt her hands curl into fists of frustration. "I don't understand. Knowing how you must feel about him, why would Dustin allow you to breed any of your mares to King's Ransom?"

"First of all, I didn't know that Emerald Enterprises was Dustin Rhodes. The original sale of the farm was handled through a broker, and neither Dustin's name nor Ellery's ever appeared on any of the documents. As for Dustin, either he's just gotten cocky and doesn't think he'll be discovered, or maybe he thinks I've buried the hatchet. After all, I have been able to put myself back on my feet. It took several years, mind you, but I was able to start again. I didn't lose everything when I sold the farm, and I managed to keep two good mares and a stallion."

"And from those three horses, you started again?"

"Yes. Fortunately I'd already established myself as a breeder. The three good horses and my reputation gave me a decent start."

"And. . .and your wife?"

"She left me immediately. I suspected that she'd followed Ethan. . .who I later found out was Ellery, to America. When Stasia filed for divorce, I didn't fight her.

"I spent the next several years working to reestablish myself."

"And you never forgot taking your revenge on Ellery," Tiffany whispered as thunder rumbled in the distant hills.

"No. That's the reason I came here. When I heard that Ellery had married, I assumed that it was to Stasia." Zane walked back to the lake and stared across the black water, watching as the raindrops beat a staccato rhythm on the clear surface. "Of course later I learned that he had married a woman by the name of Tiffany Chappel."

"And you wondered what had become of your ex-wife."
Tiffany felt a sudden chill as she finally understood Zane's
motives. He had come looking for Stasia....

"Yeah, I wondered, but I found that I really didn't give
a damn." He shrugged his broad shoulders. "The next thing
I heard about Ellery Rhodes was that he, along with his famous horse, had been killed. My fever for revenge had
cooled, and I decided to put the past behind me."

"Until you found the horse you think is Devil's Gambit."

"The horse I *know* is Devil's Gambit."

Zane hazarded a glance at the threatening sky before
looking back at Tiffany and noticing that she was shivering.

"Come on," he suggested softly. "We'd better get inside
before we're both soaked to the skin."

Tiffany refused to be deterred when she was so close to the
truth. Her emotions was as raw as the wind blowing over the
mountains. Everything Zane was suggesting was too farfetched, and yet parts of his story were true. Even Dustin
had backed him up. She ran shaky fingers through her hair
and watched his silhouetted form as he advanced on her and
stared down at her with bold gray eyes.

"When I figured out the scam that Ellery and his brother
had pulled, I knew he had to be stopped. Using one stud in
place of another, and falsifying the death of Devil's Gambit is a scandal of international proportions."

"Then you think that Ellery is still alive?" she murmured, feeling lost and alone.

"That, I'm not sure of."

"Dear God," she whispered, sagging against him. Had
she just made love to a man while still married to another?
Guilt and fear darkened her heart. "I don't think he's
alive," she murmured.

"Because Dustin says so?" he asked cynically.

"Yes. And because I don't believe that Dustin or Ellery would have let another man die in that trailer." The image of the truck carrying Devil's Gambit, as well as Ellery, charred and twisted beyond recognition, filled her mind and she shuddered.

Zane placed comforting arms over her shoulders and kissed her rain-sodden hair before urging her forward, toward the path that led to the house. "You have to face the fact that your husband might still be alive," he whispered.

"I...I don't—"

"Shh!" Zane whispered, cutting off her thought. He cocked his head to one side and listened.

"What?" Tiffany heard the faint sound rumbling in the distance, barely audible over the rising wind. With a sickening feeling, she recognized the noise. "Oh, no!" The sound became louder and more clear. Thundering hooves pounded the wet earth, charging through the pastures with lightning speed. "One of the horses is loose," she said, turning toward the direction of the sound and trying to break free of Zane's arms.

"Wait." Zane restrained her just as the black horse broke through the trees and bolted toward the lake. He raced to the edge of the pond with his ebony tail hoisted and his long legs stretching with boundless energy.

"Moon Shadow," Tiffany whispered, her heart pounding with dread as she watched the magnificent creature rear and whirl on his hind legs when he reached the water's edge.

Tiffany started toward him, all her thoughts centered on the horse and how he could injure himself by slipping on the wet grass. Zane's fingers tightened over her arm. "I'll go after the horse, you call the police."

"The police?" Tiffany's mind was racing with the stallion.

"If he gets out and onto the road, it could get dangerous. Not only for him, but for motorists as well."

"Oh, God. I don't think he can get out," she said, trying to convince herself. Shielding her eyes against the rain, she squinted into the darkness, searching the black night, trying to recall the boundaries of the farm. The horse splashed in the water and started off at a dead run to the opposite side of the pond.

"What's on the other side of the lake?" Zane pointed in the direction in which Moon Shadow disappeared.

"Nothing...some trees, it's all fenced."

"No gate?" He started to follow the stallion, his long legs accelerating with each of his strides.

"Yes, but it should be closed."

"Good. With any luck, I'll be able to catch him." Zane chased after the horse while Tiffany turned toward the buildings near the house.

Her heart was pounding as she ran through the open field, stumbling twice when her heels caught in the mud. Once, when she fell, she heard her dress rip, but didn't bother to see how bad the damage was. All her thoughts centered on Moon Shadow. *Who had let him out? Was it carelessness on the part of the stable boy or...what?* At the sinister turn of her thoughts, she raced more quickly. *No one would let the prized stallion out on purpose!*

Once she made it to the stallion barn, her heart hammering, her lungs burning for air, she noticed that the door to Moon Shadow's stall was swinging outward. It caught in the wind and banged loudly against the building. Other stallions within the building stamped nervously and snorted at the strange sounds.

Tiffany hurried inside and with numb fingers, flipped on the lights, flooding the building with illumination. The horses moved restlessly in their stalls.

As quickly as her trembling fingers could punch out the number, she called Mac. Rain peppered the roof of the barn as she counted the rings...three, four, five..."Come on," she urged. Finally the trainer answered.

"'Lo," Mac called into the phone.

"Moon Shadow's out," Tiffany explained breathlessly to the trainer. "His stall was unlatched and he bolted."

Mac swore loudly. "Where is he?"

"I don't know," she replied, trying to remain calm. Her chest was heaving, her words broken, her heart thudding with fear. "He took off past the old barn and the pond."

"God in heaven," Mac whispered. "We've been workin' on that fence on the other edge of the lake."

Tiffany swallowed hard against the dread creeping up her throat. "Is it down?" she whispered, her fingers clenched around the receiver.

"I don't think so...." He didn't sound too sure.

"What about the gate?"

"It should be closed."

"But you're not certain?"

Mac swore roundly and then sighed. "I'll be right over. Is anyone else around?"

"Just Zane. Everyone went home for the night."

"I'll call John and a few of the other stable hands that live close. We'll be at the house in ten minutes."

"I'll meet you there."

She hung up and then dialed the number of the local police. Within minutes she was explaining her situation to the officer on the other end of the line.

When she had finished with the phone call, Tiffany hurried outside and listened to the sounds of the night. The rain was beginning to sheet and run on the pavement. It gurgled in the gutters and downspouts. In the distance, faint to her ears, she heard the sound of running hoofbeats...on asphalt.

"Oh God," she swore in desperation. *Moon Shadow was on the road!*

Tiffany began running down the long driveway toward the county road that bordered the farm. She heard the truck before she saw it, the loud engine reverberating through the night.

"No," she cried, spurred even faster. Her legs were numb, her lungs burning. Headlights flashed between the trees bordering the farm, and the roar of the truck's engine filled the night.

She heard the squeal of locked brakes, and the sound of the truck's dull horn as it slid out of control on the wet pavement.

"Moon Shadow!" Tiffany shrieked over the deafening noise.

A stallion squealed, the truck tore through the trees, crashing against the solid wood until finally there was nothing but silence and the sound of the pouring rain.

"Oh, God, no," Tiffany whispered as she raced to the end of the drive. Tears blurred her vision and her voice seemed distant when she screamed. *"Zane..."*

Chapter Eleven

Tiffany raced down the slick pavement of the county road, mindless of the rain running down her back. The smell of burning rubber filled the night and the truck's headlights angled awkwardly up through the broken branches of the giant oaks, like a pair of macabre searchlights, announcing the place of the accident.

As she approached, all she could hear was her own ragged breath and running footsteps. "Zane, dear God, where are you?" she screamed, listening for a sound, any sound indicating there was life in the wreckage. Her mind filled with a dozen bloody scenarios involving Zane and Moon Shadow, but she pushed her horrible thoughts aside and dashed toward the jackknifed truck.

"Goddam it, man, what the hell was that horse doing loose?" a gravelly voice demanded. The truck driver was crawling out of the cab and swearing profusely. Rain poured down upon him, and the broken branches of the trees snapped as he stepped onto the road.

Zane must be alive! Who else would be absorbing the angry trucker's wrath?

Tiffany made it to the wrecked truck. Her heart was thudding wildly in her chest, and she had to gasp for air. The truck was lying on its side, the cab at an awkward angle. It looked like some great downed beast with a broken neck. In her mind's eye Tiffany saw another truck, the rig that had taken Ellery and Devil's Gambit from Florida to Kentucky, the one that had rolled over and burst into flame, killing both horse and driver. Her stomach turned over at the painful memory.

From inside the cab the sound of a CB's static pierced the darkness and brought her thoughts crashing to the present.

"Zane?" she cried, looking into the darkness, searching for any sign of the man and the horse.

"Hey, lady! Over here!" The large truck driver commanded her attention by calling out in his gravelly voice. "What're you doin' out here? Jesus, God, you're soaked to the skin!"

"Zane... My horse—"

"That black son of a bitch? He's your goddamn horse?" His agitated swearing continued. "Christ, woman, can't you see what that horse of yours did? He ran right up the road here—" the trucker pointed a burly arm toward the bend in the road "—like some demon. Scared the hell out of me, let me tell you."

"He got out.... I'm sorry...." She looked around frantically, dread still taking a stranglehold of her throat. "Where is he...? Where is Zane?"

"Who the hell is Zane? The horse?"

"No!"

"Tiffany," Zane shouted from somewhere in the thick stand of oak and fir trees near the road. Tiffany's head snapped in the direction of the familiar sound, her heart nearly skipped a beat and relief washed over her in soothing rivulets.

Without another glance at the truck driver, who was busy clearing debris from the road and placing warning flares near his truck, Tiffany hurried toward the familiar welcome of Zane's voice.

Then she saw him. Wet, bedraggled, mud-streaked and walking toward her. He was leading a lathered Moon Shadow, who skittered and danced at all the commotion he had inadvertently caused. "Oh, God, Zane," she cried, "you're alive."

Without further thought, she ran to him and threw her arms around his neck. "I thought...Oh, God, I heard the horse and the truck. I was sure that..." Tears began running freely down her face, and she sobbed brokenly, clinging to him.

"Shh." He wrapped one strong arm around her and kissed her forehead, smearing mud on her face. "I'm all right, and I think Moon Shadow will be, too. But you'd better have the vet look at him; he's limping a little."

"What happened?" she asked, refusing to let go of the man she loved, letting her body feel his, confirming that he was here, alive and unhurt. Rain glistened in his ebony hair, sweat trickled down his jutted chin and a scarlet streak of dried blood cut across his hollowed cheek. Still he was the most ruggedly handsome man she had ever known.

"The fence was down. I followed Moon Shadow through it and called to him, but he wouldn't listen."

"Of course," Tiffany replied, patting the horse's sweaty neck fondly. "He never does."

"He just took off down the road. Bolted as if he were jumping out of the starting gate. I heard the truck coming and tried to stop him by cutting across a field. That's when I got this." He pointed to the ugly slash on his face. "When I realized I didn't have a prayer of catching him in time, I called to the horse and yelled at the truck driver, waving my arms, hoping to catch his eye. Even though I was farther down the road, I thought the driver might see my shirt before the black horse. Anyway, Moon Shadow jumped over the ditch and ran into the trees just as the truck hit the brakes.''

"Hey, you think I could get some help over here?" the furious trucker shouted.

Zane went to help the driver just as Mac's old Dodge rumbled down the road. After parking the pickup some distance from the mangled truck and trailer, Mac scrambled out of the Dodge. "Holy Mother of God," he whispered as he eyed the wrecked truck. He expelled a long whistle and grabbed the lead rope from the front seat of his pickup. "What the devil happened?"

Then he saw Moon Shadow. Knowing that Zane and the trucker were doing everything that could be done with the truck, Mac walked over to Tiffany and snapped a lead rope onto Moon Shadow's wet halter. "Well, Missy," he said, eyeing the wrecked truck. "It looks as if you've had yourself quite a night." His eyes narrowed as he surveyed the anxious stallion.

"One I wouldn't want to repeat," she admitted. "Zane says Moon Shadow's walking with a misstep," she said. "Left hind leg."

"Let's take a look at him." Mack talked to the horse while he ran his fingers down his back and along each leg. "Yep, it's a little tender," Mac decided. "But I don't think anything's broken, probably bruised himself, maybe a pulled tendon. I'll take him back to the barn, cool him down and check for any other injuries." He tugged on the rope, and Moon Shadow tossed his great black head. "I always said *you* should have been the one named Devil's something or other," Mac grumbled affectionately to the nervous stallion.

The sound of a siren pierced the night and increased in volume. Bright, flashing lights announced the arrival of the state police. A young officer parked his car, leaving the lights flashing in warning, and walked stiffly toward the crumpled truck. "What happened here?" he demanded.

"One of the horses got out," Zane replied, tossing a broken branch off the road.

"And I damned near hit him," the trucker added with a shake of his head. "Just lucky that I didn't."

The officer's suspicious eyes moved from Zane to Tiffany. "Are you the lady who called?"

"Yes."

"*Before* the accident?"

"That's right. I was afraid something like this might happen."

The officer studied the wreckage and whistled. "Where's the horse?"

"Over here." Mac led Moon Shadow to the officer. The black stallion shied away from the flashing lights of the police car, and reared on his back legs. The lead rope tightened in Mac's hands, but he began to talk to the horse and gently led him away from the crowd.

"Blends in with the night," Officer Sparks remarked, watching the nervous black stallion shy away from the crumpled vehicle. The policeman turned his hard eyes back on Tiffany. "How'd he get out?"

"Someone left the stall door unlatched, and he found a hole in a fence we're repairing."

"Wait a minute, let's start at the beginning." He walked back to his car, reached for a note pad on the dash and began writing quickly.

"Why don't we do this inside," Zane suggested, "where it's warmer and drier?"

The young officer pursed his lips together and nodded. "Fine. Just let me take a few measurements and report what happened on the radio. Then we'll call a tow company and see if we can get this rig moved."

Three hours later the ordeal was nearly over. After two cups of coffee and what seemed to be a thousand questions, the police officer was satisfied that he could accurately report what had happened. The trucker had taken the name of Tiffany's insurance company and had left with the towtruck driver, who had driven up with a truck similar in size to the wrecked rig. Moon Shadow was back in his stall and Mac had attended to his injury, which turned out to be a strained tendon. With Zane's help, Mac had applied a pressure bandage and called Vance, who had promised to stop by in the morning and examine the horse.

"You're sure Moon Shadow's all right?" Tiffany asked the trainer. She was just coming back into the kitchen. After the police officer and the trucker had left, she had gone upstairs, showered and changed into her bathrobe. Her hair was still wet, but at least she was clean and warm.

"He'll be fine," Mac assured her. He was sitting at the table and finishing his last cup of coffee.

"Where's Zane?"

Mac scowled at the mention of the Irishman. "He went to clean up. Same as you." He looked as if he were about to say something and changed his mind. "He knows horses, that one."

"Who? Zane?"

"Aye."

"I think he's worked with them all his life." Tiffany poured herself a cup of the strong coffee and took a sip as she leaned against the counter. "Mac, is something bothering you?" Tiffany asked, her brows drawing together in concern. "Is Moon Shadow all right?"

Mac was quick to put her fears to rest. "Oh, I imagine he'll have a few stiff muscles tomorrow, and it won't hurt to have Vance take a look at him. But I think he'll be fine."

"Great," Tiffany said with a relieved sigh.

Just then, Zane strode into the kitchen, wearing only a clean pair of jeans and a T-shirt that stretched across his chest and didn't hide the ripple of his muscles as he moved.

He had washed his face and the scratch there was only minor.

"Another cup?" Tiffany asked, handing Zane a mug filled with the steaming brew.

"Thanks."

Mac rotated his mug between both of his hands and stared into the murky liquid. He pressed his thin lips together and then lifted his head, eyeing both Tiffany and Zane.

"Now, Missy," he said, "who do ya suppose let Moon Shadow out?"

Tiffany was surprised by the question. She lifted her shoulders slightly. "I don't know. I think it was probably just an oversight by one of the stable hands."

"Do ya, now?"

"Why? You think someone let him out on purpose?" Tiffany's smile faded and a deep weariness stole over her. So much had happened in one day and she was bone tired.

Mac reached for his hat and placed the slightly damp fedora on his head. "I checked the stallion barn myself earlier. Moon Shadow was locked in his stall."

Tiffany dropped her head into her hand. "I don't want to think about this," she whispered quietly, "not now."

"I think you have to, Missy," Mac said. "Someone deliberately let the stallion out."

"Buy why?"

"That one I can't answer." His gaze moved to Zane. "You wouldn't know anything about it, would you?"

Zane's gray eyes turned to steel. "Of course not."

"Just askin'," Mac explained. "You were here when it happened." He rubbed his hand over his chin. "And the way I understand it, you had a grudge against Ellery Rhodes."

"That was a long time ago," Zane replied.

"Aye. And now you're here. Pokin' around hopin' to buy the place." He shot a warning glance to Tiffany.

"Mac," she said, horrified that he would consider Zane a suspect. "Zane caught Moon Shadow tonight. If it hadn't been for him, the horse might be dead."

Mac rubbed the tired muscles in the back of his neck and frowned. "I know you're a fine horse breeder," he said to Zane. "You have the reputation to back you up, but sometimes, when revenge or a woman's involved, well...a man's head can get all turned around."

"I would never do anything to jeopardize a horse," Zane stated calmly. "And I care too much for Tiffany to do anything that might harm her." His voice was low and deadly. His indignant eyes impaled the old trainer.

Mac managed to crack a smile. "All right, Sheridan. I believe you. Now, can you tell me what you think is going on around here? It seems to me that someone is trying to sabotage the operation. Who would do that? Maybe a man interested in buying a farm and gathering a little revenge to boot?" With his final remark, Mac pushed his chair away from the table. The legs scraped against the wooden floor. After straightening his tired muscles, he turned toward the back porch. He paused at the door, his hand poised on the knob, and glanced over his shoulder at Tiffany. "And just for the record I'll be sleeping in the stallion barn tonight. Wouldn't want to have another 'accident,' would we?"

"You don't have to—"

"I'm sleeping in the barn, Missy," Mac insisted. "That's all right with you, isn't it?"

"Of course, but really, there's no need...."

Mac tugged on the brim of the fedora over his eyes before stepping outside. Tiffany heard his footsteps fade as he walked down the back steps.

"Mac's grasping at straws," Tiffany said, feeling the need to explain and apologize to Zane. She lifted her palms and managed a frail smile. "He...he's just trying to find an explanation."

"And I'm the logical choice."

"Everyone else has been with the farm for years, and, well, Mac's a little suspicious when it comes to strangers."

Zane set his empty cup on the counter and rammed his hands into this pockets. His eyes narrowed, and his lower jaw jutted forward. "And what do you think, Tiffany?"

She lifted trusting eyes to his. "I *know* you didn't let Moon Shadow out."

"So who did?"

"God, I don't know. I'm not really sure I want to. I'm just so damned tired..." She felt her shoulders slump and forced her back to stiffen. "If I had to guess I'd say that it was probably just some kids who broke into the place and thought they'd get their kicks by letting the horse out."

"Not just any horse," he reminded her. "Moon Shadow."

"He's been getting a lot of attention lately."

"How would the kids know where to find Moon Shadow?"

"His picture's been in the paper."

"And at night, to an untrained eye, Moon Shadow looks like any other black horse."

"But—"

"What about your security system?" Zane demanded. "You said yourself that the fence was down."

"Wouldn't that dog of yours bark his head off if a stranger started poking around the place?" he demanded, daring her to ignore the logic of his thinking.

"I...I guess so."

"You see," he surmised, "there are too many unanswered questions. I don't blame Mac for thinking I was involved." He raked his fingers through his hair and let out an exasperated sigh.

"He's just worried...about me."

"So am I." Zane's arms circled her waist and he leaned his forehead against hers. "Someone's trying to ruin you and I think I know who."

Tiffany squeezed her eyes shut and shook her head, denying his suggestion before he had a chance to speak. "Dustin," she thought aloud, "you think he's behind all this?"

"No question about it."

"But he's in Florida—"

"Is he?"

Tiffany hesitated. She hadn't actually seen Dustin get on a plane. "Journey's End races the day after tomorrow."

"And Dustin was here this morning." His strong, protective arms drew her close. "If you do have a saboteur, sweet lady, I'm willing to bet on your brother-in-law."

"Just because one horse got out—"

"And four foals died."

"No!" Tiffany tried to jerk away but couldn't. His powerful arms flexed and imprisoned her to him.

"And the story was leaked to the press."

"It wasn't leaked; we never tried to hide what was happening with the foals." She sprang instantly to Dustin's defense. No matter what else had happened, Dustin was the man who had helped her when Ellery had died. "Dustin himself was concerned about the story in the papers. That's why he came back."

"So he claimed."

"You're just trying to find someone, anyone, to blame all this on!"

"No, Tiffany, no," he whispered, his breath fanning her damp hair. "I'm trying to make you understand the only logical explanation. If you think Dustin's so innocent, what about Devil's Gambit and King's Ransom?"

"I...I can't explain that."

"What about the fact that Ellery may still be alive?"

"But he's not—"

"We're not sure about that," Zane said slowly, making no attempt to release her. She sagged wearily against him. "But we both know that Dustin posed as a rival bidder, interested in Ethan Rivers's horses, when in fact Ethan was Ellery and Dustin was his brother. Dustin admitted to bidding on his own horses, just to drive the prices up."

Tiffany's throat went dry. "But I just can't believe that Dustin would try and ruin our operation. It doesn't make any sense. He owns part of the farm."

Zane's voice was firm. "Has it ever occurred to you that Dustin might want to own it all? Hasn't he already offered to buy you out?"

"Only because he thought it was too much for me," she whispered, but the seeds of distrust had been planted, and she hated the new feelings of doubt that were growing in her mind. Three weeks ago she would have trusted Dustin with her life. Now, because of Zane's accusations, she was beginning to doubt the only person she could call family. She shuddered, and Zane gathered her still closer, pressing her face against his chest.

"I'm not saying that Dustin doesn't care for you," he said, gently stroking her hair.

"Just that he's using me."

"He's the kind of man who would do just about anything to get what he wants."

She shook her head and stared out the window. Raindrops ran down the paned glass. "Funny, that's just what he said about you."

Gently Zane lifted her chin with his finger, silently forcing her to look into his eyes. "I've done a few things in my life that I'm not proud of," he admitted. "But I've never cheated or lied to anyone."

"Except me?" Tears began to scald her eyes.

"I didn't lie about Stasia."

"You omitted the facts, Zane. In order to deceive me. Call it what you will. In my book, it's lying."

A small muscle worked in the corner of his jaw, and he had to fight the urge to shake her, make her see what was so blindingly clear to him. He couldn't. He'd wounded her

enough as it was. Tiffany seemed to stare right through him.
"I've never wanted anyone the way I want you, Tiffany,"
he whispered. "I wouldn't do anything that would ever
make you doubt me."

Her throat tightened painfully, and she squeezed her eyes
against the hot tears forming behind her eyelids. "I want to
trust you, Zane. God, I want to trust you," she admitted.
"It's just that you've come here when everything seems to
be falling apart..."

"And you blame me?"

"No!"

"Then look at me, damn it!" he insisted. Her eyes opened
and caught in his silvery stare. "I love you, Tiffany Rhodes,
and I'll do everything in my power to prove it."

She held up a protesting palm before he could say anything else. She felt so open and raw. Though he was saying
the words she longed to hear, she couldn't believe him.

He took her trembling hand and covered it with his.
"You're going to listen to me, lady," he swore. "Ever since
I met you that first morning when Rod Crawford was here,
you've doubted me. I can't say that I blame you because I
came here with the express purpose of taking your farm
from you...by any means possible."

Her eyes widened at his admission.

"But all that changed," he conceded, "when I met you
and began to fall in love with you."

"I...I wish I could believe you," Tiffany whispered.
"More than *anything* I want to believe you." Her voice was
raspy and thick with emotion. She felt as if her heart were
bursting, and she knew that she was admitting far more than
she should.

His fingers tightened over her shoulders. *"Believe."*

"Oh, Zane..."

"Tiffany, please. Listen. I want you to marry me."

The words settled in the kitchen and echoed in Tiffany's
mind. Her knees gave way and she fell against him. "I want

you to be my wife, bear my children, stand at my side...."
He kissed the top of her head. "I want you to be with me
forever."

She felt the tears stream down her face, and she wondered if they were from joy or sadness. "I can't," she
choked. "I can't until I know for certain that Ellery is
dead."

Zane's back stiffened. "I thought you were convinced."

"I am." Her voice trembled. "But what if there's a
chance that he's *alive*?"

His arms wrapped around her in desperation, and he
buried his head into the hollow of her shoulder. "I'll find
out," he swore, one fist clenching in determination. "Once
and for all, I'll find out just what happened to your husband."

"And if he's alive?" she whispered.

"He'll wish he were dead for the hell he's put you
through."

She shook her head and pushed herself out of his pos-
sessive embrace. "No, Zane. If Ellery's alive, he's still my
husband."

"A husband who used and betrayed you." Anger stormed
in his eyes, and his muscles tensed at the thought of Ellery
Rhodes claiming Tiffany as his wife after all these years. *The
man couldn't possibly be alive!*

"But my husband nonetheless."

"You're still in love with him," he charged.

"No," she admitted, closing her eyes against the traitorous truth. "The only man I've ever loved is you."

Zane relaxed a bit and gently kissed her eyelids. "Trust
me, Tiffany. Trust me to take care of you, no matter what
happens in the future." He reached for her and savagely
pressed her body to his, lowering his head and letting his lips
capture hers.

Willingly, her arms encircled his neck, and she let her body fit against his. The warmth of him seemed to seep through her clothes and generate a new heat in her blood.

When his tongue rimmed her lips, she shuddered. "I love you, Zane," she murmured as her breath mingled and caught with his. "And I want to be with you."

He leaned over and placed an arm under the crook of her knees before lifting her off the floor and carrying her out of the kitchen. She let her head rest against his shoulder and wondered at the sanity of loving such a passionate man. Zane's emotions, whether love or hate, ran deep.

Carefully he mounted the stairs and carried her to her bedroom. Rain slid down the windows and the room was illuminated only by the shadowy light from the security lamps near the barns. "I never wanted to fall in love with you," he admitted as he stood her near the bed and his fingers found the knot to the belt of her robe. Slowly the ties loosened, and he pushed the robe over her shoulders to expose the satiny texture of her skin.

She was naked except for a silky pair of panties. Zane kissed her lips, the hollow of her throat, the dark stiffening tips of each gorgeous breast as he lowered himself to his knees.

She wanted to fall to the floor with him, but his hands held her upright as slowly he removed the one scanty piece of cloth keeping her from him. His fingers lingered on her skin and rubbed her calves and thighs as he kissed her abdomen, moistening the soft skin with his tongue. His eyes closed, and Tiffany felt his eyelashes brush her navel. Tingling sensations climbed upward through her body, heating her blood as it raced through her veins.

The heat within her began to turn liquid as his tongue circled her navel. Tiffany's knees felt weak, and if it hadn't been for the strong arms supporting her, she would have slid to the floor and entwined herself with him.

Zane's hands reached upward and touched the pointed tip of one swollen breast. It hardened expectantly against the soft pressure of his fingers and Tiffany closed her eyes against the urge to lie with him. Zane groaned against her abdomen, and his hot breath warmed her skin.

"Zane," she pleaded, the sound coming from deep in her throat as her fingers caught in his black hair. "Love me."

"I do, sweet lady," he murmured against her skin, his warm hands pressing against the small of her back, pushing her closer to him.

As if in slow motion, he forced her backward, and she fell onto the bed. Her hair splayed against the comforter in tangled disarray. Her cheeks were flushed, as were her proud breasts with their alluring dark peaks.

As she watched him, Zane quickly removed and discarded his clothes. When completely naked, he came to her. Lying beside her elegant nude body, he caught his fingers in the silken tresses of her hair and rolled atop her. Corded male muscles strained against hers as he captured one blossoming nipple in his mouth. His tongue slid enticingly over the soft mound, and she cradled his head against her, moaning in contentment as he suckled. Her breasts, swollen with desire, ached for his soothing touch, yearned for the tenderness of his lips and tongue.

"Tiffany, I love you," he vowed as his hands roved over her skin, exploring the exquisite feel of her. His lips murmured words of love against her ear, forcing the heat within her to expand until she could stand the torment no longer.

"Please," she whispered into his ear, her fingers running over the smooth skin of his upper arms and back, feeling the ripple of solid muscles as he positioned himself above her. "Now!"

The ache in his loins throbbed for release, and he took her eagerly, becoming one with her in the heated splendor of his love. His lovemaking was violent, explosive, as he claimed her for his own and purged from her body forever any thoughts of the one man who had betrayed them both.

Tiffany soared to the heavens, her soul melding with Zane's as the clouds of passion burst open and showered her in hot bursts of satiation. She shuddered against his hard male frame; her love for him was complete and infinite. Tiffany knew that no matter what the future held, she would never stop loving him.

"I love you," she heard him vow again and again. Listening to the wonderful sound, she smiled and curled her body close to his to fall into a deep, exhausted sleep.

It was barely dawn when Tiffany awakened. She reached for Zane, but he was gone. The bed sheets were cold. Thoughts of the night before began swimming in her sleepy mind; then she heard him walk back into the room.

"Zane?" she murmured, groggily trying to focus her eyes.

He came to the bed and sat on the edge near her. "I didn't mean to wake you."

He was completely dressed, as if he were leaving. "What's going on?" she asked, glancing at the clock. It was only five-thirty. Even Mac didn't start work until after six.

"I have to go."

"Where?"

"Back to San Francisco."

She looked into his eyes and saw the sadness lingering in the gray depths. "Why?" she asked, forcing herself into a sitting position. She tugged at the comforter to cover her naked breasts and then leaned forward so that her face was near his. Something was wrong. She could feel it. In the course of a few short hours, Zane's feelings toward her had changed. Her heart, filled with love of the last few hours, twisted painfully.

"I have things I have to do," he said. "You'll just have to trust me."

"Does this have anything to do with Dustin?" she asked, shivering from the cold morning air.

"I don't know." He placed a warm hand on her shoulder. "Just trust me, okay?"

She nodded and forced a frail smile. "You'll be back?"

He laughed and broke the tension in the room. "As soon as I can. If I'm not back in a couple of days, I'll call."

"Promises, promises," she quipped, trying to sound lighthearted. He was leaving. Her heart seemed to wither inside her.

"I left the phone number of my hotel on the note pad in the kitchen. If you get lonely—"

"I already am." Lovingly she touched the red scratch on his face. "My hero," she whispered with a seductive smile.

"Hardly."

She curled her hand around his neck and pulled his face next to hers.

"Look, lady, if you don't cut this out, I'll never get out of here," he growled, but a pleased grin stole over his angular features to charmingly display the hint of straight white teeth against his dark skin."

"That's the idea."

Zane let out an exasperated sigh. "Oh, Tiffany, what am I going to do with you?"

"I don't know," she murmured against his ear as her fingers began working at the buttons of his shirt. "Use your imagination."

An hour later he was gone, and Tiffany felt more alone than she ever had in her life. She was more alone than she had been on the morning her mother had abandoned her, for then she had still had Edward, and when her father had died, she had married Ellery. When Ellery was suddenly killed, Tiffany had relied on Dustin.

Now, as she cinched the belt of her robe more tightly around her waist and stared out the window at the rain-washed countryside, Tiffany was completely alone. She had no one to rely upon but herself. She shivered more from dread than from the morning air, and she watched as Zane's car roared to life and disappeared through the trees.

Chapter Twelve

After Zane had gone, Tiffany found it impossible to return to bed. Instead she dressed and walked outside, stopping only to scratch Wolverine behind the ears. The dog responded by wagging his tail enthusiastically.

"Some hero you are," Tiffany reprimanded fondly. "Where were you last night when I needed you?"

She refilled Wolverine's bowls and walked to the stallion barn. The rain had become no more than a drizzle, but the ground was still wet, and when she ventured off the pavement, her boots sunk into the soaked earth.

Mac was already up and checking on Moon Shadow's injury.

"So how is he?" Tiffany asked, patting the black stallion's neck and forcing a smile at the grizzled old trainer. Mac had slept in his clothes and it was obvious from the way he was walking that his arthritis was bothering him.

"Moon Shadow?" He pointed a thumb in the direction of the horse's head. "He's fine."

"And you?"

"Getting too old for all this excitement."

"Why don't you take a day off?" Tiffany asked. "You deserve it."

"Not now, Missy," he said, shaking his head. "What would I do while the missus knits and watches those soap operas? Nope. I'm better off here. 'Sides, I want to see what Vance has to say after he looks this old boy over." Mac gently slapped Moon Shadow's rump, and the stallion snorted and tossed his head in the air.

"I thought I'd check on Shadow's Survivor next," Tiffany said.

"Good idea."

Mac walked with her and Wolverine trotted along behind. The rain had stopped and the clouds were beginning to break apart, promising a warm spring day. Tiffany realized for the first time that the flowering trees were beginning to bloom. Pink and white blossoms colored the leafless trees with the promise of spring.

"Say, Missy," Mac said as they approached the foaling shed.

"Yes?"

"I noticed that Sheridan's car is gone."

"He left early this morning."

"Because of what I said last night?"

"No." Tiffany shook her head and smiled sadly.

"I was out of line."

"You were concerned. We all were...are." She ran her fingers through her hair and squared her shoulders. "Something's got to give, doesn't it? We can't go on this way much longer."

Mac frowned and reached for the handle of the door. "You're right—it's time our luck changed, for the better."

They walked inside the foaling shed and heard the soft nickering of Alexander's Lady. A tiny nose attempted to push through the rails of the stall. "Here's our good news,"

Tiffany said with a smile as she tried to reach out and touch the skittish filly. "Maybe I should change her name to that. How does Good News strike you?"

"Better'n Shadow's Survivor or whatever the hell you came up with before," the old man chuckled.

"I don't know...."

"She's your horse, Missy. You name her whatever you like." Mac grinned at the sprightly little filly. "Just wait, little one," he said to the inquisitive young horse. "As soon as we get the okay from the vet, you'll get your first look at the world."

The rest of the day was filled with more good news. Two owners called to say that their mares had delivered healthy foals sired by Moon Shadow, and Vance Geddes checked Moon Shadow's leg injury and gave the stallion a clean bill of health.

"As soon as that tendon heals, he'll be good as new," Vance predicted after examining the stallion.

"He sure knows how to get into trouble," Tiffany complained with a fond look at the horse in question.

"Maybe it's not the horse," Vance suggested.

"What do you mean?"

"Seems to me, he had a little help getting out of the stall last night."

"I suppose."

"Got any ideas who unlatched his stall door?" Vance asked, placing all his veterinary supplies back in his case and walking out of the stallion barn.

"No. I thought it might be vandals, but Zane seems to think it was an inside job, so to speak."

"Somebody with a grudge?"

Tiffany lifted her shoulders. "I couldn't guess who."

"You got any trouble with employees?"

"Not that I know of."

"Haven't fired anyone, a stable boy...or maybe done business with someone else, made a competitor angry?"

"No." She sighed wearily and spotted Louise's car rumbling down the long drive. "I've thought and thought about it. I'm sure I've made a few enemies, but no one that would want to hurt me or my horses.... At least I don't think so."

Vance put his bag into the truck and grimaced. He turned his kindly bespectacled eyes on Tiffany. "Just be careful, okay? Anyone who would let Moon Shadow out would do just about anything to get what he wants."

"If only I knew what that was," she said anxiously. "Any. news on the foals' deaths?"

"Not yet," Vance said, sliding into his pickup, "but I've got a couple of new ideas. They're long shots...probably end up in dead ends, but maybe..."

"Keep me posted."

"Will do." Vance had just pushed his key into the lock and was about to start the engine, but Louise shouted at him. "Hey, wait!" the housekeeper called as she bustled up to Vance's truck. She was waving a newspaper in the air. "Look, here, on page one." She proudly handed Tiffany the sports section from the *Times*. In the lower left-hand corner was a picture of Journey's End along with the article written by Nancy Emerson.

Tiffany's eyes skimmed the columns of fine print and her face broke into a smile. Then, slowly, she reread Nancy's report, which did bring up the subject of the dead colts but also concentrated on Moon Shadow's career as well as his two strongest progeny, Devil's Gambit and Journey's End. The article ended on an upbeat note, suggesting that Moon Shadow's victories on the racetrack and as a proved sire overshadowed the unfortunate deaths of the four foals.

"Wonderful," Tiffany said, feeling a little relief. "At least we got a chance for rebuttal."

"Now," Vance stated, "if we can just come up with the reason those foals died."

"You think you're on to something?"

"I'm not sure," Vance replied. "I'll let you know in a couple of days. Like I said—it could be another dead end."

"Let's hope not," Tiffany prayed fervently.

"Come on, you two," Louise reprimanded. "Things are turning around, just you wait and see."

"I don't know about that," Tiffany replied.

"Why? What happened?"

"Moon Shadow got out last night. It looks as if someone did it deliberately."

"What!" Louise was more than shocked.

As the two women walked toward the back porch, Tiffany explained the events of the evening before and Louise clucked her tongue in disbelief.

"But who would do such a thing?" Louise wondered once they were in the kitchen.

"That's the mystery."

"You got any ideas?"

"No...but Zane seems to."

Louise's eyes sparkled. "That one, he'll figure it out. Just you wait and see."

When the telephone rang, Tiffany expected the caller to be Zane, but she was disappointed.

"Hello, Tiff?" Dustin asked through the fuzzy long-distance connection.

"Dustin? Where are you?"

"In Florida and, well, brace yourself for some bad news."

Tiffany slumped against the pantry, the receiver pressed against her ear. Her fingers curled over the handle until her knuckles showed white. "What happened?" she asked, dread steadily mounting up her spine.

"It's Journey's End," Dustin said.

Tiffany's heart pounded erratically, and she felt as if her whole world were falling apart, piece by piece. "What about him?"

"He was injured. Just yesterday, while working out. From everything we can tell, he's got a bone chip in his knee."

"Oh, God," Tiffany said, letting out her breath in a long sigh. When would it end? She ran shaking fingers through her hair and wished that Zane were with her now.

"It looks bad, Tiff. I think his career is over—"

"Before it really began."

"We can retire him to stud."

"I guess that's about the only thing we can do," she reluctantly agreed, her shoulders slumping. "Other than the knee, how is he?"

"The vet says he'll be okay, but we'd better not count on him racing anymore. It wouldn't hurt to have Vance look at him when he gets home."

"How is Bob Prescott taking the news?"

There was a long silence on the other end of the line. "That's a little bit of a sore point, Tiff. I think Prescott ran him knowing that something was wrong."

"No!"

"I can't prove it."

Tiffany felt sick inside. "Let me talk to him," Tiffany demanded, rage thundering through her blood. The last thing she would stand for was anyone on her staff mistreating a horse.

"Too late."

"What?"

"I fired him."

"On suspicion?" Tiffany was incredulous.

"He's been involved in a couple of shady things," Dustin said. "I just didn't want to take any more chances."

"But who will replace him?"

"I'm talking to a couple of guys now. Big-name trainers...I'll call you after I meet with them."

"I don't know—"

"Look, I've got to go. I'll make all the arrangements to send Journey's End home."

"Wait. Before you hang up."

"What?" Dustin demanded impatiently.

"Last night someone let Moon Shadow out of his stall."

There was silence on the other end of the line. "What do you mean 'someone let him out'?" Dustin asked, his voice cold.

Tiffany gave a brief account of the events of the evening and Dustin's voice shook with rage. "Zane Sheridan was there again? What does he want this time? Don't tell me he's still pressuring you into selling to him."

"No, Dustin, he's not," Tiffany replied.

"Then why the hell is he hanging around?"

"Maybe he enjoys my company—"

"I'll bet. If you ask me, he's the culprit who let Moon Shadow out. He's probably trying to make it tough on you so you'll sell him the farm." Dustin swore descriptively.

"I don't think so."

"That's the problem, isn't it—sometimes you just don't think. Period."

With his final words, Dustin slammed down the phone, and Tiffany knew in her heart that everything Zane had said about her brother-in-law was true. A deep sadness stole over her, and she spent the rest of the day locked in the den, going over the books, hoping to block out the bitter truth about Dustin and what he had done.

Dustin would be back on the farm with Journey's End by the end of the week. When he arrived, Tiffany planned to confront him with the truth.

Four days later, she still hadn't heard from Zane. Things had settled into the usual routine on the farm, and she had spent her time working with Mac and the yearlings.

The fence had been repaired, and there had been no other disturbances on the farm. Moon Shadow was healing well, and Mac had prepared a neighboring stall in the stallion barn for Journey's End. "A shame about that one," the old trainer had remarked when he learned about the accident. "Sometimes fate seems to deal out all the bad cards at once."

Later that night, Tiffany was seated in the den going over the books. The house was dark except for the single desk lamp and the shifting flames of the fire burning noisily against dry oak. Tiffany felt cold and alone. The portrait of Devil's Gambit seemed to stare down from its position over the mantel and mock her. Where was Zane? Why hadn't he called?

She tried to force her attention back to the books and the red ink that was beginning to flow in the pages of the general ledger. The farm was losing money. Without Moon Shadow's stud fees or any income from Journey's End's racing career, Tiffany had little alternative but to sell several of the best yearlings.

The rap on the French doors surprised her, but she knew in an instant that it had to be Zane. She saw his haggard face through the glass, she opened the doors with trembling fingers and flung herself into his arms.

He stepped in with a rush of cold air that chilled the room and fanned the glowing embers of the fire and billowed the sheer draperies. "Thank God you're here," she whispered against his neck before lifting her head and studying the intensity of his gaze.

The look on his face was murderous. Dark shadows circled his gray eyes, and a weariness stole over his features making the angular planes seem more rugged and foreboding. He looked as if he hadn't slept in weeks.

"Zane?" she whispered as his dark eyes devoured her.

"It's just about over," he said as he closed the door and walked over to the fire to warm himself.

"What is?"

"Everything you've been going through." He reached for er and drew her close to him. "I wish I could make it eas-r for you—"

"Easier?"

"Shh." He brushed his lips over hers, and his hands ocked behind her back, gently urging her body forward ntil her supple curves pressed against him and he groaned, s if in despair. She felt her body respond to his and heard he uneven beat of her own heart when he kissed her hun-rily and his tongue touched hers. Her fingers lingered at his eck, and she felt the coiled tension within him, saw the train on his face.

"What happened?" she asked, when at last he drew his ead back.

"It's a long story."

"I've got the rest of my life to listen," she murmured.

Zane managed a wan smile. "Oh, lady, I've been waiting or four days to hear you say just those words," he whis-ered, his arms tightening around her. "God, I've missed ou." He kissed the curve of her neck, his lips lingering near er earlobe, before he gently released her.

"So tell me."

He rammed his fingers through his black, windblown hair nd poured them each a drink, "I found Stasia," he admit-ed roughly, Tiffany's heart nearly missed a beat. "It wasn't ll that easy, and if she'd had her way, I never would have ocated her."

He walked over to Tiffany and handed her a snifter of randy, before taking a long swallow of the warm liquor and itting on the hearth, hoping that the golden flames would arm his back.

"How did you find her?"

"A private investigator by the name of Walt Griffith."

His gray eyes searched hers. "I had him do some check-g on you, too—"

"What!"

He smiled devilishly and his eyes twinkled. "I didn't fig ure you'd like it any more than Stasia did. But it was nec essary. To find Ellery."

Tiffany nearly dropped her drink. Her hands began t shake as she lifted the glass to her lips.

"I'm getting ahead of myself," Zane said. "Walt foun Stasia living with some artist-type in Carmel. When I ap proached her she was shocked, but managed to fall rig back into character—she agreed to tell her side of the E lery Rhodes story for a substantial fee."

"You paid her?" Tiffany was outraged.

Zane's eyes rested on her flushed face and he smiled "Believe me, it was worth it."

Tiffany wasn't so sure. "What did you find out?"

"About the accident that supposedly killed Devil' Gambit."

Tiffany's heart was pounding so loudly it seemed to ech against the cherry-wood walls. "Wait a minute," she in sisted as the cold truth swept over her in a tidal wave o awareness. "What you're saying is that—"

"Stasia was Ellery's mistress. Even when he was marrie to you, he was having an affair with my ex-wife. Seems tha they were hooked on the excitement of carrying on whe there was the danger of being discovered."

"I..." Tiffany was about to say that she didn't want t believe it, but she knew it was the truth. She'd come to th same conclusion herself once she had talked to Dustin. Th affair explained so much about Ellery that she had neve understood.

"So Ellery?" she asked breathlessly.

"Was killed in the accident," Zane assured her.

"I...never wished him dead," Tiffany whispered, walk ing across the room and sitting next to Zane on the hearth

"I know. You just had to know the truth." Zane looke into her eyes and smiled. "It's going to be all right, yo know."

"God, I hope so."

"We'll be together."

Tiffany's eyes filled with tears of happiness. "Then you're right—everything will work out."

"Stasia admitted that the horses were switched," he said, continuing with his story. "Ellery had thought that the insurance forms had already been processed—"

"The ones that were waiting for his signature?"

"Yes. No one but Ellery, Dustin and Bob Prescott knew that Devil's Gambit had pulled a ligament after his last race."

"Not even Mac?"

"No."

"When?"

"While exercising a few days after his last race. It looked as if Devil's Gambit, the favored horse, wouldn't be able to race in any of the Triple Crown races. If Ellery could make it look as if Devil's Gambit had died in an accident, when in fact it was really another, considerably less valuable horse who was killed, he could breed Devil's Gambit under an alias in another country, collect stud fees and get the insurance money to boot. It was better odds than just putting him out for stud before he'd really proved himself."

"Oh, God," Tiffany said with a long sigh. Nervously she ran her fingers through her hair.

"It wasn't a foolproof plan by any means and it was extremely risky. But Ellery enjoyed taking risks—remember the stunts he and Dustin would pull in Europe when he posed as Ethan Rivers?"

Tiffany nodded, her stomach turning over convulsively. What kind of a man had she married? How had she been so blind?

"There was always the chance that Devil's Gambit would be recognized because of the Jockey Club identification number tattooed on the inside of his lip. And of course there

was the remote possibility of something going wrong wit
Ellery's plans.''

Tiffany had broken out in a cold sweat. She wrapped he
arms around herself as she relived the horrible night whe
she was told that Ellery and Devil's Gambit were killed.

"Everything backfired when Ellery was trapped in th
truck and killed along with the switched horse, which, by th
way, Bob Prescott supplied. It seems that the trainer wa
involved in the scam with Ellery and Dustin.''

"And all this time I've let him work with our horses...
God, how could I have been so stupid?''

"There's no shame in trusting your husband, Tiffany,
Zane said softly and kissed the top of her head before smi
ing. "In fact, your next one will insist upon it.''

She felt his warm arm slide around her waist. "And Du
tin—what about him?'' she asked.

"He decided to gamble and carry out Ellery's plan.''

"With Bob Prescott?''

"Right. Stasia claims he was absolutely furious that th
insurance forms hadn't been signed, and that you, not he
as the new forms indicated, would get the settlement.'' Zan
shrugged and finished his drink in one swallow. "But b
that time it was too late.''

"So what are we going to do?''

His arm tightened possessively around her, and his fin
gers toyed with the lapels of her robe. "For now, go to bec
Tomorrow we'll deal with Dustin.''

"How?''

"I have it on good authority that he'll be here with Jou
ney's End. Come on.'' He pulled her gently to her feet an
walked her to the stairs. "I haven't slept in days—'' he sli
an appreciative glance down her body "—and somehow
get the feeling that I'll have trouble again tonight.''

They mounted the stairs entwined in an embrace. Once i
her bedroom, he let his hand slip inside her bathrobe an
felt the shimmery fabric of her nightgown. "I've bee

vaiting for so long to be with you again," he whispered into
er ear as he untied the belt of the robe, pushed it gently
ver her shoulders and let it drop unheeded to the floor.

True to Zane's prediction, Dustin arrived around nine. He
narched into the kitchen and stopped abruptly. The last
erson he had expected to see was Zane Sheridan. Dustin's
omposure slipped slightly and his broad shoulders stiff-
ned. His jeans and shirt were rumpled from the long, cross-
ountry drive, and three day's growth of beard darkened his
hin. In contrast, Zane was clean-shaven and dressed in
resh corduroy pants and a crisp shirt. His hair was neatly
ombed, and the satisfied smile on his face made Dustin's
air stand on end.

The differences in the two men were striking.

Dustin cast a worried glance in Tiffany's direction before
lacing his Stetson on a hook near the door.

"'Morning, Dustin," Zane drawled. He was leaning
gainst the counter sipping coffee while Tiffany made
reakfast.

Dustin managed a thin smile. "What're you doing here?"

"Visiting." Zane took another long drink.

The meaning of Zane's words settled like lead on Dus-
in's shoulders. "Oh, no, Tiffany," he said. "You're not
etting involved with this bastard, are you?" He hooked a
humb in Zane's direction.

Zane just smiled wickedly, but Tiffany stiffened. "I don't
ee that it's any of your business, Dustin. Is Journey's End
n the stallion barn?"

"Yes."

"With Mac?"

"He was there and that veterinarian, Geddes."

"Good."

Dustin became uneasy. "What's going on?"

Zane propped a booted foot on a chair near the table.
"That's what we'd like to know." Zane's gray eyes glittered

ominously, and Dustin was reminded of a great cat about t
spring on unsuspecting quarry. His throat went dry.

"Tiffany?" Dustin asked.

She turned to face her brother-in-law and he saw the di
appointment in her eyes. *She knows. She knows ever*
thing! Dustin's palms began to sweat, and he tugged at th
collar of his shirt.

"I think you need to answer a few questions, Dustin. Di
you let Moon Shadow out the other night?" she charged.

Dustin's gold eyes narrowed treacherously, but he r
fused to fall into any of Sheridan's traps. "Of course no
I...I was in Florida."

"It's over, Rhodes," Zane cut in. "I checked the flight
You were booked on a red-eye."

"No—I mean, I had business in town...."

Tiffany's shoulders slumped, but she forced her gaze
bore into Dustin's. "Zane says that Devil's Gambit is aliv
in Ireland, that he's siring foals while King's Ransom
taking all the credit." Dustin whitened. "Is it true?" Ti
fany demanded, her entire body shaking with rage and di
appointment.

"I don't know anything about—"

"Knock it off," Zane warned, straightening to his fu
height. "You're the primary owner of Emerald Ente
prises, which happens to own a farm where King's Ranso
stands. I saw Devil's Gambit and I've got the pictures t
prove it." His face grew deadly. "And if that isn't enoug
proof to lock you up for the rest of your life, Stasia is wil
ing to talk, for the right price."

"None of this is happening." Dustin turned his gold eye
on her. "Tiff, you can't believe all this. Sheridan's just o
for revenge, like I told you.... Oh, my God," he said as h
recognized the truth. "You're in love with the bastar
aren't you? What's he promised to do, marry you?" He sa
the silent confirmation in her eyes. "Damn it, Tiffany, don

be a fool. Of course he proposed to you. He'd do anything to steal this farm from you.''

"The only time I was a fool, Dustin," Tiffany stated, her voice trembling with rage, "was when I trusted you."

"I helped you—when your world was falling to pieces, I helped you, damn it."

"And you lied. About Devil's Gambit and about Moon Shadow." Her eyes blazed a furious shade of blue. "You let me think that Moon Shadow was the cause of the dead foals and you leaked the story to Rod Crawford."

"What are you saying?" Dustin demanded.

"That the jig is up. Vance Geddes has discovered that the only unhealthy foals sired by Moon Shadow were all conceived during one week—a week you were on the farm," Zane said, barely able to control his temper. "He hasn't discovered what you injected the mares with yet, but it's only a matter of time before he knows just what happened."

"That doesn't mean—"

"Give it up, Rhodes!"

Dustin turned furious eyes on Tiffany. "You've got it all figured out, haven't you? You and your lover! Well, I'm not going to bother to explain myself. It looks as if I'm going to need an attorney—"

"I'd say so," Zane stated. "The police are on their way. They've already rounded up Bob Prescott, and I'm willing to bet that he sold you out."

Dustin visibly paled. He lunged for Tiffany; his only chance of escape was to take Tiffany hostage.

Zane anticipated the move and as Dustin grabbed for Tiffany, Zane landed a right cross to Dustin's cheek that set him on his heels.

"Don't even think about it," Zane warned as Dustin attempted to get up. In the distance, the sounds of a police siren became audible. "I'd be thinking very seriously about an attorney myself, if I were you," he said.

When the police arrived, they read Dustin his rights and took him in for questioning. As he left he was still rubbing his jaw and glaring angrily at Zane.

"I've waited a long time for that," Zane admitted. He stepped onto the back porch and watched while the police cars raced out the drive with Dustin in custody.

"I just can't believe it's over," Tiffany murmured, her eyes looking over the rolling hills that she'd grown to love. "And to think that Dustin was behind it all...."

Zane tilted her chin upward and looked into her worried eyes. "Like you said, it's over." He kissed her tenderly on the eyelids and tasted the salt of her tears, before leading her back to the den. "I came here intending to ruin you," he admitted roughly. "I wanted to buy this farm no matter what the cost." He took out the legal documents that John Morris had prepared. After showing her the contract of sale, he tossed it into the fireplace, and the coals from the previous night burst into flame against the crisp, white paper. "It was all so damned pointless," he said. "All I want is for you to be my wife."

"And I will be," she vowed.

"Even if it means living part of your life in Ireland? We have to bring Devil's Gambit home, you know."

"It doesn't really matter where," she said. "As long as I'm with you."

Zane folded her into the protection of his arms. "I'm not a patient man," he said.

"Don't I know."

"And I'm not about to wait."

"For what?"

"To get married. The sooner the better."

"Anything you want," she said, her blue eyes lingering on his handsome face.

"Anything?" With a wicked smile, he urged her slowly to the floor with the weight of his body. "You may live to regret those words."

"Never," Tiffany whispered as Zane's lips covered hers and she entwined her arms around the neck of the man she loved.

The Silhouette
Cameo Tote Bag
Now available
for just $6.99

Handsomely designed in blue and bright pink, its stylish good looks make the Cameo Tote Bag an attractive accessory. The Cameo Tote Bag is big and roomy (13″ square), with reinforced handles and a snap-shut top. You can buy the Cameo Tote Bag for $6.99, plus $1.50 for postage and handling.

Send your name and address with check or money order for $6.99 (plus $1.50 postage and handling), a total of $8.49 to:

**Silhouette Books
120 Brighton Road
P.O. Box 5084
Clifton, NJ 07015-5084
ATTN: Tote Bag**

SIL-T-1R

The Silhouette Cameo Tote Bag can be purchased pre-paid only. No charges will be accepted. Please allow 4 to 6 weeks for delivery.

N.Y. State Residents Please Add Sales Tax

Offer not available in Canada.

Silhouette Books

brings you the best
in contemporary romance.

SILHOUETTE ROMANCE—
contemporary romances that depict all the
wonder and magic of falling in love.

SILHOUETTE DESIRE—more sensual,
provocative stories of modern women in
realistic situations.

SILHOUETTE SPECIAL EDITION—
longer contemporary romances,
emphasizing emotion as well as heightened
romantic tension. And SILHOUETTE
SPECIAL EDITIONs are sensuous and
believable love stories.

AND NOW

SILHOUETTE INTIMATE MOMENTS—
love stories with the one element no one
else has tapped: excitement. They are
longer, more sensuous romance novels
filled with adventure, suspense, glamour
or melodrama.

AMERICAN TRIBUTE

Where a man's dreams count for more than his parentage...

Look for these upcoming titles under the Special Edition American Tribute banner.

LOVE'S HAUNTING REFRAIN
Ada Steward #289—February 1986
For thirty years a deep dark secret kept them apart—King Stockton made his millions while his wife, Amelia, held everything together. Now could they tell their secret, could they admit their love?

THIS LONG WINTER PAST
Jeanne Stephens #295—March 1986
Detective Cody Wakefield checked out Assistant District Attorney Liann McDowell, but only in his leisure time. For it was the danger of Cody's job that caused Liann to shy away.

AM-TRIB-1

Silhouette Special Edition

AMERICAN TRIBUTE

AMERICAN TRIBUTE

RIGHT BEHIND THE RAIN
Elaine Camp #301—April 1986
The difficulty of coping with her brother's death brought reporter Raleigh Torrence to the office of Evan Younger, a police psychologist. He helped her to deal with her feelings and emotions, including love.

CHEROKEE FIRE
Gena Dalton #307—May 1986
It was Sabrina Dante's silver spoon that Cherokee cowboy Jarod Redfeather couldn't trust. The two lovers came from opposite worlds, but Jarod's Indian heritage taught them to overcome their differences.

NOBODY'S FOOL
Renee Roszel #313—June 1986
Everyone bet that Martin Dante and Cara Torrence would get together. But Martin wasn't putting any money down, and Cara was out to prove that she was nobody's fool.

MISTY MORNINGS, MAGIC NIGHTS
Ada Steward #319—July 1986
The last thing Carole Stockton wanted was to fall in love with another politician, especially Donnelly Wakefield. But under a blanket of secrecy, far from the campaign spotlights, their love became a powerful force.